When the Magnolia Blooms

The resemblance of any character in this novel to any person, living or dead, is not intended. The characters, events, and locations are completely fictional. However, since we all have a dark side, each of us just might see ourselves in one or more of the people that reside in the fictional community of Falls City, Georgia.

WWW.EPISKOPOLS.COM
Books for Clergy and the People They Serve

Copyright © 2006 Dennis R. Maynard.
All rights reserved.
ISBN: 1-4196-4103-4

To order additional copies, please contact us.
BookSurge, LLC
www.booksurge.com
1-866-308-6235
orders@booksurge.com

DENNIS R. MAYNARD.

WHEN THE MAGNOLIA BLOOMS

Book Two in the Magnolia Series

BOOKSURGE PUBLISHERS
2006

When the Magnolia Blooms

Steele Austin is filled with youthful enthusiasm. This idealistic Episcopal priest accepts a call to one of the oldest and most prestigious pulpits in the state of Georgia. His idealism continually conflicts with the determination of the parish leaders to keep things just the way they have always been. Steele, on the other hand, is equally determined to battle bigotry and prejudice, even when masked in tradition.

In this, the second book in the Magnolia Series, Steele finds himself in the middle of a murder investigation. He is the only person that believes the accused is innocent. This puts him at odds with his good friend, Chief Sparks.

Almeda Alexander, one of Steele's foremost antagonists, finds love. It is a love, however, that unites her in a strange bond with the young priest.

And through it all, the work of the Church goes on. Miracles of work and mercy do occur. You won't want to miss this, the second installment, of life in Falls City, Georgia.

BOOKS BY
DENNIS R. MAYNARD

THOSE EPISKOPOLS
This is a popular resource for clergy to use in their new member ministries. It seeks to answer the questions most often asked about the Episcopal Church.

FORGIVEN, HEALED AND RESTORED
This book is devoted to making a distinction between forgiving those who have injured us and making the decision to reconcile with them or restore them to their former place in our lives.

THE MONEY BOOK
The primary goal of this book is to present some practical teachings on money and Christian Stewardship. It also encourages the reader not to confuse their self-worth with their net worth.

FORGIVE AND GET YOUR LIFE BACK
The book teaches the forgiveness process to the reader. It's a popular resource for clergy and counselors to use to do forgiveness training. In this book, a clear distinction is made between forgiving, reconciling, and restoring the penitent person to their former position in our lives.

BEHIND THE MAGNOLIA TREE
When the Gospel of a young Episcopal priest conflicts with the secrets of sex, greed, and power in an old southern community, it can mean only one thing for the youthful outsider, even if he is ordained. His idealism places him in an ongoing conflict with the bigotry and prejudice that are in the historical fabric of the community.

WHEN THE MAGNOLIA BLOOMS
This is the second book in the Magnolia Series. Steele Austin finds himself in the middle of a murder investigation. Those antagonistic to his ministry continue to find new ways to attempt to rid themselves of

the young idealist. And through it all, the work of the Church goes on. Miracles of work and mercy do occur.

PRUNING THE MAGNOLIA

To be released in the summer of 2007, the third book in the Magnolia Series. Steele Austin's vulnerability increases even further when he uncovers a scandal that will shake First Church to its very foundation. A most unusual pastoral situation cements him in an irrevocable bond with one of his most outspoken antagonists. You won't want to miss this third visit to First Church and Falls City, Georgia.

All of Doctor Maynard's books can be viewed and ordered on his website
WWW.EPISKOPOLS.COM

ACKNOWLEDGEMENTS

I am most grateful to all the people that bought my first novel, _Behind the Magnolia Tree_. I am especially grateful to those of you who wrote me letters, notes, e-mails, or telephoned me with words of encouragement. Many of you have been quite insistent that I continue the story with this sequel. One of my favorite notes read, "_What will keep me up to 4:00 a.m.? I stayed up reading your novel. I laughed and I cried. I could not put it down. It's a real page turner. Now, send me the sequel and send it to me now!_"

It was also quite gratifying to receive notification from book clubs across the country that chose to read and discuss my book. Likewise, several parish Rectors gave the book to their staffs and Vestries to read and discuss.

The list of those who have voluntarily promoted _Behind the Magnolia Tree_ to others is lengthy. I am particularly grateful to Shirley and Dick May of Canyon Lake, Texas; Jaunita Wells of Salina, Kansas; Michael and Carol Evans of Greenville, South Carolina; Clayton and Ginya Trier, and Trudy MacGregor of Houston, Texas; Matthew and Hope Meek of Reno, Nevada, Chris Koonce of Dallas, Texas, and Jim and Jo Ann Marshall of Richardson, Texas. Several of these good folks took the time and effort to write a review of the novel for the online book stores. Again, I am grateful to you.

Encouragement and opportunity to promote my novel has also come from my brothers and sisters in the clergy. I am grateful to Gary Jones and Janet Allen of Richmond, Virginia; Jim Taylor of North Charleston, South Carolina; Timothy Dombeck of Greenville, South Carolina; Laurence Gipson of Houston, Texas; John Goddard of Reno, Nevada; Rick Sanders of Augusta, Georgia; and Robert Certain of Palm Desert, California.

My wife, Nancy, has read and re-read my manuscripts and made multiple suggestions that have greatly improved this work. In a very real way, she has lived in Falls City, Georgia with me. Much of the excellence in this book is due to her many contributions. Sean Cary, my publishing consultant with Booksurge Publishing, has been an invaluable asset. He has been an efficient and effective guide through the entire process. He is a delight to work with.

And last, but not least, I am grateful to each of you that have taken the initiative to venture into Falls City and meet the good folks at historic old First Church. I trust that they have both entertained and frustrated you as much as they have The Reverend Steele Austin.

P.S. If you know Oprah Winfrey, please give her copies of my books. Even if you don't know Oprah or another famous book promoter, thanks for continuing to recommend my books to your family and friends. Word of mouth is the best advertisement an author's work can receive.

This Book Is For Nancy.

FORWARD

There have been two universal responses to the first book in this Magnolia Series. The first response is that most every reader thinks that they know one or more of the characters that reside in Falls City, Georgia. I have literally received e-mails and notes from people coast to coast who believe that they recognize the residents of this fair city as citizens in their own. Let me repeat, you don't know them!

But then again, you just may know someone very much like them. The classic roles of Lay Pope, Keeper of the Treasury, Keeper of the Traditions, and Clergy Antagonist are most likely being played out by a real person in your parish, synagogue, garden club, neighborhood association, country club or community. While the roles may be universal, the people portrayed on these pages are figments of my imagination and creativity.

Mentally moving to Falls City, Georgia and meeting the various folks that live there is a lot like getting to develop multiple personalities. The various members of the community begin to live in my head. I get to listen in on their conversations with one another. The story line unfolds through their interaction. And the beauty for me is that I get to have these multiple personalities reside in my psyche and no one tries to medicate me. To the contrary, I get to record their voices and their stories on paper. A novel is born.

The beautiful thing about a novel is that the reader gets to look inside the various personalities that come to life on its pages. We get to see their hurts, their fears, their secrets. We literally get an emotional MRI of their inner selves. We gain insight into the very things that motivate them to do the things that they do.

Every spiritual person struggles with two crucial components of their journey. These two aspects, summarized by Jesus, are love of God and love of our neighbor. Loving God, who we cannot see, is done with relative ease. Loving the neighbor that we can see is the more difficult struggle. When we sin against God the consequences fall primarily on us and no one else is injured. The repercussions of our sins against our neighbors often ricochet through entire communities. Our faithfulness to God is more often than not a source of holy pride. Homiletical challenges to increase our faithfulness to God are welcome words. More often than not we resist the charge to love our neighbors as we love ourselves. Confronting the consequences of not doing so is one of the most difficult aspects of the soul's work.

This brings us to the second reaction to this storyline as it was first revealed in _Behind the Magnolia Tree_. Some readers have found it difficult to believe that members of a church could be so conflicted. The negative, even cruel, by-products of the parish in conflict are directed at the clergy. This may indeed be one of the darkest secrets in the religious community. Every congregation has two versions of its history. The first version is contained in the narratives known as The Living Room Stories. These are the stories that the congregation loves to repeat. They are the stories that bring back fond memories. They are also the stories that make the congregation look good. They include ministry successes, moments of spiritual renewal, and beloved clergy who have become larger than life itself. They are the stories of the congregation's love for God.

Congregations also have Kitchen Stories. These are the stories that are uttered with hushed voices in the kitchen. These stories mirror the shadow side of the congregation. These are the stories of the congregation in conflict. They mirror the congregation's efforts to love the neighbors that they find unacceptable. Stories of the abuse of the clergy and their mistreatment are interwoven in those conflicts. This is especially true if the clergy person is challenging the members to take a closer look at themselves and include those they find less desirable.

The stories of abused clergy are included in the Kitchen Stories. These whispered stories recount the verbal and/or emotional abuse that was inflicted on a member of the clergy and their families. Invariably they include the names of a handful of parish leaders who had a singular purpose; they wanted the clergy person removed. They wanted the parish to return to its previous comfort zone. Sadly, these leaders are often armed with Bible quotes and an air of arrogant self-righteousness. It is understandable that the faithful would prefer that a novel about the Church eloquently recount our Living Room Stories. They would suggest that Kitchen Stories are best left in the kitchen. I fear the books in this

Magnolia series will disappoint those who delight in recounting Living Room Stories and prefer to whisper the Church's Kitchen Stories.

I've heard it said that a novel is never finished. I find this to be true. I haven't finished this story; I have merely abandoned my characters for the present. I fear that they continue to speak to me and a third book in this Magnolia Series is already taking formation in my mind. In a year or so you'll hear that a third visit to Falls City, Georgia is being released. _Pruning the Magnolia_ will continue to give life to these leading citizens that have earned my admiration and my devotion.

And now, once again, I can hear the church bells ringing in the bell tower at historic old First Church. The congregation is gathering. The choir is lining up behind the processional cross. There is just a hint of incense in the air. The clergy with their robes blowing in the breeze are hurrying to take their places as well. The doors of the church are standing wide open. It's time for us to go in. Welcome back to historic First Church. Let me help you find a seat. We're so glad that you're here.

Happy Reading,
Dennis Maynard
Rancho Mirage, California

CHAPTER 1

The Reverend Rob McBride was getting older. He didn't like it. Stopped at the traffic light, he studied his face in the rearview mirror. His hair was turning gray. He didn't mind that so much as the gray hair that was now streaking his eyebrows. The wrinkles on his face were more visible. He didn't find the worry lines attractive or signs of wisdom, good living, or anything else. He glanced down at his belly hanging over his belt. There was a time when he could give up desserts or skip a meal and lose five pounds. Now he could starve himself and still gain weight. He hated growing older. He longed for his youth. He wanted back all the years that he had given to the Church. He would begin again. He would do something different. He would not waste his youth on ideals that could never become a reality.

The light changed and he pressed down on the accelerator. The car had a delayed reaction before starting to move. He had bought the Ford Taurus six years ago. It was two years old when he bought it. He wished that he had the money to buy a new car, but he hadn't had a raise in salary at St. Mary's in almost five years. The mission parish that he had served for the past twenty-two years was having some hard times. But then again, it had always had hard times. After all, it hadn't even come close to becoming a self-sustaining parish and it didn't appear that was a likely possibility in the foreseeable future.

St. Mary's was started on the south side of Falls City by old First Church; the historic church dominated the two major intersections downtown. If the truth were ever to be told, St. Mary's was started as a polite way to move some of the less desirable Episcopalians out of First Church and into a congregation more to their suiting. The mill had brought in some folks best described as blue-collar. Even though some of them were life-long Episcopalians, they simply didn't fit in with the aristocracy at First Church. So, with the blessing of the Bishop, the Vestry at First Church bought property closer to the houses the mill workers lived in and built them a multi-purpose building to use for worship, education, and fellowship. The Bishop was then called on to "select the volunteers" that would begin this holy work. Of course, the Bishop had discerned that God was calling them to begin this new church so that the Diocese could be expanded and God's Kingdom on earth could grow.

Rob McBride was fresh out of seminary. He was to be ordained at the Cathedral in Savannah. In spite of the sultry day, the Cathedral itself was filled to overflowing as the Bishop ordained three new priests. The air was thick with the smell of incense as he prostrated himself on the floor. The congregation chanted the Veni Creator over him and the other two ordinands. "Come Holy Spirit our souls inspire. Enlighten with celestial fire." The brand new Father McBride was already filled with the Holy Spirit. He was certain that God had called him to the priesthood. He was equally certain that God had great plans for him. Family and friends alike filled the Cathedral, all believing that one day in the future they would be attending yet another ordination for their particular new priest. One day, they were certain their favorite son would be ordained a Bishop.

The Bishop appointed Rob to serve the newly formed congregation of St. Mary's. As Vicar of a mission congregation receiving financial support from the Diocese, Rob would report directly to the Bishop. The Bishop that appointed him to St. Mary's was convinced that Rob would turn it into a thriving, self-supporting parish in just a few short years. He believed success was inevitable. Rob was young, attractive, enthusiastic, and talented. There were a lot of people moving into the neighborhood around the new mission church. It was a winning combination. St. Mary's Mission would become St. Mary's Parish and Rob would be elected the first Rector.

Seventy-five people were at worship on the first Sunday the new congregation gathered. Sixty-one were in church last Sunday. Oh, he had tried. He had read all the books that promised sure-fire formulas for attracting new members to a congregation. He had listened to all the successful Rectors that the Bishop brought to the clergy conferences to inspire and enlighten the troops. He had tried all their recommendations. Greeters at the door on Sunday mornings, nametags, welcome baskets, new member coffees, and door-to-door visitation. He embraced every program that came down the pike, hoping it would be the one to turn them into a mega-church.

He tried the currently popular parish renewal weekend. A large team of enthusiastic lay people from other congregations in the Diocese literally swelled his little church to overflowing. That is, for one Sunday. There were tearful witnesses and rousing music. Then, those who had faithfully supported the congregation through the years were converted yet one more time. The Sunday following the renewal weekend attendance was up a little, but all the visitors had returned home. The following Sunday things were back to the routine.

He then got active in a renewal retreat program housed at the Diocesan Camp. It was a similar format with rousing music and stimulating teachings. But he was never able to transfer the weekend experience back to the parish. There were church growth plans from Africa to England. He tried them all. His faithful members all attended, but as far as attracting hundreds of the unchurched, well, he just kept turning over the same people.

In reality it was difficult to be a small mission in the shadow of First Church. Any of the well-educated and consequently prosperous new members to the community invariably would find their way downtown. After all, it had a grand campus, the worship facility itself was absolutely gorgeous and lined with beautiful stained glass. They even had some Tiffany windows above the altar which tourists from all over the southern states would come to see. The choir was led by paid section leaders and the congregational singing was supported by a well-voiced pipe organ. Instrumentalists from the local college were employed to play for all the big services.

The little electronic organ that the congregation at St. Mary's struggled with each week was exceeded only by the organist. The only organist that Rob could find was the part-time organist at Rose Garden Funeral Home. She wasn't an Episcopalian and struggled with the mass music. Her upbringing was Southern Baptist. She had a way of making the most brilliant composer's work sound like an Irish pub song. The routine hymns sounded like they were more suited for a skating rink. The little volunteer choir of six to eight people at St. Mary's struggled with an anthem each week. There were actually a couple of pretty decent voices in the choir that could offer an occasional solo. But then, there was Mary Stewart. Mary was seventy years of age, rather full-figured, and liked to use her enormous lung power to pilot her soprano vocal chords into a high-pitched warble. At one time, she had sung in the choir at First Church. She left that church, she said, "because she could not stand that new Rector, Misturh Austin." She would literally spit his name and then roll her eyes.

Her voice was shrill and not at all pleasant. Rob actually looked forward to the Sundays that she wasn't present. Mary Stewart believed her gift was indispensable, so she made certain that there were very few Sundays that the choir would have to struggle through without her. What is it about every small church choir? It seems that every one of them is being held captive by a warbling soprano.

Anyone who was anyone attended First Church. If by chance one of Rob's members did get a promotion, say to management level, they would soon leave his little flock and move over to First Church. The same was true of any of his teachers, professors, or entrepreneurs. Just as soon as they made their mark professionally they also outgrew St. Mary's. On those rare occasions when one of his members did get accepted for membership at the Country Club or the all-male Magnolia Club, a transfer to First Church inevitably followed within days.

Things had become even more competitive since Steele Austin had become Rector at First Church. He had opened up the congregation and made it more user-friendly to all types of people. The blue-bloods at First Church didn't like it and Steele was being put through the wringer. Rob felt like Steele was holding his own. Not only were some of the unchurched in Falls City going to take a closer look at The Reverend Austin and his unique style of ministry, but he had also started to make a dent in the Presbyterian, Methodist, and Baptist congregations in town. The Diocesan Journal showed that he presented over one hundred people for membership confirmation last year.

Rob had tried to get out of St. Mary's on several occasions, but something always happened. He just could not figure it out. He would fill out the questionnaires. His references would call him and let him know that they had been contacted and that the various search committees were really excited about his candidacy. He and Esther would go on the interviews. He thought they hit it off with each committee and Vestry that took him through the interview process. On more than one occasion, the chairman of the committee would take them back to the airport and leave them with the assurance that in just a few days they would be receiving the anticipated telephone call. The same phrase was used over and over again; the words still rang in his ears. "Father McBride, if I should call you in a couple of days with a Letter of Call from our Vestry, would you be inclined to accept it?" Over and over again he stated, "With enthusiasm." Repeatedly over the past fifteen years such a telephone call never came. Rob had memorized all the rejection letters. They were basically the same.

> *Dear Father McBride,*
> *We are so thankful that you agreed to be a part of our process. After much prayer, we have discerned that you do not possess the unique gifts that our parish is looking for in a Rector at this time. Please know that you will remain in our prayers as you continue your discernment process. We ask you to join with us in celebrating the new ministry of NN who has agreed to serve as our next Rector.*
> *Best Regards,*
> *Blah, Blah, Blah*

A couple of years ago, a Rector invited Rob to join him as his associate priest up in Atlanta. The two men really hit it off during the interview process. The Rector was excited about having Rob join him and Rob was equally excited about the possibility of the two of them working together. The wives hit it off as well. Esther and Rob returned to Falls City after the last interview, fully prepared for a move to Atlanta. This time the Rector didn't send a letter. He picked up the telephone and called Rob.

A cold shiver ran up Rob's spine as he recalled the telephone conversation. "Rob, I can't call you as my associate. The only thing I can tell you is that your Bishop isn't recommending you. In fact, he is suggesting that you haven't been completely truthful with me." Rob's stomach turned over as he thought about the next comment. "Your Bishop says that he has some information about you that, should it become public, it could cause tremendous embarrassment to me and to this congregation. He would not give me the specifics of the information, but he strongly encouraged me to remove your name from consideration and to continue my search. I am sorry, Rob. I really like you, but I'm not in a position to take such a risk."

At first Rob tried to protest. He assured the Rector that his record was clean. He had never done anything that would put him in a bad light. He simply didn't know what the Bishop was talking about. The only thing he could figure was that someone had slandered him to the Bishop and the Bishop had believed them. The Rector again apologized, but he told Rob that without a positive recommendation from his Bishop, he just could not proceed.

Rob made an appointment with the Bishop. He began by expressing his disappointment that he had not been successful with any of his searches for a new position. He asked the Bishop if he had any thoughts as to why he had been so systematically rejected for every new position that he considered. The Bishop tried to reassure Rob that he was an excellent priest and that most likely the reason that he had been unsuccessful in his searches was because God wanted him to remain at St. Mary's. "You're doing a wonderful job there," Bishop Peterson hummed. "The people love you and I love having you there. God must still have more work for you to do. Why don't you just focus all of your energy on St. Mary's? Let's see if you can't present her as a self-supporting congregation at the next Diocesan Convention."

Rob didn't ask the Bishop specifically about his comments to the Rector in Atlanta. He had heard the other clergy talk about Rufus Petersen. He knew that he wasn't a man to be trusted. He also knew that the only ideas he really liked were his own. It was at this point that Rob turned to Steele Austin. He needed a pastor. He needed a confidante. He thought that he might be able to find both in Steele.

They met for coffee in a café adjacent to the local drugstore. Steele Austin wasn't as tall as Rob thought he might be. In fact, they were about the same height. Steele might even be a little shorter than Rob except for the notorious western boots that he was wearing. Rob had certainly heard the uproar about The Reverend Mister Austin's choice in clothing. Black clerical shirt, no jacket, blue jeans, and cowboy boots made up this priest's signature clothing. Not at all what would be expected of the Rector of such a prestigious parish in the Diocese. Most Rectors of large, prestigious parishes Rob had known wore custom-made clerical shirts with French cuffs, the finest suits that money could buy without being ostentatious, and black shoes. Never, oh never, would any of them be seen in jeans and boots.

Steele's skin was a little darker than what Rob had expected. He had been told that he had some Indian blood, but Rob thought at first he just sported a tan well. On closer examination he could see the features that in fact were Steele Austin's heritage.

Rob needed to talk so he began pouring his heart out to Steele soon after the waitress had poured their coffee. He told him about the revelation the Rector in Atlanta had given him. He told him about his own conversation with Bishop Petersen. His frustrations poured out. He felt trapped in his job. He was never going to get out of St. Mary's if Rufus Petersen had anything to say about it. He was strapped for money. His wife Esther helped as a librarian at the local community college. They only had one son. He was in the University of Georgia. He had wanted to go to Vanderbilt, but they simply couldn't afford to send him there, even with financial aid.

Rob felt himself on the verge of tears as he opened his grief to Steele. "I know that Esther is unhappy. She keeps up a good front, but she has to buy all of her clothes at the bargain basement and at the thrift house. She makes some of her things. She never goes to the hairdresser or gets a manicure. We seldom can go out to dinner. When we do go to a movie it has to be a matinee and we smuggle in our own popcorn and drinks. We haven't been on a real vacation in ten years. The closest we have come to any recreation is the annual clergy conference, but that's held at the Diocesan Camp. That camp doesn't even come close to being a second rate hotel."

As he talked, the depth of Rob's depression became even more evident. "Hell, Steele, we don't even own the house that we have lived in for the past twenty-two years. It belongs to the church. If I am ever able to retire, we will be homeless and unable to do much more than rent a cheap apartment somewhere. I haven't had a raise in five years." Rob took a long sip of his coffee while he studied the face of the man he had taken into his confidence. Steele was looking back at him. He didn't break eye contact. He simply reached across the table and put his hand on Rob's arm. "You said Esther was unhappy."

Rob nodded. "She keeps up a good front, but there's not much to smile about. We had wanted to have more children, but we simply could not afford it. We could barely take care of one child. I know that Esther is really hurt that we couldn't afford to have at least one more child...

maybe a daughter. She works. I work. I've even thought about getting an early morning paper route to help with the finances."

Rob sat back in his seat and rubbed his moist eyes. We each try to share the cooking and housework. She reads at night and I watch television or read. There's no passion between us anymore. I still care for her, don't get me wrong. There's just no passion. Sex is actually more work than it's worth. I would just as soon go to sleep. It's just not worth it. I guess she feels the same way because she doesn't complain. I think she's just as depressed as I am. We really aren't living like a husband and wife in love. We live more like roommates caught in a trap that neither one of us can escape. Although..."

Steele waited in silence. Then he encouraged Rob, "Go on."

"Esther is still an attractive woman. I have caught her flirting with other men."

"Are you sure she's flirting?"

"Now you sound like her. She says she's just being friendly, but Steele, I know flirting when I see it."

Rob became silent again as though lost in his thoughts. He stared out the window as words rolled out of him as though he had never considered them before. "She's very secretive. She doesn't like sharing what she does each day. She gets defensive if I ask her. She says she's simply going to do the things that are on her list."

Again, Rob became silent. He looked back at Steele. "I'm going to say something to you that I've never said to another person. In fact, I've resisted acknowledging these feelings to myself." Rob swallowed hard. His hands started shaking. He wrapped them around his coffee cup. A tear rolled down his cheek. "Sometimes... sometimes... I feel it down here in my guts..."

"Yes, Rob, go on. You're in a safe place."

"Steele, sometimes I get the feeling that there is someone else in my marriage. I mean, add these feelings in my gut to her continual flirting and hell, it's like she wants to have sex with every man she meets except me."

"Have you talked to her about it?"

Rob signaled the waitress for a refill of his coffee. "Yeah, I've been pretty confrontational on a couple of occasions. She just laughs it off and tells me it's all in my head. She says I'm just being ridiculous."

Rob again stared out the window. "Now with no hope of getting out of St. Mary's, it's like I have come to a dead-end. My job is going nowhere and my marriage is dead or at least terminally ill. I'm just so lonely. I feel trapped in a loveless marriage and a dead-end job."

Steele waited quietly until Rob had vented all his frustrations. "Rob, I don't know what I can do to help you find a new position. I only know one other Bishop and I have reason to believe that he has Rufus Petersen's number. With your permission I'll share your story with him. He may or may not have a position for you in his Diocese, but I know that he won't let Rufus Petersen stand in his way when it comes to attracting good priests. I also know that all of those guys have their cronies. Maybe he can put in a good word for you with one of the other Bishops in his particular circle. I don't think that Peterson is the most respected purple shirt in the House of Bishops anyway.

As for you and Esther, I think you're in a very dangerous place. You need to talk. You need to do some things to reignite your love for each other. You're unhappy. She's unhappy. The tragic road you're on is a case-study right out of any marriage handbook on dysfunctional relationships. Don't let that happen. But most of all, Rob, I'm worried about you. Loneliness is the most desperate of all feelings. Please don't do anything stupid until we can figure all of this out."

Rob nodded his agreement. "I know that you're right. I'm afraid it's gotten to the point that I don't care enough to try anymore."

Steele and Rob stood. Steele patted Rob on the back, "Don't lose hope. Don't stop trying. Together, we can figure something out."

Rob asked Steele if he wanted to see St. Mary's. Steele nodded and accepted Rob's invitation to ride with him over to the church. They took a tour. It was brief. St. Mary's consisted of one multi-purpose building. Steele spotted the Bishop's throne sitting in the tiny sanctuary. He chuckled that the Bishop's chair was almost bigger than the altar. Rob told him that Bishop Petersen had picked out the chair himself and had it delivered to the church.

They stood silently before the altar. Steele could tell that Rob was on the verge of breaking. "Steele, what am I going to do? I'll never get out of this place. Rufus Petersen is going to block every opportunity that presents itself. I mean, there are some good people here at St. Mary's and they have hung in here with me, but this little mission has stabilized. It's never going to be any more than it is right now. Deep down, I think the people here blame me."

Rob's chin began to quiver. "And my marriage, Steele, I think it's over. I really think it's over for Esther. I think she stopped loving me a long time ago." Rob sat down on the altar step. Steele sat next to him. "I'm trapped. I feel like I'm in a deep dark hole and there's no way for me to get out. I really think I'm dying down here."

Steele put his arm around Rob's shoulder. "You're depressed, Rob, that's clear. I can understand why you feel the way you do, but Rob, you've got to promise me that you're not going to do anything stupid. Promise me that you won't hurt yourself. Promise me that you won't do anything to hurt Esther. Do you promise?"

Rob wiped his eyes, "I promise."

"Rob, I just need you to work with me. I want to meet Esther. Let's just see if we can't get the two of you some help. Rob, God isn't going to leave you in that hole."

"I really hope you're right." Rob looked deep into Steele's eyes. "My friend, I just don't know how much more I can take."

CHAPTER 2

Steele Austin walked with a decided determination down the hallway to the parlor. There was one thing that he now knew for certain. He was absolutely exhausted with the turmoil that the Altar Guild was causing in his life. He was tired of impromptu Altar Guild meetings. He refused to be treated like a sixth grader being summoned to the principal's office for throwing spit balls in math class. He knew that the ladies who had been chosen to serve on the Altar Guild were the crème de la crème of Falls City. Not only did they run the Debutante Society, the Cotillion, the Women's Club, and the Junior League, but they were silent partners in control of every business enterprise in the city and most of the state of Georgia. Their husbands were in charge, but these women were in control. Nevertheless, he'd had enough. Boundaries had to be set.

He entered the finely appointed parlor. The first thing that he noticed was that it had been completely redecorated. He couldn't help himself. He blurted, "When was the parlor redecorated? I don't recall the Vestry authorizing any funds for that purpose. What happened to all of the old furniture? Ladies, this must have cost a fortune. Just look at that rug." Steele's gaze was fixed on a large oriental rug. He knew something about the price of such rugs. He was looking at thousands of dollars on the floor of a room that traditionally was used only on occasion by the ladies here present.

"Misturh Austin," Steele turned his head toward the sound of the all too familiar voice. It was Mrs. Gordon Smythe. She had been the directress of the Altar Guild for three decades. One thing was certain. She would be directress until the day she was buried in the family plot in the churchyard outside Steele's office window. No one in this room or any heir apparent on the horizon would dare challenge her for the title. "Misturh Austin, I need you to come over here and sit down next to me."

"Mrs. Smythe," Steele remained standing at the entrance to the room. "Mrs. Smythe, I asked a question. Would you be so kind as to inform your Rector on the facts surrounding this redecoration?"

"Well, all right." Clearly she was disgusted with him already. "There is no need for you to concern yourself with such trivial matters. We all know just how busy you are and that there are many demands on your time. We didn't bother you with our decorating project because no church funds were used. We used Altar Guild money for our little project. All of us felt that the parlor was getting a bit shabby and it just wasn't suitable any longer for us to use as a place for our meetings."

Steele felt his face growing red. "Just a couple of corrections, Mrs. Smythe. The Altar Guild money is church money. You're a part of the church. What you have belongs to the church. And second, as your Rector, I believe I should be informed when the Altar Guild is contemplating spending thousands of dollars redecorating a room that is used only once or twice a month by a small segment of this parish. I think you should have also gotten the consent of the Vestry for such a project."

Laughter rose up in the room. Steele could feel his anger boiling. Another familiar voice interrupted the laughter. "Ladies, ladies," it was Mrs. Howard Dexter. Steele looked over at the woman who was doing all she could to bring her own laughter under control. She was so short her feet dangled off her seat, just barely touching the floor. She was always overly made up. Steele thought she would make a great advertisement for a clown college. Her lips were painted bright red and she had far too much rouge on her cheeks. Her two front teeth protruded over her bottom lip. This caused her to speak with a bit of a lisp. Every time Steele saw her, she reminded him of the beaver on the old Ipana toothpaste commercials. "Ladies, please," she continued. "Misturh Austin, most of the men on the Vestry are married to one of the ladies in this room. Each of them heard of our decision as they were intended to — over breakfast."

"Misturh Austin," it was Mrs. Smythe again. "Please come and sit down. We have several things to discuss with you."

Steele didn't know whether he was more angry or more humiliated, but he knew he wasn't going to sit down. "No, Mrs. Smythe, I'll not be sitting down. As you stated earlier, I am a very busy man. I didn't see this meeting on the parish calendar so I didn't place it on my own. I suggest that in the future if you want to meet with me, you ask my secretary if the meeting time is convenient for me. If the time is available, she will place it on my calendar and the calendar of the parish."

"But Misturh Austin, we just need to ask you a couple of questions that carry some urgency. Can't you spare us just a minute of your time?" Mrs. Smythe wasn't pleading, but at least she was making some attempt at being courteous.

"Okay, but I prefer to stand because my answers will be brief." Steele placed his hands on his hips. He knew that the stance communicated defiance, but that is exactly what he felt.

Mrs. Smythe continued, "We are quite concerned that the Robert E. Lee Corporal is missing. Would you know anything about that?"

"What on earth is the Robert E. Lee Corporal?"

"Well, just prior to the War of Northern Aggression, General Lee attended worship in this church and he made his communion here. The Rector at the time instructed that the altar cloth on which the General's communion was blessed be designated as the Robert E. Lee Corporal. He further instructed that it be withdrawn from customary use and utilized only on very special occasions. And that has been our practice for well over a century."

"Frankly, Mrs. Smythe, I've never heard that story and further didn't even know that the Robert E. Lee Corporal existed."

Mrs. Howard Dexter spurted, "Perhaps if you could refrain from some of your more unusual activities in Falls City and devote some time to learning the traditions of this parish you would have heard of this blessed cloth."

Steele didn't look at her or even acknowledge that he heard her comment. "I would think that anything as valuable as the Robert E. Lee Corporal would be kept in the parish vault. If it's not in the vault, perhaps in the parish safe deposit box in your husband's bank, Mrs. Dexter. Surely none of you would have left it lying around for just anyone to pick up. Have you looked in all the places that we keep the other parish valuables?"

There was an uncomfortable silence in the room. After some shifting in their chairs and some embarrassed glances at one another, Mrs. Howard Dexter broke the silence. "My yard man tells me that Crazy Vera was down at the beer bar crying about her cat being buried in the churchyard. She said that you wrapped it in a white cloth before burying it."

"Yes, I did bury Vera's cat. I wrapped it in an old cloth that I found in the bottom drawer of the Sacristy. It could not have been the Robert E. Lee Corporal because I know that you ladies are very serious about your responsibilities. You would never have left anything that valuable just lying around in a musty drawer. The cloth I wrapped Vera's cat in looked more like an old dish towel needing to be discarded. No, I know that no member of the First Church Altar Guild would treat such a valuable altar cloth in that manner."

Again, there was an uncomfortable silence in the room. Steele observed some sheepish looks quickly exchanged between several of the women. Again, it was Mrs. Howard Dexter that broke the silence. "Misturh Austin, we on the Altar Guild have yet one more matter to discuss with you. You reported in the parish newsletter that you have employed a new priest. I'm sure that all of us can appreciate your need for assistance with your many duties, but Misturh Austin, there is a dreadful rumor going about the community. Personally, I have reason to believe that it was started over at the Presbyterian Church; nevertheless, the gossip is that you have hired a *Negara* priest to work with you here at First Church. Please, reassure us that it's only a rumor and contains no substance whatsoever."

"Yes, Mrs. Dexter, part of what you have heard is untrue."

"Oh what a relief," she began to fan herself with her hand. I was so afraid that there just might be some truth to that ugly rumor. Now I'm convinced that it was started over at the Presbyterian Church. Some of those people are so envious of our good fortune." There was a general murmur of agreement around the room.

"No, ladies," Steele held up his hand as he interrupted them. "I haven't called a Negro priest to work with us, but I have called an African American priest who is very well qualified for the ministry we have mutually agreed upon."

"Oh, no! You've got to be kidding. Please, please tell us you're not serious." Mrs. Gordon Smythe came straight up out of her chair. She began waving her finger at Steele. "This parish has suffered through a lot of your silliness, but I assure you, Misturh Austin, we will not tolerate this bit of nonsense. Just where do you plan to get the money? I know the Vestry hasn't agreed to fund this position. Ladies, I'm absolutely speechless." She sat down in her chair with an exasperated look on her face. Clearly everyone in the room was upset. Every woman present was shaking her head and murmuring phrases, while not profane, did include some most unladylike words.

Again, Mrs. Howard Dexter rose to the occasion. "I'm here to tell you right now that none of us will care for this African priest, as you choose to call him. I'll not be left in the church alone with him. Misturh Austin, no member of the Altar Guild will feel safe. Ladies, can any of you imagine having to wash his vestments for him or even helping him get vested?" Again, there were murmurs and nods of agreement.

"Now listen to me, ladies," Steele once again fought to keep his anger under control, but he knew his voice was shaking. "Father Drummond is a well-educated priest of our Church. He has served with distinction on the Eastern Seaboard. We should count ourselves fortunate to have him come to First Church."

"Fortunate?" Mrs. Dexter interrupted. "You simply have to be beside yourself. You're not thinking clearly about this subject, Misturh Austin. Let us help you."

"No, Mrs. Dexter, let me help you." Steele waited until he had everyone's attention. "Listen to Father Drummond's qualifications. Actually, I should call him Doctor Drummond. He has a Ph. D. from Princeton School of Theology. He did his undergraduate work at the University of Virginia and his Master's Degree is from Andover Newton. He served on the staff of the National Cathedral in Washington D.C. and most recently at a very large and prestigious parish in Atlanta."

Mrs. Smythe was clearly exhausted with the entire subject. "Misturh Austin, you aren't listening to us. We aren't arguing with his credentials or his ordination. Our displeasure is with his color. We have no *Negara* members so we don't need a *Negara* priest."

Steele was exhausted. "Ladies, I have called Doctor Drummond to this parish and he has accepted. He will be overseeing the Soup Kitchen and several other outreach projects I have in mind for the poor in this community. His ministry will not cost the parish one cent. I'm going to use the income from the endowment that Chadsworth Alexander left to the Rector's discretion."

"Does Almeda Alexander know about your scheme?" Mrs. Dexter shouted at Steele.

Steele looked around the room. Almeda was conspicuously absent. "No, I've not discussed it with her as yet. Almeda is out of the state right now, but I have an appointment with her just as soon as she returns. I'll be discussing Doctor Drummond with her as a courtesy and out of respect for her husband's memory. As you know, ladies, the income from that endowment stipulates that it can be used at the Rector's sole discretion. I am accountable only to the auditors in Atlanta." Steele took a deep breath. Clearly, he wasn't going to change their minds. "Ladies, Doctor Drummond will share his first Sunday with us in one week. I pray that you'll open your hearts and your homes to him and to his ministry."

"Is he married? Does he have a family?" Mrs. Dexter spit the words at Steele. Steele noticed that she had lipstick on her two front teeth, but then if his memory served him correctly, she always had lipstick on her teeth. He wondered if anyone had ever told her.

"No, Doctor Drummond is a widower. He hasn't remarried."

"What are you saying, Misturh Austin?" Mrs. Gordon Smythe came up out of her chair again. "No single woman in this parish will be safe. How dare you bring a single *Negara* man into this parish? You have put every woman in this parish in harm's way, but particularly our single women. Just what has gotten into you? You know how *Negara* men are."

"No, Mrs. Smythe, I don't have a clue as to what you're talking about."

"Well, then spend some time with our husbands. They'll tell you how they have to protect their wives and daughters. Or better yet, just pick up a copy of the newspaper or watch the nightly news. You'll see who the rapists and murderers are."

Steele desperately wanted to respond to her comments, but decided just to bring the entire issue to a close. "Doctor Drummond is a priest of this Church. He has been for over twenty-five years. He is a man of mature years and has a distinguished record of ministry."

"Are you trying to tell us that this Negara priest is a Ho-mo-SEX-u-All?" Mrs. Dexter stood with her hands on her hips. "Now we have to worry about our acolytes."

Steele felt his face grow hotter than he ever remembered in his entire life. His eyes became teary. His throat was quivering and his chest was ready to explode with anger. He stood silent for a long time listening to the other ladies run every nightmare scenario that could be imagined. After several minutes devoted totally to regaining his composure, Steele spoke again. "Doctor Drummond is a priest of mature years. He is a very distinguished gentleman. I haven't inquired as to his sexual orientation nor do I plan to do so. Ladies, I regret that there's nothing I can say to persuade you to open your hearts and minds to him. I can only pray that in time, as you get to know him, you'll see Christ at work in him and in his ministry."

Again, Steele stood silent and made eye contact with every woman in the room. Then he turned to Mrs. Smythe and addressed his closing comments to her. "In the future, when you schedule meetings of the Altar Guild, please clear the date and time with my secretary. Then send me, in writing, a proposed agenda listing the topics you wish to have covered at the meeting. It will be my intention to remove from the agenda any items that are unrelated to the work of the Altar Guild. I will then have my office mail out the notice of the meeting along with an agenda listing the appropriate items for review or decision."

"We have never done it that way before. Our previous Rector always found time for us."

"I'm not your previous Rector. I am your current Rector. I will find time for you. I will find time to be your pastor. I will find time to be your teacher. I will find time to be your Rector and assist you with the ministry of this Guild. I will not, however, be summoned, ambushed, or have decisions questioned that are totally unrelated to the work of the Altar Guild." Steele didn't blink. He gave Mrs. Smythe a determined look.

"But," she started.

Steele put his hand up and turned toward the door. "No buts, ladies. I expect you to clear your meeting times with my secretary and to send me a proposed agenda. Good day, ladies. God bless each of you."

With that Steele walked out the door and down the hallway toward his office. He was torn between anger and laughter. He knew that this would not be the final word on the subject. He had a Vestry meeting tomorrow night. He knew that he would have to go through this one more time. The face of Horace Drummond entered his mind. "Oh God," Steele prayed. "I hope I've not done that dear man a disservice by bringing him to this parish." For the first time, Steele wondered if he shouldn't reconsider his decision. This time his idealism would not only get him and his family in trouble. This time he just might be risking the career of a brother priest.

CHAPTER 3

The delegation from Falls City has just arrived. I have them cooling their heels out in the waiting room."

Bishop Rufus Petersen looked up from the novel he was reading. He loved a good story filled with all the horrors of war. The one that he was currently reading took place during the Second World War. It included all the intrigue that goes with spying behind enemy lines. The danger and brutality had captivated him. He was sitting in the crimson wing-back chair that he had placed next to a big window in his office. His feet were resting on the footstool. The combination of crimson furniture and purple carpet gave his office the look of Roman Royalty. In fact, a Roman Emperor would be envious of the office of Rufus Petersen. He was pleased with his surroundings. He really didn't want to be disturbed, but he had been anticipating these visitors.

"I'm telling you, Bishop, this group is up to no good. I think that you should send them back to Falls City with their tails between their legs."

His secretary was pointing her finger at him. He rose from his chair. "And I don't pay you to have an opinion about the people who want to see me." The Bishop reached for his white clerical collar lying on the side table. He'd removed it so that he could be more comfortable while he was reading. He put it around his neck and attached it with the pearl collar buttons on his purple shirt.

"Now, Bishop, you and I both know that Father Austin and the good people at First Church have been through enough. That group of vigilantes out there isn't here to do him any favors."

Bishop Petersen shot her a disapproving look. "Your opinion doesn't count. You're a secretary. I'm the Bishop. Please try to keep our roles straight. Now, go get my guests and bring them in here. And then, make a fresh pot of coffee and bring it in here as well."

She stared at him for a moment, but he continued to ignore her as he put his suit jacket on and adjusted his pectoral cross. She shrugged her shoulders and turned to walk toward the door. "If you ask me, it just ain't right that you keep listening to the malcontents down there at First Church."

Those words hit his hot button. He shouted at her, "No one asked you. Now do as I have told you."

"Bishop Petersen, it's so good of you to take the time out of your busy schedule to see us." Ned Boone extended his long, skinny arm and bony hand to shake that of the Bishop. "I believe that you know Henry Mudd. Henry is the Junior Warden in our congregation. And, of course, you're well acquainted with Colonel Mitchell. Colonel Mitchell is in charge of our ushers at First Church and has been for over thirty years."

"Yes, yes, welcome. It's so good to see all of you." The Bishop gestured for the men to take seats opposite his desk. He walked to the other side of his desk and sat in the large purple desk chair. "If memory serves me right, Colonel Mitchell, you've been a delegate to Diocesan Convention for just about as many years as you've been in charge of the ushers. Isn't that about correct?"

Colonel Mitchell nodded, "Yes sir, I've been a delegate to Diocesan Convention every year but one for the past twenty-eight years. There was one year that I had to have my gall bladder removed. I was so distressed that my illness kept me from serving my church and you, Bishop. But that was just for one year and you all seemed to do just fine without me."

"Well, you were missed and I just hope that won't happen again." Rufus Petersen beamed. "I know that I can always count on your vote to help me with my programs. I want you to know that I appreciate it."

"Don't mention it, Bishop. I'm just grateful that I can play some small part in the life of our Diocese."

The Bishop turned his gaze to Henry Mudd. "And, Henry, you've just got to catch me up on your beautiful wife and daughters. Are they all well and happy?"

Nodding, Henry Mudd smiled, "Thank you for asking, Bishop. My girls will all be pleased to know that you asked about them. My wife is doing quite well. Of course, she stays very active with her church work, the girls' school activities, and her many community service responsibilities."

"Well, please do give her my regards and hug your sweet little daughters for me. Tell them that the hug is from their Bishop. You might also tell them that I said that it was okay for their Bishop to hug them, but they're not to let any little boys do so."

His comment was followed by some polite laughter that was interrupted by his secretary. "Knock, knock, the Bishop requested that I bring you some freshly brewed coffee." She entered, carrying a large silver tray with a silver coffee service on it and four china cups with saucers. The cups had the Bishop's seal stamped on them in gold.

Colonel Mitchell stood to take the tray from her. Bishop Petersen motioned for him to sit back down, "She can handle it, Colonel. Keep your seat."

"Oh, it's not all that heavy. I'll just put it here on the desk. Now, I need to warn you before I pour you a cup that it's very hot." She continued to pour each of them a cup of coffee and hand it to them. "I brought out some extra sugar. I know that all of you men will want to sweeten up..."

"That will be all." The Bishop interrupted her and gave her a stern look. She returned the look. When she got to the door, she once again turned and waved her finger at the Bishop. He increased the severity of his look and waved for her to shut the door.

"You'll just have to excuse my secretary, gentlemen. I'd fire her, but I'm afraid I would get hit with a racial discrimination suit."

Ned Boone's neck stretched up over his collar and bowtie. "I have to confess, Bishop. I was surprised to see that you had a black woman as your secretary."

Bishop Petersen lifted both his hands from his desk, "Political correctness. It's all about political correctness. Even here in the South, we've got to try to keep up."

The four men sat in silence sipping their coffee. The Bishop broke the silence, "If I recall correctly it was you, Ned, that called for this appointment. What can I do for you?"

Ned put his coffee cup and saucer on the Bishop's desk. "Right Reverend, Sir, I trust that you'll understand that we only have the best interest of the church at heart. What we're here to discuss with you is very painful for all of us. None of us are here by choice. But Bishop, we just can't sit back and watch our beloved parish suffer any longer."

"If I could add something," Henry Mudd reached into the briefcase sitting on his lap and brought out a folder. "In this folder are the names of all the people in our parish that have talked to one of the three of us. They share our concern for First Church. We speak on their behalf. Would you like to see the list, Bishop?"

"No, no, that won't be necessary." Bishop Petersen smiled. He knew what was coming and he was enjoying it. "Let's just say that I recognize that the three of you are the voice of many others."

"Thank you, Bishop. As you might guess, we're concerned for the future of our parish. Frankly, Bishop, I just don't think that we can survive another year under the leadership of our current Rector. He's absolutely destroying our congregation. I can't tell you the number of our long-time faithful members who simply don't attend services anymore."

"But the parochial report showed that attendance at First Church is growing."

"If I could speak to that issue, Bishop?" Colonel Mitchell twisted uncomfortably in his chair. "I usher every Sunday and as you know, the ushers are responsible for recording the attendance at worship. Now, it's true that we have a lot of visitors and that certainly contributes to the increase in attendance being reported. But, sir, it's the faithful members who've been at First Church for years that are not in attendance."

Ned joined in. "I can name several of our old members that simply aren't in attendance any longer. There's the Carters, the Bartletts, the Bradleys, the Mortons...

Colonel Mitchell interrupted, "The Mortons joined the Presbyterian Church, didn't they, Ned?"

"No," Ned shook his head. A look of disgust returned to his face. "I saw Bill Morton at Sam's Coffee Shop last week. He told me that they were attending the Presbyterian Church, but they have no intention of joining. They're just going there until First Church gets rid of its current Rector. Once he's gone, they'll return."

The Colonel continued, "I tell you, Bishop, it's just not the same. Hell, the faces of the faithful members of our parish that have been the stalwarts of our congregation for decades just aren't there anymore. They simply can't stand this sorry excuse for a Rector. It just breaks my heart."

The Bishop nodded, "I have to agree. I know all those people that you mentioned. It grieves me to think that they can't be comfortable in their own parish."

"Pledges!" Henry Mudd blurted. "We also need to tell you about the pledges." Once again he was shuffling through his briefcase in search of a folder. "It's true that the parish report to the Diocese will show that we have an increase in giving, but that's not the total picture. I have a list of people here who have been members of our parish for generations who no longer include First Church in their charitable giving." He put the folder on the Bishop's desk. The Bishop opened it.

"This is very distressing." The Bishop shook his head. He then looked at each of the men and gave them a distraught look. "I've known some of the people on this list most of my life. They've been the glue that's held First Church together. And now they don't support the parish financially. Is that what you're telling me?"

They all three nodded and spoke in unison, "Yes, Bishop."

The Bishop closed the folder. He turned in his chair to look out the window. This was one of his favorite meeting techniques. He hoped it would communicate to the observers that he was in prayerful reflection. Rufus Petersen wanted to be known as a man of prayer. He wanted to be remembered as a great spiritual leader. He put his hands on his chest and began thumping his fingers gently together as though he were lost in deep thought. He turned back to look at the men. The Bishop put his hands on his stomach. He sat silently tapping the Episcopal Ring that he was wearing with the fingers of his other hand. He wanted to make sure that his visitors had noticed this symbol of his authority. Then again, it would be hard for anyone to miss. Rufus Petersen had personally designed the ring that was placed on his finger at his ordination as a Bishop. It was every bit as large as the hand of a newborn baby. Once he was satisfied that all present had admired his ring, he asked the question that he knew they wanted to hear. "What do you propose that we do? How can we fix this?"

Ned Boone stood and began pacing the floor. "I think better if I can stand."

"Go ahead."

"Thank you, Bishop." Ned stopped to look at the pictures of the Bishop's service of ordination hanging on the wall. "If we didn't have you as our Bishop, I just don't know what we would do. I just thank God that you're our Bishop. We have complete confidence in your leadership."

Bishop Petersen smiled broadly and then blushed slightly. "Thank you."

Ned stopped to look at him. "It's not our intention to put you in a difficult situation, Bishop. We just have to do something about the Rector and we need your help and guidance."

"I know. I don't have to remind you that I wasn't happy when you called him. I thought that there were plenty of other good candidates out there. We had a couple of men right here in this Diocese that I recommended. I had my reservations about Steele Austin the minute I saw his name cross my desk. I'd already heard some things about him that were not very favorable."

"That's why we're so grateful to have you as our Bishop. You're a leader that knows how to get things done." Henry Mudd poured himself another cup of coffee. "May we also remind you, Bishop, that none of us were on the Vestry that employed the current Rector?"

The Bishop turned his chair to once again look out the window. After a minute, he turned back to face the men. "Well, this won't be the first time that the solid folks in a parish have had to correct a mistake made by a Vestry and I don't guess it'll be the last. Now, what is it you want me to do?"

"Steele Austin has to go." Ned Boone was growing weary of all the politeness. "He needs to be removed as Rector and yesterday wasn't too soon to get it done."

"Do you have grounds for removal?"

Ned Boone was confused. "Do you have to have grounds for termination? I mean, you're the Bishop. I understand that he works for you. We want you to fire him. The three of us, along with all the other faithful members of First Church, will support you."

"Well, Ned, it's just not that simple. In order for a Bishop to remove a Rector, you've got to have grounds."

"Like what?"

"Oh, clergy are most vulnerable to rumors around sex and money. Heresy is just a little more difficult to make stick. So the most common attacks on priests involve the first two things I mentioned." They all sat silent for a minute. Then the Bishop continued, "Ned, Henry, Colonel, we've gone through all this with your Rector once before. Rumors and allegations were reported, investigated, and none were substantiated. I just think you're going to have to try another tactic."

"What do you suggest?"

"Oh, I think the three of you are smart enough to figure that one out."

The three men looked at each other. "We were really hoping you could help us. Isn't there anything you can suggest?"

The Bishop smiled sheepishly. "Do any of you remember when ol' Bob Frank left Saint Joseph's Parish here in Savannah?"

Colonel Mitchell chuckled, "I sure do. There were a number of rumors floating around that departure."

"Exactly," the Bishop rubbed his hands together. "The leaders of that congregation were in a situation very much like yours. They were unhappy with his leadership, but they didn't have grounds for getting rid of him."

"So what did they do?" Ned Boone was listening intently.

"Well, they simply wore him down. They just stayed on his back like fleas on a junkyard dog. They never let up. His every move was questioned. His every word was critiqued. His leadership style was evaluated. His personality flaws were magnified. And then, of course, there were rumors."

"What kind of rumors?" A plan was beginning to formulate in Ned Boone's mind.

"Oh, you know the kind. Use your imagination."

"Were any of them true?"

The Bishop chuckled. "They were rumors. They don't have to be true. They don't even have to originate with you. You can say you're just repeating what you've heard."

Colonel Mitchell stood, "Gentlemen, I want to be rid of Steele Austin as much as any of you, but I just don't know if I can go along with destroying a man's priesthood. If we follow through with all of this then that's exactly what we're going to do. There just has to be another way."

"Sit back down, Colonel." The Bishop motioned for him to be seated. "No one wants to destroy Austin, but we've just got to get through to him. I think that you men have evaluated the situation correctly. If First Church is to return to its former greatness, he has to go. I believe that you can put some things into play that will frustrate him. Hopefully, he will become so frustrated he will leave on his own accord. You'll need only to receive his letter of resignation."

Colonel Mitchell resumed his seat. "Well, that's something I could live with. It would be best for everyone if it was his decision to leave."

"Exactly, and you only have to move things around so that he will decide to leave."

"He has a lot of supporters." The reservations were still evident in Colonel Mitchell's voice. "If there is any hint that we are forcing him out it will only further divide the congregation. How will we put the congregation back together? I already have people who won't speak to me at church. They've labeled me as anti-Austin."

"Look, Colonel. The reason that your parish is divided right now is sitting in the Rector's office. Remove the problem and the people won't have anything to fight about. There won't be a split in your parish between the pro-Austin group and the anti-Austin group. Remove Austin and the groups disintegrate. Your parish will return to normal. You'll be one big happy family again."

"Oh, I don't know if it's going to be that easy."

The Bishop leaned back in his chair and put his hands behind his head. "A few minutes ago we were talking about Saint Joseph's. Once that Rector left, I went in there and had a healing service for the congregation. Everyone reconciled. They called a new Rector and everything is just fine now."

"Oh, I was told that a lot of people left that parish after the last Rector resigned. I know for a fact that a lot of them left because they felt like there was a group that forced him out." Colonel Mitchell lowered his voice. He didn't resume eye contact with the Bishop, but looked down at the floor. "And Bishop, at the banquet at the last Diocesan Convention I was sitting with some of the people from Saint Joseph's and they were telling me that they weren't too thrilled with their new guy. In fact, if my memory is correct, that parish has complained about every Rector they've had. I think they treated more than one of their priests pretty severely."

The Bishop chuckled uncomfortably. "I think there's a group in every parish that will find something wrong with any Rector. I'm convinced some of them would complain if Jesus Himself were their Rector. They would probably say that He shines too brightly at the altar."

The men chuckled nervously. Then Colonel Mitchell continued. "You may be right. I think a service of healing and reconciliation would be a good thing to do once the Rector leaves. It just might do the trick. You can include me on any plan to encourage him to move on. I know that's the best thing for First Church and in my heart I really believe that it would be the best thing for him as well."

The Bishop stood and began shaking each of their hands as they stood in turn. "Then, we all are in agreement. You know what you have to do. Bring me his letter of resignation and I'll sign off on it."

When the Bishop came to Colonel Mitchell he shook his hand, but the Colonel didn't make eye contact with the Bishop. The Bishop put both of his hands on his shoulders. The Colonel looked at him. "Everything is going to be just fine. You're only doing what's best for First Church. And you're right. This is also what's best for Steele Austin."

The Colonel's lower lip began to quiver. The Bishop sensed that he was on the verge of tears. "Gentlemen, before you go, let's have a prayer together." The three men knelt on the floor in front of the Bishop. Bishop Petersen pontificated, "Strengthen these men for the work and ministry that you've called them to do. Keep them ever mindful of the sacrifices that they must make for the church that they love. And now, send them forth with the assurance that this is Your will and Your plan for their parish." Bishop Petersen then made the sign of the cross on each of his new warrior's foreheads and blessed them.

CHAPTER 4

Mrs. Almeda Alexander studied the old magnolia tree that graced the front lawn of historic First Church. She estimated that the tree must be at least forty feet high if not closer to fifty. It was as tall as the roof line of the church, but not as tall as the steeple. At its base it had to be twenty-five feet across. The tree was perfectly formed. There were no spaces between the branches. It was thick with leaves. And on this beautiful morning it was thick with blossoms.

Almeda felt a special kinship with this particular tree. The deep green wax leaves glistened in the morning sun. The large white blossoms appeared to be strategically placed about the tree to enhance its beauty. On the outside, like her, the tree looked magnificent. Everything was in order. Deep inside the branches, hidden from the sunlight, were secrets so deep and dark they could only be found by dismantling the tree itself.

According to Almeda's estimates the tree was at least one hundred years old. She was just sure that it was the oldest and largest magnolia tree in Falls City, if not all of south Georgia. She smiled to herself. If that is true, when I was born that tree was already thirty years old.

Since Chadsworth's death, Almeda had restricted her social attire to black. Today she chose a black full-brimmed hat to protect her face from the late summer sun. She had most carefully examined her reflection in the floor length mirror in her dressing room this morning. She had feared that her grief had taken a toll on her. She was relieved to see that her beauty had not faded.

Almeda turned to look back toward the Alexander family plot. She could see the bouquet of roses that she had picked from her garden just yesterday and placed on Chadsworth's grave. The roses still looked fresh despite the heat. She must remember to stop and make sure there was plenty of water in the container.

Almeda did miss her husband, even though they seldom saw each other while he was alive. His business demanded that he spend a great deal of time in Atlanta. "Oh just who do you think you're kidding?"

Almeda startled herself by mumbling those words out loud. She looked around to make sure no one heard.

A tear streamed down her cheek as she recalled their last telephone conversation. Just minutes before he walked into that shower and put a gun in his mouth, her Chadsworth had telephoned her. She could tell that something was amiss, but she couldn't get him to reveal it to her. He was so sweet to her on the telephone that day. She felt so close to him as they talked. Those few precious moments on that telephone just may have been the most intimate they had shared in their entire marriage. He asked her to forgive him, but for what? She shook her head as she painfully recalled that she now knew all too well the answer to her own question.

She had been married to a man for forty years who had been living a double life. In Falls City he was the respectable married church elder. In Atlanta, not only was he queer, but his long time lover was a *Negara*. Slowly and with the help of an Atlanta private investigator she had been able to put all the pieces together. She had no desire to make public the secrets that Chadsworth had taken to his grave, but she needed to know for her own peace.

The detective discovered that he had been arrested twice for soliciting male prostitutes. He had been arrested once in Atlanta and once in Falls City. She now knew that it was the Rector, Steele Austin, that had used his Discretionary Fund to bail Chadsworth out of jail here in Falls City. She had further discovered that Chadsworth had a house in Charleston. She shuddered, "a love nest, I suppose." Her husband for all those years had a very active sex life, but not with her. Had he not taken his own life in the Ritz Hotel in Atlanta he would have died with AIDS. Yes, the police report recorded that he had called 9-1-1 and stated that they would find a suicide victim in the shower of his hotel room. He told them to handle the body with care. The victim had AIDS.

Before his death, Chadsworth took great care to make sure that she would never want for anything financially. From his grave he continued to protect the Rector that had been his pastor and friend. He also made arrangements for the Rector to have a generous endowment that he could administer at his sole discretion. She knew she would have to carry out all of Chadsworth's instructions. If she failed to do so, an Atlanta attorney had made it clear to her that he had evidence of her many indiscretions during her marriage to Chadsworth. If she failed to follow Chadsworth's final instructions to protect The Reverend Steele Austin and to leave Chadsworth's secret in his grave, her own secrets would be made public.

A shudder ran up her spine. She reasoned that Chadsworth's secret was safe. Here in Falls City he had proven himself to be a man's man. He went on all the hunting and fishing trips with the other leading men in the community. He was an excellent golfer and was part of a foursome that played at the Country Club on a regular basis. He was a leader in the community and in this parish. She didn't know anyone who had ever suspected that they were anything but a happily married couple with two sons.

Yet another unexpected tear ran down her cheek. She was caught off guard by the feelings that welled up in her as she reflected on her life with Chadsworth. In spite of everything, she knew that she really loved him. No, more, she was in love with him. She treasured the moments that they had together. Chadsworth had been a wonderful father when the boys were small. He was present with her for most all their school plays and activities. Christmas, Halloween, and their birthdays were all celebrated with Chadsworth playing the role of the proud father. She loved him and she knew that he loved her. Maybe he hoped that by loving her he could change. Maybe if she had only loved him more she could have changed him? She shook her head and wiped the tears from her cheeks. "Nonsense," she muttered.

She moved the hose that was watering the magnolia to a new spot. To her knowledge the only person in Falls City that knew Chadsworth's secret was the Rector. For some strange reason she trusted him. Until Chadsworth's death she didn't particularly like Steele Austin, but Chadsworth trusted him and left her a letter assuring her that she could trust him as well. It was Chadsworth's dying wish that she do everything in her power to support the Rector and protect him from those who wished him ill. Chadsworth's secret was safe with Father Austin, she felt certain. Again, she glanced toward his grave. She whispered, "Chadsworth, my darling, rest in peace. Your secret is in good hands."

God knows she wanted her own secrets protected. Maybe in a strange sort of way she was now being punished for her lack of judgment. All those years ago, her mother had shown her how to get Chadsworth Purcell Alexander the Third drunk and then to trick him into marrying her. Chadsworth was almost ten years younger than she was at the time. He was a young man of means and of considerable promise from Falls City, Georgia. She shuddered; he just might have been her last chance to escape the trailer park and a life of waiting tables for onion farmers in a greasy diner.

She had betrayed Chadsworth with other men on more than one occasion during their marriage. She always justified it on the grounds that Chadsworth didn't seem to want her, at least, he didn't want her that way. He always provided well for her financially, but there just wasn't any affection. All these years she had thought that she was the one keeping secrets. It wasn't until after Chadsworth's death that she learned otherwise.

Almeda sat down on the steps of the church. In her mind's eye she relived the events that would change the way she lived forever. Two days after his death a registered letter arrived for her. It was from Chadsworth. He wrote it right before he took his own life. In it he let her know that he knew about her several indiscretions. He advised her that he had pictures, videos, and complete detective reports. These were being kept by his Atlanta attorney. That attorney would be coming to see her exactly one week after his funeral. In the interim, she needed to know that her secrets would remain a secret as long as she kept his confidence. If she did anything to disgrace his memory, all of her secrets were to be made public. Almeda shuddered.

The envelope also included a copy of the arrangement that Chadsworth had made with Howard Dexter to name Almeda as Chair of the Board of his bank. Chadsworth's considerable fortune would remain in Howard Dexter's bank so long as Almeda was Chair of the Board. And, at first the second part of the agreement had confused her, but now she understood all too clearly. The second part of the agreement stipulated that both Almeda and Howard Dexter were to do everything in their power to protect The Reverend Steele Austin and his family. He was to enjoy his tenure as Rector of First Church for as long as he wanted. They were not to interfere in any way with the terms of the trust that he had left for the Rector to use at his discretion for ministry with the poor.

In spite of herself, Almeda had developed a warm spot for Steele Austin. Oh, she had not agreed with a single thing that he had done since his arrival. But he had been a pastor to her Chadsworth and he had been a pastor to her. That meant a lot to her. When it came to good judgment, however, Steele Austin seemed to have a considerable deficit. Almeda stood and walked to the other side of the magnolia tree so that she could look down the length of the cemetery. She looked past Chadsworth's grave to the lower part of the cemetery. There she could make out the headstone for old Willie. My God, what was the man thinking? Who would have ever thought that any Rector of First Church would bury the *Negara* sexton in the churchyard? Again, she felt a shudder run the entire length of her body.

At first she thought her eyes deceived her so she put her hand to her forehead so as to shade her eyes from the bright sun. She squinted in an effort to see more clearly the flowers that were on Willie's grave. "Uhh...," she grunted. Her eyes had not deceived her. "Artificial flowers," she uttered with disgust. There on Willie's grave was a bouquet of artificial flowers. She reasoned further that they were most likely plastic. Any person of taste and distinction would have used silk flowers at the very least. This just would not do. She would give that Steele Austin a piece of her mind on this matter. This is exactly the sort of thing that begins to happen when you lower the burial standards in the First Church Cemetery.

She planned further. After she had finished giving the Rector a thorough tongue lashing, she would then call the Vestry and insist that they implement a policy that only fresh flowers could be placed on the graves of those buried in the cemetery. Of course, such a policy had not been needed up to this point. Sophisticated people of class and breeding knew instinctively not to put artificial flowers on the graves of those they loved. And none would have ever considered plastic flowers. Only the lower classes and the colored would do such. Now, because the Rector had buried a *Negara* in the church cemetery a policy must be adopted. God only knows who or what he will try to bury in this precious soil next.

Almeda turned back to look at the magnolia tree. She had not been happy with Steele Austin for starting a Soup Kitchen. He tried to convince her to volunteer. She agreed to visit, but she would not volunteer. When she entered the Soup Kitchen it wasn't at all what she had expected. Oh, she had expected to see the smelly men in desperate need of bathing and perhaps some rehabilitation. She wasn't prepared to see the young mothers with their children at the Soup Kitchen. Her eyes welled up with tears even now as she thought about those precious little children gulping down fresh glasses of milk and eating peanut butter sandwiches as though they had never eaten before.

The Rector had introduced her to a grimy looking man named Duke that was a regular at the Soup Kitchen. At first she was disgusted by him. He was filthy. His voice and his demeanor, however, were of a well educated gentleman. He was articulate and quite knowledgeable on a great many subjects. And play the piano, that man could really play the piano. He didn't play that honky-tonk stuff. No, his repertoire was sophisticated. He played a wide range of classical music most every day while the *guests*, as Steele Austin insisted on calling them, ate their lunch.

One day Duke told her his story. It was filled with pain and grief. A few years ago he had lost his only son in a drowning accident. Then his wife, overcome with heartbreak, had taken her own life. Duke was left all alone with only drink and drugs to comfort him, but they became his undoing. Almeda knew that Steele Austin was a pastor to Duke just as he had been a pastor to her Chadsworth and to her.

Many of the leaders at First Church had not been very receptive to Steele and his unique style of ministry. She had to admit to herself that before she had gotten to know him she wasn't very keen on the man either. She didn't agree with all the mean things that had been done to Steele Austin and his family. She was pretty sure that it was Howard Dexter who had asked the Klan to come in and put a good scare in them. She really didn't think anyone would hurt them. At the time, she thought it would be in the best interest of all concerned if Steele Austin would simply resign his position and return to Oklahoma. Had she known all that Steele was doing for her Chadsworth, she might have felt different. Well, she felt different now.

Almeda looked at her watch. It was time for her appointment with the Rector. She had come early just to check on the grounds. She had long ago appointed herself as a committee of one to oversee the church grounds. She made sure that all the flowers were planted and well cared for by the church sextons. She had also fought to maintain the beauty of the magnolia tree. If it had not been for her vigilance, every bride and her mother would have butchered that tree for garlands to decorate the church for weddings. Because she had taken her responsibilities seriously, the tree was protected and the branches remained in place.

She walked toward the entrance of the parish house. She knew that the Rector was using some of the income from the trust that Chadsworth had left to employ a *Negara* priest. Her telephone had been ringing constantly since she had returned home from her trip to New York City. Some of the callers were in tears, desperately begging her to intervene and to reason with Steele Austin not to do this. She knew better than to try. Steele was a determined man. She could hear him remind her of the terms of the agreement Chadsworth had set up. She wondered if Steele Austin knew about her secrets. Had Chadsworth shown him the pictures, the videos, the detective reports? Was he privy to the consequences she would suffer if she tried to interfere?

"Misturh Austin, I have agreed to come by and meet your *Negara* priest as a courtesy to you and out of respect to my Chadsworth's memory." She walked across the carpeted floor of his office to the chair opposite Steele Austin's desk. She held her head high and managed her look of superiority. That look isn't taught in any school, but any lady of means soon learns how to both make eye contact with another person and look down on them simultaneously. "I can only continue to express my personal displeasure in your decision, but out of respect for my dear late husband's wishes, I will not interfere."

"I really appreciate your tolerance, Almeda."

"Tolerance?" Almeda chuckled. "You dear man, you do have a way with words. This has nothing to do with tolerance. It has everything to do with patience."

"Well, for whatever reason you've agreed to come here to meet Doctor Drummond..." Almeda didn't let him finish.

"Let's just get on with it. Where is your Doctor Drummond?"

Steele picked up the telephone and pushed the extension for his secretary. "Will you advise Doctor Drummond that Almeda Alexander is here? Ask him to step down so that I can introduce her to him."

"I have read all about this *Negara* priest in the church newsletter..." This time it was Steele who interrupted.

"Almeda, please stop referring to him as a *Negara* priest. He is African American. He is extremely well educated. He has a distinguished record of service in the Episcopal Church. And I feel fortunate that he has agreed to work with me."

"Umm," Almeda chuckled again. "All right, your African American priest, I understand that he is about twice your age."

"Yes, he is in his sixties." Just then there was a knock on the door. The door opened and Doctor Drummond entered.

Almeda turned in her chair so that she could look at him. She started to stand to greet the priest, but her legs quickly went out from under her. She was like a school girl. She actually felt her face blush. There, coming across the room toward her, was one of the best looking men she had ever seen in her life. He was tall, physically trim, and had beautiful hazel-colored eyes. His brown face was crowned with a beautiful mass of curly salt and pepper hair.

"Mrs. Alexander, I am so pleased to finally be able to meet you."

His voice was deep. It had a polished baritone quality to it. There was a slight hint of an English or perhaps a Caribbean accent. He was immaculately dressed in a black suit and he was wearing a grey clergy shirt with his clerical collar. Almeda thought that his entire presentation echoed a person of learning and culture. Almeda tried to speak, but she simply could not get her throat unfrozen. She feared that she was going to make an absolute fool of herself. Almeda glanced back toward Steele Austin. The Rector was standing with a confused look on his face.

"Are you all right, Almeda?"

She regained her composure, "Oh, ahh, yes I am fine. It's a pleasure to meet you, Doctor Drummond." She was at a loss for words. She simply could not remember the last time that she had felt this foolish. She couldn't think of anything to say.

Steele saved her. "Almeda, I just wanted the two of you to meet. Do you have any questions for Doctor Drummond?"

"No, I don't have any questions." Almeda searched her mind for something to say. "Is there anything I can do to help you feel more welcome at First Church?"

Steele rushed to answer Almeda's question. "I'm glad that you asked. There is one thing that you could do to help me make Doctor Drummond feel more welcome."

"Oh, what could that be?" Almeda tried not to stare. She feared that if she made further eye contact with the handsome man standing before her he would be able to read her mind. And the thoughts flashing through her mind at that instant should not be revealed to anyone.

Steele continued, "Bishop Petersen is refusing to accept Doctor Drummond's Letter Dimissory from Atlanta. He is really unhappy with me about this call and has indicated that he will only license him to function in this Diocese for one year."

Almeda looked back at Steele, "I don't understand."

Without a Letter Dimissory Doctor Drummond could be forced to leave after one year. Also, I can't enroll him in the Diocesan Health Insurance Program. He basically is a guest without the full rights and privileges of a priest resident in this Diocese."

"I am confused. How can I help you with that, Misturh Austin? That all sounds awfully ecclesiastical and I really don't know much about such things."

Steele winked at Doctor Drummond. "I think that if you and Howard Dexter made a conference call to Bishop Petersen and asked him to accept Doctor Drummond's credentials as a full priest resident in this Diocese it would be accomplished."

Almeda smiled, "Now I understand. Consider it accomplished, Misturh Austin, the call will be made this afternoon." Almeda stood again and turned to face Doctor Drummond. Once again her legs grew weak and her stomach was filled with butterflies. Her voice actually quivered as she extended her hand. "It's a pleasure to meet you, Doctor Drummond."

"Please, call me Horace."

"And you call me Almeda."

Steele Austin took a quick survey of the two of them. His new assistant was looking deep into Almeda Alexander's eyes and she was returning the favor. Perhaps it was his imagination, but he surmised that he was observing some clear signs of flirtation. He also concluded that the flirtation was mutual. He felt a big smile cross his own face as he watched them. Dear God, your ways are so mysterious and the wonders you perform so marvelous.

CHAPTER 5

Bishop Rufus Petersen was not a happy man. But then he had never been a very happy man. Nature had played a pretty ugly, but genetically predetermined, trick on him. He never grew to be very tall or strong in physical stature. He was branded as a "sissy" very early in his childhood. For this, he took a lot of teasing throughout his years of education. He was continually subjected to all the "fat jokes" and he was the constant recipient of boyish pranks.

The fact that his family carried a fine blood line representing the best that Georgia aristocracy had to offer had not helped him either personally or professionally. He did go to Woodbury Forest Prep School, the University of Virginia, and Virginia Theological Seminary. His credentials were impeccable, but the emotional bruising that he had taken most all of his life remained with him.

Rufus was ordained in the Diocese and appointed Vicar of a small mission outside of Savannah. He spent his entire priesthood in tiny congregations. He was never elected the Rector of a single parish, not even a small one. He did endear himself to the previous Bishop and when it came time for that Bishop to retire, he named Rufus heir apparent.

The search committee returned three names for the Diocese to consider. One was the Rector of a large parish up in Atlanta. He had a national reputation as a preacher, administrator and leader in the greater Church. The second was Rector of an even larger parish in Mobile. Like the first nominee, this one too was well known throughout the south for his leadership ability. He was a stellar candidate and most folks were shocked to discover that he would even allow his name to be considered for such a small Diocese. The third candidate on the slate to be presented at the convention was Rufus. The retiring Bishop made sure that his choice was one of the nominees.

The Convention had been especially called to elect a Bishop. It was being held in one of the larger churches up in Augusta. Rufus had not done well in the pre-convention meetings. The other two candidates were quite articulate and held before the delegates two very exciting, but similar visions for the future of the Diocese. Rufus had stammered when asked questions during the "dog and pony" events. He could not articulate his vision for the Diocese. His one strength was that he was clearly opposed to change of any kind.

The delegates to the Diocesan Convention are divided into two groups. The clergy cast their ballots together. The lay representatives do the same. To elect a Bishop requires a concurrent majority of the clergy and the lay delegates casting votes. On the first ballot the candidate from Mobile was the clear front runner. Rufus was a distant third. He had only a handful of votes from the clergy and not many more from the lay people. On the second ballot the candidate from Mobile was very close to being elected by the clergy. The only votes that Rufus had on this ballot from the clergy were those of the retiring Bishop, his loyalists, and of course, his own. It appeared that on the third ballot the laity would follow the clergy lead and the priest from Mobile would be elected. The candidate from Atlanta was maintaining a strong second place. Someone suggested to Rufus that he withdraw from the election process, but he refused.

The retiring Bishop was presiding at the Convention to elect his successor. After the second ballot he called for a thirty minute recess. He then marched to the back of the room where he took the clergy who were the floor chairs for the candidate from Atlanta outside onto the front lawn of the church for a meeting. Observers say that he was very angry and that he was pointing his finger at each of them. It was also reported that following the meeting on the lawn, these same nervous and red-faced delegates were seen moving about the Convention floor whispering into the ears of those supporting the candidate from Atlanta. While no one knows for sure what they were saying to their fellow supporters of the priest from Atlanta, the results speak for themselves.

The retiring Bishop called for ballots to be cast the third time. Those supporting the candidate from Mobile naïvely believed that he would be elected on this ballot and were prepared for a celebration. However, when the results from the third ballot were posted on the overhead projector they were in for quite a surprise. Every one of the votes for the priest from Atlanta had been shifted over to Rufus Petersen. In the twinkling of an eye he had gone from a distant third place runner to the winner.

In a shrewd political maneuver orchestrated by the retiring Bishop of the Diocese, Rufus Petersen had been elected a Bishop, with a concurrent majority in both houses. The organist immediately did a fanfare leading into a hymn of praise and the Convention stood to blame God for electing Rufus a Bishop.

Rufus managed the Diocese the only way he knew how. He did so through manipulations, control, temper tantrums, public humiliation of his priests and if need be, any underhanded means he needed in order to accomplish God's purposes.

Rufus wasn't a happy man and on this day he was particularly unhappy. He had received a conference call from Almeda Alexander and Howard Dexter. He was given little choice in the matter except to admit Horace Drummond as a full priest in the Diocese. He was caught between a rock and a hard spot. Not twenty minutes before he received that telephone call he had met with a delegation from First Church. Henry Mudd, Ned Boone and Colonel Mitchell had made the appointment. These three had come to appeal to the Bishop to help them move Steele Austin out of First Church and back to Oklahoma. They objected to his leadership style. They didn't think he was a very spiritual person. He seemed far too concerned with money and power. He was just a bad fit. They assured the Bishop that they were not just speaking for themselves. They were also speaking for the vast majority of the congregation who felt as they did.

After that meeting and before the telephone call, Rufus was sure that he now had all the support that he needed to get rid of Steele Austin. That braggart had been nothing but a thorn in his flesh since he arrived. Once before he was ready to drive the final nail in Steele's coffin, but that was before Almeda Alexander was able to get Howard Dexter in her pocket. Rufus still wasn't sure how that all came about, but he knew it had something to do with money. Before Howard became so deferent to Almeda, he too wanted Austin out of First Church. Now, you would think he was the president of the Steele Austin Fan Club.

Rufus Petersen knew he had to make the telephone call. He didn't want to do so. He was so angry that Steele Austin had beaten him at his own game that his hand was shaking as he pushed the buttons on the telephone.

When Steele's secretary put the call through, Steele responded, "Good Morning, Bishop."

"Father Austin, I'm going to get right to the point." Rufus didn't recognize his own voice. He was so angry it was actually quivering. "I've decided to accept the Letter Dimissory for Horace Drummond. Just tell him to write the Bishop in Atlanta and have his office send his credentials to me."

"That's wonderful news, Bishop Petersen," Steele was elated. "You won't regret it."

"Now listen to me!" the Bishop shouted at the top of his voice. His voice was a strong shrill. "I already regret it. I don't know how you pulled it off, but I caution you not to ever use Almeda Alexander and Howard Dexter to get your way with me again. Do you understand what I'm saying? I guarantee you that if you triangle against me a second time, there will not be a Diocese in this entire Church open to you; I will make sure of that. Are we clear?"

Steele sat silently not saying a word.

"Father Austin, did you hear me?"

"Is there anything else, Bishop?"

"Yes, you need to know that I just had a meeting with Henry Mudd, Colonel Mitchell, and Ned Boone. They were the representing several of the leading members of First Church."

Steele wasn't surprised that Henry Mudd and Ned Boone had gone to complain about him to the Bishop, but he hadn't heard much from Colonel Mitchell. Steele's mind rushed over the encounter that he had with Colonel Mitchell on his first Sunday in the parish. Colonel Mitchell was clearly a traditionalist who didn't want anything changed. It was also clear that he didn't like Steele Austin. Each time he had run across Colonel Mitchell or his name, he had wondered what possessed his parents to give him a given name that was longer than his last name. C. Hollingsworth Mitchell. I wonder what the C. stands for? The Bishop's voice interrupted his thoughts.

"What is this nonsense I hear about you opening a Medical Clinic? Why can't you just be satisfied running a parish? Surely there are sick people you need to be visiting, or can't you do something to build a stronger Sunday School? First you open a Soup Kitchen and now a Medical Clinic. Just where is it going to end with you?"

Again, Steele chose not to respond and he just listened as the Bishop threw another one of his infamous temper tantrums. Steele had seen him in action before. His response to this scene had grown from shock, to amusement, to pity. He now genuinely felt sorry for Rufus Petersen. Oh, he didn't trust him for a milli-second and he knew that he should never turn his back on him, but he could not help but feel sorry for the man. He must be absolutely miserable living in constant fear of not being in total control.

Again, the Bishop's voice brought him back to the telephone. "I know I'm wasting my breath on you. You're hell bent on self-destruction, Steele Austin, and there isn't a thing that I can do to stop you. One thing for sure is that I'll not help you when the time comes. You're making a bed of nails down there and I intend to watch you lie on it. Good day, Father Austin." And with that there was a click on the other end of the telephone as the Bishop hung up the receiver.

Bishop Petersen sat in his chair shaking. Nausea was washing over him. He felt light-headed. He couldn't stop himself from shaking and his eyes were moist with anger. His doctor had warned him about his blood pressure. He had never been a violent man, but if he could get his hands around the throat of Steele Austin at this moment... He sat back in his chair and closed his eyes. He took some deep breaths and tried to regain his composure.

After a few minutes, he pushed the intercom and spoke into it. His long-time secretary entered the room. To this day he didn't know why he had hired her and he was even more confused as to why he kept her. He had gotten caught up in the political correctness that was sweeping the House of Bishops. If you didn't have at least one person of color on your staff you were suspect. Since the only staff he had was a secretary, well, he felt he might as well follow suit. Besides, it would make him look more open minded... tolerant. But since hiring her he'd had plenty of second thoughts. Not about her color, but her behavior. She was absolutely brazen. She was constantly arguing with him and didn't know how to keep her own counsel. Still, he put up with her. Maybe he enjoyed her bantering.

"I want you to open a file on Horace Drummond. The Bishop in Atlanta will be sending his Letter Dimissory to us."

"My oh my," she chuckled. "Horace Drummond, he is a fine specimen of manhood. I may just have to start commuting to Falls City to go to church on Sundays. I wouldn't be surprised if the women didn't start chartering buses from all over the diocese just to go down there on Sundays to stare at that hunk of burning love."

"Don't you start with me." The Bishop rose up out of his seat. "Now just go back to your desk and do what I have asked you to do."

"Oh, yes surh Masturh, yes surh." She began bowing and backing out of his office. "It jus' ain't right for an old black woman like me to have even a moment of visual pleasure, no surh, no surh. I'sa movin'. I'sa understand. No eye candy for me, no surh." She backed all the way through the door and then he heard the laughter just roll out of her. "Horace Drummond, oh my, oh my, things are beginning to look up around here." And then she laughed some more.

He sat back down at his desk and opened the bottom drawer. He pulled out the flask that he kept there and brought it to his lips. As the whiskey washed over his tongue and warmed his throat, he shook his head. "That damn Steele Austin has done it again. I'll get him. I'll figure out a way to send that Okie packing. Maybe not today and it may not be tomorrow, but one day soon, Steele Austin, I'll hang you out to dry." He took a deep breath followed by another swallow of whiskey. He leaned all the way back in his chair. He put his feet on his desk. He shut his eyes. He sat silent. He was just starting to doze off when... a big smile crossed his face.

CHAPTER 6

Rob McBride drove his car to the Atlanta Hartsville Airport. He parked in the long-term parking garage. He checked his luggage at curbside, cleared security and boarded the Delta Airlines flight to Los Angeles. Bishop Petersen was giving him a gift. He wanted him to attend a Church Growth Seminar in Pasadena targeted for the small church. The Bishop wanted Rob to learn what he could and then make a presentation on the conference topics to the Vicars and Rectors of the other small churches in the Diocese at the next clergy conference.

Rob settled back in his seat. It had been years since he had been on an airplane. He had never been to California. He tried not to show his excitement at getting away from Falls City and just having some time to learn and relax. He hoped that he would have some time to see the sights. Steele Austin was happy for Rob and had given him some money out of his Discretionary Fund to use over and above the cost of his hotel and meals. He told him to use it as he saw fit.

When the plane landed in Los Angeles, he gathered his luggage from baggage claim and then looked for the shuttle that was to take him to the conference. When he boarded the shuttle there were about fifteen other priests wearing clerical collars on the bus. The conference attendees were staying at the Sheraton Hotel in Pasadena. The conference was being held in one of the meeting rooms. Rob didn't make much of an effort to converse with the priest sitting next to him. He wanted to look out at California. It was all he had heard it was. The freeway was congested and the bus lumbered along, alternating between moving freely and coming to a complete stop in the traffic. The mountains and flowers along the roadside were different from the ones he was familiar with in Georgia. There were flowering oleander bushes planted in the median of the freeway. The palm trees were tall, straight, and a signature of the area suitable for any postcard.

At the hotel, Rob checked into his room. He had a large king-sized bed. A great view of the mountains was off in the distance. There was a beautifully landscaped garden around the swimming pool directly below his room. He opened the doors leading to a small balcony off his room so he could smell the cool air. He had hoped to see some orange trees on his way to the hotel, but none were in sight. He was still hopeful.

After his shower, he went down to the conference room where the opening reception was to be held. He picked up his packet of materials at the registration table and walked into the meeting room. At the far end there was a video screen and a podium. In the back of the room there was a display of books and tapes on how to grow a congregation. The middle of the room was set up for the opening banquet. Off to the side, he could see that people were gathered around a bar and some tables covered with fruits, cheeses, and breads.

Rob decided to use some of the money that Steele had given him to buy himself a drink. To his surprise the drinks were free. He noticed most everyone had a glass of white wine in their hand. He decided to follow suit. "When in Rome," he thought. Rob took his name tag from his packet and placed it on his jacket. It was now time to socialize. He didn't know a soul, but it appeared everyone was making an effort to get to know one another. Rob walked toward a group of people standing in a circle not far from him.

Then he saw her looking at him. At first, he thought she was looking at someone behind him. He looked over his shoulder, but no one was there. She was definitely looking, no, staring at him. She had piercing blue eyes that flashed at him even before he reached the group. A big smile issued from her lips and he smiled back. She moved toward him. "You look lost."

"I don't know a soul."

"Where are YOU ALL FROM?" She giggled. "I know you're not from Connecticut with that accent."

"Do I really have an accent? I mean, is it that noticeable?"

She giggled, "Oh, it's noticeable, but I think it's rather endearing. Now just where are you all from?"

Rob felt himself blush. "I'm from Falls City, Georgia."

"I know about Georgia, but where's Falls City?"

"It's south Georgia, near the Florida border."

He couldn't believe this beautiful woman had singled him out for a conversation. She was striking. She was just the kind of woman that would turn the head of every man and woman when she entered a room. Not only was she beautiful, but she impressed Rob as a real lady. He kept staring into her deep blue eyes. She didn't break eye contact. She stared back with equal intensity. Rob knew he was flirting and he knew she was flirting. Perhaps it was the wine on an empty stomach, but he just didn't care. He had been so lonely for so long. He had felt so undesirable ... so unattractive. No, it was even more than that. There was chemistry between them. Their conversation flowed with ease. She laughed at his attempts at humor. She listened to him like he had not been listened to in years. She complimented him on his hair and his broad shoulders. It was as though he had known her all of his life or at least in another life. Her name was Melanie - Melanie Mason.

"M & M, hard on the outside. Soft on the inside." She laughed again at his attempt to be funny.

"That's for me to know and if you're a lucky man, you just might find out."

They sat next to each other at the opening banquet. It was as though they were the only ones at the table. Neither one of them ate much. To do so would have required that they stop looking at each other. It would have required that they stop conversing. She had been married once for just a few days. The marriage had been annulled. She discovered that her new husband was stealing from her after only a couple of days of marriage. He was an addict. He had stolen some of her jewelry to sell for drugs. She had not dated much since her annulment. She was the Volunteer Coordinator for an Episcopal parish in Beverly Hills. She loved what she did.

Rob guessed that she was at least fifteen years younger than he was if not more, but that just didn't seem to matter. It certainly didn't seem to matter to her. At first he was surprised when she pressed her leg against his underneath the table. He pulled his leg away from her, thinking that he was crowding her. She simply reached underneath the table with her hand, pulled his leg back, placed her leg next to his and patted it. Her knowing smile reassured him that it wasn't an accident. While the rest of the table was enjoying their dessert and coffee, she again took his hand and placed it on her leg underneath the table. She slid her hand in his. They intertwined their fingers. It was a perfect fit. Her hand felt so small, so smooth inside his.

After the welcoming remarks were concluded, the attendees all stood and sang the words to a church growth hymn that were projected on an overhead. Melanie held his hand as they walked out of the banquet room. She suggested that they go down to the hotel bar. They found a table for two in a corner. They sat and stared at each other and listened to the pianist play show tunes. This time he held both of her hands in his on top of the table.

He broke the long silence, "You know that I'm married."

"I know. And you're a priest." She looked down at their hands locked together. "Are you happily married? Rob, I need the truth. I have only known you for, let's see." She looked at her watch. "Four hours and twenty-two minutes. Are you happily married? I want the truth. Don't tell me what you think I want to hear so that I will sleep with you tonight because that's not going to happen. I'm not a pick-up. My God, I've never done in my life what I've done with you already in just one evening. I've certainly never been this attracted to a married man or a priest. Are you happily married?"

Rob shook his head, "No, I haven't been happy in my marriage for years. There is very little conversation and even less affection. We are like ships passing in the night. I'm not happy and neither is she."

"Is she pretty?"

"Her name is Esther. And yes, she's pretty." This time Rob grimaced. "When we were first married I thought she was the most beautiful woman I'd ever seen. But she's not that way anymore. She has sort of let herself go. She doesn't take care of herself in the way that a husband or a wife would like their spouse to do. She can out-eat me and if truth be told out-drink me as well. She never exercises. She works as a librarian at the community college. If you were casting a librarian for a play, she has the perfect look, but don't get me wrong. She would be the pretty librarian. Even..." He paused, "yes, she would be cast as the pretty, sexy looking librarian."

"Do you find her sexy? I mean, do you still make love to your wife?" She asked. "Do you find her desirable?"

"It's not very passionate. A kiss or two, oh, I don't know. It hardly seems worth the effort."

"You must find her desirable or you wouldn't make the effort?"

"I guess I'm hoping that we might find each other again, but the truth is..." Again, he paused as though lost in his thoughts.

Melanie waited patiently. "The truth is..." She patted his hands, attempting to pull his thoughts out of him.

He looked back at her and removed his hands from hers. He leaned back in the booth and took another swallow from his drink. Again, he looked at her. "The truth is I don't feel very desirable to her. She openly flirts with other men in my presence. It's so humiliating. I feel so embarrassed by her behavior, but worse, I don't think she finds me attractive anymore. I told a priest friend of mine the other day that I think she wants to have sex with every man but me. It's been going on for a long time. At first it really hurt; now, well now, I'm just numb. I fear that I've reached the point that I just don't care. When I see her flirting, I just walk away."

"What are you going to do?" Melanie probed, "Have you thought about leaving her?"

"Sure I've thought about it, but I'm a priest." Rob didn't want to sound like he was making excuses or giving her a line. The truth would sound like both. Still he decided to risk it. "Yes, I've thought about leaving her, but I would have to give up my priesthood. Bishop Petersen, my Bishop, is totally opposed to divorce. The day a priest files for divorce is the day that he must resign."

"Nice guy," she said, shaking her head.

Rob chuckled, "Rufus Petersen can be called many things, but nice guy isn't one of them. In all honesty, Melanie, Esther and I need each other financially. I get paid so poorly that when I took my income tax to H & R Block a few years ago, they suggested that I was eligible for food stamps. My wife makes more money than I do, but even at that, it takes both of our salaries to live. I would not have come to this conference if the Bishop had not paid for it out of the Diocesan funds. One of my fellow priests, a friend, the one I mentioned to you a minute ago, gave me some spending money out of his Discretionary Fund."

The waiter brought their check. Melanie grabbed it and signed it to her room. "My treat, Father McBride."

"Thanks, thanks so much. I think you're the first woman ever to buy me a drink. In fact, I think you're the first woman since my mother to buy me anything."

She stood and took his hand. "Come on, handsome, walk me home."

At the door to her hotel room she reached up and put her arms around his neck. She kissed him lightly on the lips, not giving him a chance to respond. Then she placed two of her fingers over his lips. "I'm not going to invite you in. You need to know I'm not that kind of girl. I've not been with anyone since my annulment. I've promised myself that I won't be with anyone until I find the right one. You just may be that man, Rob McBride, but it's too soon for either of us to know. I'm not going to let my own loneliness and a bottle of white wine make my decisions for me." This time she kissed him on the cheek and gave him a squeeze around the neck. "Then again, I have a hunch that you're not that kind of guy either. No, I think you're high quality – a real gentleman." She turned and walked into her room. As she closed the door she smiled at him, "Good night, Father, meet you in the hotel café for breakfast – let's say 8:00 a.m.?"

He nodded and smiled back at her. Rob McBride didn't sleep well that night. He couldn't get her out of his mind. He kept thinking about her eyes, her smile, and her laugh. Even the sound of her voice was hypnotic. He thought again about the way she rubbed her leg against his. He could feel her hand in his. When he placed his hands to his face he could still smell her perfume. It had been so long since he had felt attractive to anyone. He could still hear her call him handsome. She said it like she meant it. It felt so good to hear. Those beautiful blue eyes on that pretty face looked at him as though he was desirable. For the first time in years he felt just that way. He felt desirable.

He couldn't go to sleep. He tossed and turned for a couple of hours. Then he got up and walked through the open sliding door onto the balcony just outside his room. The cool California air smelled of orange blossoms. He sat down in one of the chairs on the terrace. He looked at the shadow of the palm trees against the night sky. The mountains surrounding the city were in the distance. Rob could not sleep, but his mind was exploding with diverse thoughts. He tried to pray. The words, "deliver me not into temptation," crossed his mind. He dismissed them as quickly as they entered. He could not pray. He had been so lonely for so long. It's a terrible thing, he thought, to be married and lonely at the same time. Melanie had brought feelings out in him that he had never before known. He liked them. He liked feeling this way. He refused to let himself feel guilty for feeling alive. She made him feel like a man. He was a handsome, virile, desirable man. He loved the way she made him feel. The stars were bright in the California sky. The moon was full and hung low over the horizon. For the first time in years, he was happy. He didn't want to lose these feelings. Throughout the night he relived his evening with Melanie. Rob did a lot of thinking that night. Not once did he think about his wife, St. Mary's, or Falls City, Georgia. All his thoughts that night were of Melanie.

Over the next week they ate every meal together. Often they would sneak away from the hotel to one of the restaurants in the surrounding neighborhood. They skipped the evening session on the second night and went to a club. They danced all the slow dances. Rob held her in his arms. She laid her head on his chest as they danced. Rob loved to dance. When they were dating, he and Esther would dance together. After she got pregnant she didn't want to go dancing. They just never resumed after the baby was born. Melanie and Rob knew that the attraction between them was growing even more intense. It was much harder the second night than the first for her to close her hotel door on him. Neither of them slept well in their empty beds. Their thoughts were of each other. They had each come to the point of genuinely hurting to be together. They each longed for the night to end and morning to come so that they could spend another day holding hands and talking.

On the last night of the conference they skipped the closing banquet in favor of a romantic restaurant. Rob hurt to be with her. She hurt to be with him. "What are we going to do?" he asked.

"I can't bear the thought of never seeing you again," the tears rolled down her cheeks. "I'm not a home wrecker, Rob. You're going to have to sort out your marriage without any influence from me."

"Falls City, Georgia is a long way from Beverly Hills." He too felt tears welling up in his eyes. "Can I telephone you?"

"I think that would be safe enough. We can also e-mail each other. What's your e-mail address?" She started opening her purse in search of a pen and her address book.

Rob chuckled. "E-mail? You've got to be kidding. I don't have a computer."

"Surely your parish has a computer you can use."

"No," he shook his head. "The parish is too poor and I'm too poor to purchase a computer. Hence, no e-mail address."

Melanie was determined, "Well, then we'll just write letters and send them snail mail. We'll talk on the telephone. When you sort things out, then we'll see if and where we go."

The walk back to the hotel was the longest walk in Rob's life. He knew that this was the last time he would see her for a very long time, if ever again. He held her close. He loved the way she felt in his arms. He saw her wipe tears from her face. He tried to keep her from seeing him wipe his own tears. At her door they kissed more passionately and intensely than ever. She buried herself in him. She allowed him to touch her and hold her in places that she had not the previous evenings. Then she broke it off. "We have to stop. I have to stop. This goodbye has to end." She turned quickly and opened the door and walked through it. Just as the door was closing she smiled at him. The tears were flowing down her face. "If I could, I would tell you that I think I love you, but circumstances make those words impossible to utter. Good night, my Rob. Please call me when you get home. Call me just to let me know that you arrived safely." Then she closed the door.

Rob McBride was in pain. He hurt for Melanie as he had never hurt for anyone. He felt as though part of him was missing and the part that was missing was in her possession, in her body, in her soul. He tried to sleep. He could not get her out of his mind. He thought of her lips, her eyes, her touch, her smell. He needed her. He longed to wrap his arms around her. He wanted to hold her in his arms. He loved the way she felt to him when he held her. When they were together he felt complete. He missed her. He felt empty without her. Sleep eluded him. He dreaded the sunrise. He feared that he would never see her again. He tried to telephone her room in the middle of the night. The operator advised him that she had already checked out.

The next morning as he handed his keys to the desk clerk and paid the incidental expenses on his account, the bellman approached him. "Are you Father McBride?"

"Yes."

"I have a package for you. It's a gift from a Miss Melanie Mason." The bellman handed him a leather briefcase. It had a red bow on it. The attached card read,

My Darling Rob,

Now you can talk to me whenever you want. Your e-mail address and account have already been set up and paid for one year in advance. Your address is hopeful@tv.net and my address is missingyou@tv. net.
You make me so happy.
Melanie

He opened the briefcase. Inside was a brand new laptop computer.

CHAPTER 7

Steele Austin had a queasy feeling in his stomach. Bishop Petersen had telephoned him and announced that he was coming to see him at 10:00 a.m. Any time the Bishop had asked to meet with Steele he had never inquired as to whether or not the time was convenient. That wasn't the way Bishop Petersen did things. "I'm coming down to Falls City on Tuesday morning at 10:00 a.m. Whatever you have scheduled, cancel it. I have someone I want you to meet. We'll be at your office at ten o'clock sharp. Make yourself available."

The queasy feeling in Steele's stomach only intensified as he thought about the Bishop's visit. Bishop Petersen had never brought anything but trouble into his life. And when Steele was in trouble and really needed the intervention of the Bishop he had been of absolutely no assistance. To the contrary, he sided with the troublemakers and those opposed to Steele's ministry at First Church. Steele was equally concerned about the mystery guest. Just who did Bishop Petersen want him to meet?

At precisely 10:00 a.m. Bishop Petersen and a young man wearing a clerical collar walked through the office of his secretary without even acknowledging her presence and walked unannounced directly into Steele's office. Steele stood in deference to the Bishop. He walked around the desk and extended his hand to Bishop Petersen. The Bishop shook Steele's hand and smiled broadly. "Father Austin, I want you to meet Richard Davis. Richard is coming to us after two years in the Methodist Church. He is a graduate of Emory School of Theology. I ordained him a deacon six months ago and I am going to ordain him a priest on Saturday at the Cathedral in Savannah."

Steele extended his hand to the young man. Richard limply shook Steele's hand and simultaneously looked over the top of his glasses at Steele while giving him a full-toothed smile. Again, Steele felt that queasy feeling in his stomach. There was something about this young man he didn't like. He spoke and managed to swallow his own words while doing so. "Father Austin, I have heard so much about you. Your work here at First Church has certainly peaked the curiosity of so many of us. I look forward to the opportunity to observe you firsthand. I hope I can develop an appreciation for your unique style of ministry."

Steele was dumbfounded. "What do you mean observe me firsthand?" He looked over at the Bishop. "I don't understand."

Bishop Petersen proceeded to walk behind the Rector's desk and sat down in Steele's chair. He leaned back and placed his hands behind his head. "I'm assigning Richard Davis to you, Father Austin. He will begin next week as your Curate. Of course, the Diocese will pay his salary and benefits. He will be assigned to you for two years as a Diocesan Curate."

Now Steele's stomach had developed a full case of indigestion. "Bishop, I've not asked for a Curate and I really don't need one. I'm not sure what I would do with Richard. I'm sure he's a fine person, but I simply don't have any need for another priest on my staff. As you know, Bishop, I have just brought Horace Drummond on..."

"Where is Doctor Drummond?" The Bishop interrupted. He walked to the door and instructed Steele's secretary to have Doctor Drummond come down to the Rector's office. The Bishop returned to Steele's chair behind his desk. This time he hesitated for just a minute before being seated and shuffled through the papers that Steele had lying on the top of his desk.

"Bishop, those papers are just some preparation that I was doing for the Vestry meeting next week."

"Yes, I can see that now." Again the Bishop sat down. "You need to know that I continue to get complaints about you starting a free Medical Clinic down here. For the life of me I just don't know what you're thinking."

Before Steele could answer, Horace Drummond walked into his office. He quickly surveyed the situation and gave Steele a puzzled look. The Bishop spoke first. "Doctor Drummond, I'm so pleased to be able to welcome you to the Diocese. I am happy that the misunderstanding surrounding your Letter Dimissory could be resolved. I just know that you'll be a fine addition to First Church and our Diocese."

Horace Drummond thanked the Bishop for his welcome and then turned to face the young man. Richard Davis extended his hand. "I'm Richard Davis. I've heard just as much about you as I have Father Austin. I can't tell you just how excited I am to have the opportunity to work with both of you. It's going to be wonderful."

"Are you joining the staff at First Church?" The puzzled look on his face was even more strained.

"The Bishop just informed me that he wants to assign Father Davis to us as a Diocesan Curate. I'm not sure what we would do with him." Steele took his cue from the look on Horace Drummond's face. "Bishop, I need you to know that I really appreciate your thinking about us here at First Church, but I fear I'm going to have to decline your offer. As you know, I'm in the process of building a clergy team here and a Diocesan Curate is just not part of that plan. I'm sure there must be another parish in the Diocese that would be all too happy to have Father Davis on their team."

The Bishop had been watching the entire scene and taking some delight in the discomfort he had generated in both Steele and Horace. He heard Steele's clumsy attempt to refuse Richard's assignment to First Church, but he had already made up his mind. "Now, now, Father Austin, you underestimate yourself. I'm not putting Richard here so much to help you as to learn from you. You have so much to offer such a promising young priest. It's not what Richard can do for you. This is about what you can do for one of our newly ordained priests and for this Diocese. Just let Richard observe the two of you at work. Let him follow you about and learn from you. He's a very bright young man and in short order I'm sure he'll begin to develop some additional programs of his own that will benefit you and the parish."

Steele and Horace shot each other questioning looks. They sat down and Richard Davis followed suit. "I am curious, Richard. Why did you leave the Methodist Church? Why would you want to be an Episcopal priest?"

"The Methodists are a Church looking for a denomination. The leaders of the Methodist Church have no courage, no conviction. They are completely without vision." The young man wasn't conversing, he was pontificating. "The Methodists are more concerned about numbers than holiness. I believe they have departed from the basic teachings of the Scriptures. John Wesley would be ashamed of the Methodist Church today."

Steele interrupted, "Those words seem awfully harsh. I know a lot of Methodists and Methodist clergy. They strike me as people with lots of courage and conviction. I've gotten to be pretty good friends with the Senior Pastor at the Methodist Church here in Falls City. He has a very effective ministry and I would certainly say that he's faithful to the teachings of Christ."

Richard Davis straightened up in his chair and leaned forward toward Steele. He looked over the top of his glasses at Steele. Steele had the incredible urge to reach over and push the man's glasses up on his face. "I can see that as an outsider you just might come to that conclusion, but I've been working inside the Methodist Church for the past two years. Let me assure you that's not the case."

Horace interrupted, "Could you be more specific? Just what is it that you find so disturbing about Methodism?"

"They've gotten completely off track. The Methodist Church used to be a Bible Church. That's no longer true. They interpret the Bible to suit their own purposes. In fact, they only use the parts of scripture that will make them popular with whatever the current trend might be. The Methodist Church doesn't proclaim God's Word to society. They are trying to conform to society."

"For example?" Horace asked.

"The Methodists preachers don't condemn sin from the pulpit. We need to open the scriptures to the people and let them know just which things are abominations to God."

"Like what?" Steele asked.

"Father Austin, I'm certain that you realize that fifty percent of all marriages end in divorce. Do you know why?"

"Continue."

"Because the Church has failed to teach women that their place is in the home. The Bible makes it clear that God created women to be wives and mothers. The clergy have failed to teach God's Word. Now, women are forsaking their responsibilities as wives and mothers for careers. It's little wonder that half the marriages don't make it."

Visions of Cro-Magnon man sitting in front of his cave flashed through Steele's mind. "Not all women want to be wives and mothers. There are thousands of professional women who make valuable contributions to the Church and society. There are thousands of others who balance both family and career."

"Just because it can be done doesn't mean it should be done, Father Austin," Richard smirked. "That's precisely my point. God's plan for women is revealed in the scriptures. We must instruct women to accept God's plan."

"How would you advise a woman that doesn't have a choice?" Horace decided to join the contest.

"Women have a choice between doing God's will or disobeying scripture." The smirk on Richard's face grew even larger.

Horace asked, "As a pastor, how would you counsel a woman that is being physically abused by her husband? She fears for the safety of not only herself, but her children as well. She has no choice but to leave her husband and find a way to support her family."

"As I said earlier, Doctor Drummond, she can choose to honor her marriage vows or she can choose to rebel against God. She promised God that she would stay married to her husband for better or for worse, until death. She must figure out a way to make her marriage work. You do realize, Doctor Drummond, women were created second! God created woman after He created man. There's a reason for this. It's a part of God's plan for the family. The Bible makes it clear that a wife is to submit herself to her husband and be obedient to him. Surely you don't want to disregard this very clear teaching in God's Word?"

Both Horace and Steele slumped back in their seats. They looked at each other and then studied the face of Richard Davis. He appeared very pleased with himself. Obviously, he felt he had won one for God. There was an uncomfortable silence in the room.

Steele leaned forward in his chair toward Richard. "I have a hunch that the role of women in society isn't your only issue."

"Sir, you're absolutely correct. I think that the Church isn't being faithful to the Bible when it fails to uphold the teachings of God when it comes to sexual perversion." Richard Davis was now red in the face. "The Bible is equally clear on this one."

"What do you regard as a perversion?"

Richard took a deep breath. "Homosexuality, Father Austin. The Bible is very clear on this one too. But then, if you are not going to teach the Bible when it comes to women, my hunch is that you don't want to teach the Bible on this one either."

Steele asked calmly, "Richard, I think that Doctor Drummond was following a reasonable line of logic with his previous question to you on the role of women. What would you say to parents who have a gay child?"

"That's easy. If the parents had done their job correctly their child wouldn't have chosen to be a homosexual. Now it's their job to fix him. They need to ask Jesus to heal him of his perversion."

"And you're absolutely convinced that people choose to be gay? Do you allow for even the most remote possibility that people are born homosexual and that they don't choose it?"

"Absolutely not!" Richard shouted. He rose up in his chair. "These aren't my answers to the choices sinners make. They are God's answers. God has spoken. It's all in the Bible. It's our job to let the people know what God has already said." Richard Davis was making wide gestures with his hands to further emphasize his point. Steele feared that at any minute he was going to whip out his pocket Bible and start reading selected scriptures to them.

Horace met Richard's posture by leaning forward in his chair. "I can assure you, Richard, that there are many passages in the Bible that we don't teach nor do we want to teach them."

"No," Richard's face grew red again. "The Bible is the final word. You cannot pick and choose. Every word of the Bible is God's Divine Word and every word must be honored."

Horace asked, "Richard, don't you think it's our duty as pastors to minister to people in whatever situation they might find themselves?"

"A prophet must proclaim God's law. If the sinners feel convicted of their sins, then they need to change their ways. Our job isn't to coddle them but to try to keep them from burning in the eternal fires of hell." Richard crossed his legs and started swinging one of his feet. Clearly, he felt in control of the conversation. "You know what I think, Doctor Drummond?"

"Please enlighten me."

"I think liberal clergy are a bunch of cowards. They're afraid to teach what's in the Bible. Instead, they hide behind the cloak of being pastors. Well, they're not being pastors. They're just afraid to tell the sinners what they need to hear. They're more concerned with their own popularity than they are with faithfulness."

Steele and Horace both leaned back in their chairs. Once again they gave each other exasperated looks. They continued to study Richard Davis. An uncomfortable silence filled Steele's office. Bishop Petersen had a smile the size of an amusement park on his face. Steele and Horace continued to study the young man in front of them. He appeared to be unmoved by their questions. His commitment to his convictions was unwavering.

Steele broke the silence. "Richard, let me ask you a reflective question. Do you really think the issues that we have been discussing are that simple? These are all complex issues that touch the lives of real people. If the first words they hear from us are words of judgment and condemnation, what hope do we have of sharing a message of hope with them? Richard, simple answers cannot be used to respond to complex questions."

Richard glanced over at the Bishop. The Bishop nodded his encouragement. Richard answered with an exasperated tone, "It's in the Bible, gentlemen. What part of *in the Bible* do you not understand? The Bible is the final word. That's the problem with the Church. We've gotten away from the Bible and started listening to the bleeding heart liberals."

Horace wasn't going to let Richard have the last word. "And what is your attitude toward those who disagree with your understanding of the Bible?"

Richard became defiant. "I don't have an understanding of the Bible, Doctor Drummond. Either the Bible is the Bible or it's just another book."

"And those who believe they also are being faithful to the Bible, but their truth differs from your truth?"

"My truth is the truth that Jesus taught. They're wrong. It's as simple as that. It really isn't all that complex. Right is right. Wrong is wrong. They're wrong. If they insist on rewriting the scriptures to suit their political purposes then I must separate myself from them. That's why I'm leaving the Methodist Church."

Horace lowered his voice to just above a whisper in an effort to control his anger. "You talk about those who disagree with you as though they were your mortal enemies. They're not your enemies, Richard. They're your brothers and sisters in Christ." Horace swallowed hard and then took a deep breath. "What is gained by demonizing those that disagree with you? Putting labels on those who have a different understanding only dehumanizes them. It's like you're at war with your fellow Christians. Don't you think that they too love the Lord and are struggling to understand these difficult issues that face people in today's world?" Again, Horace took a deep breath. "And Richard, separating from those who have a different understanding of these issues is contrary to Jesus' final prayer for the unity of His Church."

"We are at war!" Richard exploded. "They are the enemies of the Gospel. Evil must be named. Sin must be labeled. And heretics must be called to task for misrepresenting the Bible."

Steele shot a glance at the Bishop. "Where is Richard getting his Anglican studies? I know you said that he is a graduate of Emory and that is a fine school, but where are you sending him to learn Anglican theology?"

"I'm having Father White up in Savannah lead him through the basics. He has done a sufficient enough job that Richard passed his General Ordination Exam."

Richard interjected, "Father Austin, it sounds to me like you're more interested in making Episcopalians than you are in converting people to Christianity."

Steele was on the verge of exploding. This time he took a deep breath. "Richard, Episcopalians are Christians. We are a Bible Church. I just don't think we're your version of a Bible Church. It seems to me that if you're going to be a priest in the Episcopal Church you could benefit from at least one year of training in an Episcopal Seminary."

The Bishop didn't give Richard an opportunity to respond. He stood and gave Horace and Steele a look that clearly communicated that they were not to pursue the subject further.

Steele wasn't about to be detoured. "Bishop, I know that this is your call. But clearly, from this brief conversation I don't believe this young man understands the way we Anglicans do theology. There is a reason that we're called the thinking person's religion. Bishop, simplicity of thought isn't a part of our theological process."

"Well then, Father Austin, it will be part of your job to teach him." Again, the Bishop gave him a very determined look.

"Have you thought about having Richard attend one of our schools for a year of Anglican studies?" Steele was hoping against hope that the Bishop just might reconsider.

"No, that's out of the question." The Bishop waved his hand in a dismissive fashion. "I've made my decision. He's coming to join you here at First Church. I've not asked you for much, Father Austin, but I am asking you to do this for me and for this Diocese. First Church and you two priests have a lot to offer this young man. Please, in an effort to mend some of the fences between us, I'm asking you to work with me on this curacy.

Horace stood to excuse himself. "I need to check my voicemail. I've been waiting on an urgent message from one of the parishioners. It's a pastoral matter." He walked over to the telephone on the credenza behind Steele's desk. When the Bishop wasn't looking he caught Steele's eye and shook his head. Clearly, Horace had the same reservations about this situation that Steele had.

The Bishop stood to leave. "Richard will be reporting to you on Monday. I'm depending on you to have an office ready for him and to be prepared to have him exercise a full ministry here at First Church."

Steele started to offer yet one more alternative, but the Bishop stopped him. "Father Austin, just one time could we do something together without your being so difficult? I'm giving you a gift. I'm giving you a Diocesan Curate for two years. He's bright, articulate, and attractive. Your people are going to fall in love with Richard. Now just say 'thank you' so that we can go get some lunch before I have to drive back to the Diocesan Center."

Steele simply nodded and extended his hand to shake the hands of both men. Horace did the same. The Bishop and Richard left.

Horace and Steele stood looking at each other. Steele had that familiar sick feeling in his stomach. Horace broke the silence. "We've got to be careful, Steele. That young man is trouble and I think the Bishop knows he's trouble. But Steele, that fellow thinks that he's found Jesus."

Steele grinned, "You know what, Doctor Drummond? I didn't even know that Jesus was lost."

***

Today, Rufus Petersen was a happy man. He pointed his brand new Cadillac toward Savannah. He turned up the radio and began singing along to a country and western song. He kept time to the music by thumping his fingers on the steering wheel. He felt wonderful. He relived the scene he had just witnessed in Steele Austin's office. He relished the discomfort that Richard Davis had created in Steele and Horace. Yes, Rufus Petersen was a very happy man. He had a big smile on his face and the taste of victory in his mouth. There were very few things that made him smile in life. He smiled when he knew he was in control of any situation. He smiled most when he could get his revenge. Right now he was both in control and getting revenge. His smile turned into a chuckle. In just a few minutes laughter gushed from him. He delighted in the joy of it all. Yes, Rufus Petersen was a very, very happy man.

CHAPTER 8

I can't stand it, Rob! I just have to see you." The multiple e-mails, on-line conversations, telephone calls, and long letters had only brought them closer. Rob had managed to keep his wife from finding the computer that Melanie had given him. He would call California with the paid calling cards Melanie sent him. He rented a mail box at the local post office so that she could send him letters and romantic cards. Rob didn't want to think of himself as having an affair, but he knew that he had fallen in love.

He told Esther that the Bishop wanted him to go to Atlanta to talk with a small group of Atlanta clergy about the workshop on church growth he had attended in Pasadena. She didn't seem to mind and didn't even ask him any questions. Melanie had sent him some money to hire a supply priest to cover his Sunday services so that they could have a long weekend together.

"I will be staying at the Westin Hotel right by the Atlanta Airport. When you get to the lobby just pick up the house phone and ask for my room. I'll be waiting. My darling, I can't wait to see you. We've got to talk. I can't go on this way."

Rob pointed his automobile toward Atlanta. He knew that he was putting everything at risk. He was risking his marriage, and if he hurt Esther, his son would be very angry with him. He could alienate him forever. As for his priesthood, what he had done already could cost him. Bishop Petersen had no tolerance for clergy who act out sexually. Rob had been in the Diocese long enough to see clergy who messed up come and go in the twinkling of an eye.

"Melanie Mason's room please." His voice was shaking. He knew that just as soon as he walked onto that elevator, rode up, and knocked on her door, his life would never again be the same. He didn't care. He was certain of only one thing. He knew that he loved Melanie. These past few weeks had been pure agony. Physically he hurt. It hurt to be without her. He hungered just to be able to talk to her. The sound of her voice was the only thing that brought him any release. He could not eat. He could not sleep. He had lost over twenty pounds. Some of his members were speculating that he was ill with a dreaded disease. In order to get some relief from his loneliness he had started taking long walks. At least on the walks he could think about her. He could re-live their time together in Pasadena. Before long, his walks turned into long runs. There was something about wearing himself out jogging that allowed him to sleep. In his sleep, he could dream about being with Melanie.

She opened the door and threw her arms around him. They struggled together with the door as he pulled her close to him and kissed her. Their lips and their tongues were hungry for each other. He pushed the door shut with his foot and she began unbuttoning his shirt. "Oh my God, I've missed you. I want you more than I have ever wanted any man." He picked her up in his arms and carried her to the bed. She sat up on her knees on the bed and began unbuttoning her blouse. "Hurry, Rob – hurry!" He stood beside the bed and removed his shoes and socks. He quickly took off his shirt and pants. He was ready for her. She stretched out her naked body on the bed below him. She was absolutely gorgeous. Physically she was everything Rob had thought she would be.

He lay down beside her and wrapped his arms around her. He kissed her again and again. He began kissing her face and neck. He literally wanted to smother her with kisses. She pulled him to her. "Now Rob, now, I can't wait any longer." As they became one he looked down into her beautiful face. She looked back into his eyes. Tears began streaming down her face. "Oh Rob, my Rob, God forgive me," she sobbed. "I love you –I can't help myself. I'm so in love with you." His own tears dropped onto hers. They were together. They were one. The emptiness that had haunted each of them was no more.

He lay next to her, holding her naked body in his arms. Her head was on his chest. "Perhaps I should apologize," he whispered. She lifted her head in order to look up at him. She had a puzzled look on her face. "You're the only other woman I have ever been with. You may find this hard to believe, but I was a virgin when I married Esther. And, then it has been so long since – I mean – I had hoped everything... you know, I mean..."

She put a finger over his lips. "I thought it was absolutely beautiful. You were perfect. And then a devilish smile crossed her face. "I have a feeling that things will continue to improve." They both giggled. In just a few minutes, things did improve.

They stayed in bed the entire weekend. Rob wrapped a towel around his waist in order to answer the door and sign for room service. They never left their room. Their craving for each other was satisfied only for a short time before they hungered for each other again. Rob got a glance of himself in the mirror. His back and chest looked as though he had been in a street fight. In her passion, Melanie would not only scream out, but she bit and scratched him.

They made love that weekend in ways that Rob had only heard about or saw alluded to in books and movies. Clearly, Melanie was the more experienced lover, but for some reason he just didn't mind. He knew that if other men had possessed her body it didn't matter because he possessed her heart. Melanie was giving herself completely to him. He knew that she could not have ever done that with another human being. The type of uniting they were experiencing wasn't just the joining of two bodies; it was the joining of two souls.

"What are we going to do, Rob?" She began the conversation that he knew they must have. He was closing his luggage. They were both dressed. Her plane was to leave in just a couple of hours. He was going to drive her to her terminal and then he would go back to Falls City. "Rob, I will do whatever you want. If you want to stay married and stay a priest, we can go on like we are. I will be your mistress for as long as you want me. I'll fly here every few weeks and we can be together. Just tell me what you want. I just need a plan. Whatever plan you come up with I'll accept." She began to cry. "I just know that I can't live without you. I want you any way I can have you."

He sat down on the bed and pulled her onto his lap. He was on the verge of tears as well. "Melanie, I love you and I have loved every second that we've been together this weekend."

She interrupted, "Oh Rob, please, please don't tell me this is over. Please, oh God, please don't tell me that we have to say goodbye again. No, Rob, no." She began to sob.

He pulled her close to him. "No, darling, that's not what I was going to say. I wasn't going to say anything near that." He put his hands on her shoulders and pushed her back so that he could look into her face. He wiped her tears first and then his own. "Melanie, I'm an adulterer.

Worse, I'm an adulterous priest. This weekend, as wonderful as it has been, is wrong. It's a sin. You deserve so much more. I'll not degrade you or the love we share by making you my mistress. I can't live that way. Melanie, I love you and I want you to be my wife. I want to have babies with you. I know that we have only known each other a few weeks, but it's as though I've known you all my life. No, it's like I knew you in another life and I've been searching for you. Now that I've found you I'm not going to let you go."

She kissed him. A girlish smile spread across her face. "I know... me too. It's so weird. The first time I saw you enter that conference room in Pasadena I was drawn to you. I told the people I was with that I knew you. I feel so connected to you. My darling, when I'm away from you I feel lost. I feel like I have a big hole in my heart. Some part of me is in your possession and I have to be with you in order to get that part of me back."

"I'm going to ask Esther for a divorce as soon as I get back to Falls City. I'm going to do it as soon as I get home. I'll be moving out of the Rectory tonight. I won't spend another night with her in this charade. I've been unhappy for a long time and I know she's been unhappy as well. I wouldn't doubt but that she wants a divorce as much as I do."

"What about your priesthood?"

"I don't guess I'm very good at it. I've been in the same place for over twenty years and the congregation hasn't grown. I can't seem to get a better position." He grimaced, "I love it though. I love being able to take care of people who are having a difficult time. I like leading people in worship, but..." He was quiet for a moment. "I can't have both. If I have to resign my priesthood in order to have you, Melanie, then that's just what I'm going to do. I can only ask God to forgive me for the sin of loving you. I know it's a sin. I don't need Rufus Petersen to tell me that, but Honey, I don't feel like a sinner. I just feel like a man in love with the most beautiful woman in the world."

She put her arms around his neck and squeezed him. "Is there no other way? Is there no way that you can't have both of us? If you want to keep your priesthood, I'll be your mistress and you can keep your wife. I'm not jealous of her as long as I know that you really love me."

"No, I'm not going to live a lie. It's you that I want. You make me happy. You're what I have been looking for all these years. Now that I've found you I'm not going to risk losing you." She squeezed his neck again. "We do have one big problem." He dropped his face and began looking at the floor.

This time she leaned back and lifted his face with her hand so that she could look at him. "What problem? Rob, what else could there be?"

"I'm broke. I don't have any money. I don't even have a savings account. My credit card is maxed out and I've been making minimum payments on it. I think I can get a job teaching school, but that won't be much of a life for you."

She started laughing hysterically. She could not control herself.

"Melanie, this isn't funny. I will take care of you. I just don't know yet how I'm going to do it. I mean between your job and my job we ought to be able to get by. I guess since you have a job, I should move to California and try to get a job there."

She continued to laugh. He sat dumbfounded watching her. "Melanie, just what in God's name is so damn funny?"

"Oh, my darling Rob, you're so cute." Her giggles finally gave way to a smile of amusement. "Rob, listen to me. Are you ready?" He nodded. "Rob, I'm what they call loaded. My entire family is loaded. I have a trust fund that we'll never be able to deplete. We'll never have to worry about money."

He was stunned. He couldn't speak. He just sat staring at her. Then she looked anxious. "That's not a problem for you, is it? I mean, does my money change the way that you feel about me? If it does, Rob, I'll give it all away today. I don't need it. We can live in one of those little apartments in West Hollywood if need be. If you want to be poor, I'll be poor with you. Please don't let my money destroy what we have together."

This time he started to laugh. "You're rich! Damn, you're the most beautiful woman in the world and you're rich!" He stood up and took her in his arms, "And you're in love with me!" He cupped his hands around his mouth as though he were speaking through a microphone and echoed, "Today... today .... today...I'm the luckiest... luckiest... man in the world... world. And Melanie Mason is in love with me."

"Hopelessly."

"My precious Melanie, your money's not a problem for me. It's more like an answer to prayer. When I come to you in California, I'll probably have nothing but the clothes on my back. I'll not, however, be a kept man. I want to get a job. I want to do my share. I want to be able to contribute to our well being."

"Rob, that really won't be necessary."

"Yes, it is. I need to have some money of my own even if I spend every dime on you. When I buy you things to show you just how much I love you, I want to do it with my money, not yours."

"Oh, Rob, you're so wonderful!"

"I'd better get you to the airport. I'll call you after you get home. By then I will have written out my letter of resignation and mailed it to the Bishop and the Vestry. Then I'll tell Esther that I want a divorce. I'll make an appointment with a divorce attorney for tomorrow morning. I'll give everything to Esther and not ask for anything but my books and clothes. Maybe then she'll be more likely to go along with the divorce." He paused for a minute, "Melanie, what about your family? Will they accept me?"

She giggled, "My parents want what I want. They're going to love you. What about your son?"

"It's going to be hard on him. He adores his mother. He'll probably take her side. I imagine he'll think that I've lost my mind in some sort of mid-life crisis. In time, however, once he gets to know you and he sees just how happy we are together, I think he'll come around. He's a good boy."

He dropped her at the curbside check-in. They stood and embraced until the security officer blew his whistle and told him he would have to move along. "I'll call you this evening. I'll have everything set by then. When are you going to tell your parents?"

"We're having dinner together tonight. With the time difference, I should be able to tell them about the same time that you're telling Esther."

"Melanie, tell them whether you hear from me or not. Darling, it's a done deal. I love you and I'm not changing my mind. I'll not go on without you."

"I love you, Rob. You make me so happy."

She disappeared into the terminal and he began his drive back to Falls City. He knew what he had to do and there wasn't a doubt in his mind. He was going to do it. When Rob entered his house he shouted for Esther. She didn't respond. He was relieved she wasn't home. He hoped it would give him time to do the things he needed to do. He would tell her when she got home and then leave. He went immediately into his study and took the laptop computer Melanie had given him out of its hiding place. He then typed his letter of resignation.

Dear Bishop Petersen,
I know that this letter will come as a surprise to you, but I have made the decision to resign my responsibilities as Vicar of St. Mary's Mission. I am also going to ask you to grant me a leave of absence from the priesthood. I have filed for a divorce from my wife and don't want to take you or my congregation through the embarrassment of such an ordeal. Please consider my resignation to be effective as of this date. I trust you'll grant me a leave of absence from the priesthood effective on this date as well.

Faithfully,
Rob McBride

He transferred the document to a floppy disk and put it in his pocket. He would take it over to First Church later. Steele had been very generous with Rob, allowing him to use the First Church printers and copy machines. He would make a copy for each member of the Vestry. He decided to go ahead and hand address each of the envelopes and put stamps on them in anticipation of having copies of the letter. He would put them all in the mail on his way back home from First Church. He looked in the yellow pages under attorneys and wrote down the name of a divorce attorney and his telephone number on his pocket calendar. He would call for an appointment the first thing in the morning.

He then went into the bedroom to re-pack his bag and pack two more. He thought that it would be easier on Esther if he could just tell her and then leave. He would already have his luggage in the car. Melanie had given him several one hundred dollar bills to rent a place to stay for a few days. Once his divorce had been filed he would join her in California. Rob placed his suitcases on the bed in order to pack them. The bedroom was immaculate. It smelled of clean linens and lemon oil. Esther kept a clean house. He could never fault her for that. She was as neat as a pin. He used to joke that she was so meticulous with her housekeeping that if he got up in the middle of the night to go to the bathroom, she would have his side of the bed made when he returned.

Rob walked out of the bedroom and down the hall toward the kitchen. As he rounded the corner he could see Esther's legs. It looked like she was sitting on the floor. He ran into the kitchen and was jolted by what he saw. Esther was on the floor with her upper torso and head up against the kitchen cabinets. He ran to her. He felt for a pulse. Shaking, he ran to the wall telephone and dialed 9-1-1.

CHAPTER 9

The Vestry of First Church publishes an agenda and mails it to all of its members before each meeting. Steele Austin learned after his first few meetings that the agenda was never the agenda. The real meeting to set the agenda had most likely been conducted at the Magnolia Club by a handful of the Vestry just hours before the meeting itself. Since no women were on the Vestry it only made sense that the guys could get together at their all-male club and talk things over before the meeting was held. They were assured of relative security since Steele Austin wasn't eligible for membership. The membership was restricted to white protestant males who were the sons and grandsons of other white protestant males who had been members for decades.

Steele had learned to prepare himself for the concerns that would be presented once the formal agenda had been concluded. He had learned to hate the word "concerns". Tonight would be no different. Steele concluded each meeting with his usual remarks, "Gentlemen that is our agenda for the evening. The chair will now entertain a motion for adjournment." After a period of silence, someone would begin. Tonight it was Ned Boone.

Steele remembered Ned Boone well. The first time he ever saw the man was at an annual meeting that was engineered to get Steele removed as Rector. That night his then Senior Warden and close friend, Stone Clemons, told him about Ned Boone. "That S.O.B. wears people's careers on his belt like trophies. He has been instrumental in getting rid of two college presidents, a museum director, the county superintendent of schools, and one headmaster of a private school in Atlanta. He's as mean as a snake." Ned Boone got himself elected to the Vestry at that annual meeting. Howard Dexter had been antagonistic to Steele before Chadsworth Alexander died. At that same annual meeting he manipulated the process to get himself elected Senior Warden. His platform had only one plank. He would rid First Church of Steele Austin. But that was before Chadsworth Alexander left instructions that his substantial fortune would be deposited into Howard Dexter's bank on the condition that his widow be made Chair of the Board and that Howard would support the ministry of the current Rector.

Steele Austin pulled a maneuver of his own. His strongest advocate, Stone Clemons, and his retiring Senior Warden, could not serve on the Vestry again for a least one year. Steele created a new position on the Vestry. He appointed Stone to be his Chancellor to serve with all the privileges of a member of the Vestry. Stone was at the meeting in that capacity. He would have voice, but he could not vote.

Mr. Boone began. He craned his neck over his bowtie in an effort to make sure that he had everyone's attention. He didn't direct his remarks to Steele, who was chairing the meeting, but he directed his remarks to the Senior Warden, Howard Dexter, and the other members of the Vestry. "Misturh Senior Warden, I'm quite concerned about several items that I feel in good conscience I simply must bring to the attention of the members of the Vestry. There is a terrible rumor going about the community that the Rector is attempting to turn our sacred burial ground into a pet cemetery. My investigations are conclusive. Gentlemen, this is no rumor. The Rector isn't attempting to desecrate our churchyard; he has already done so. I find this very distressing."

There were several nods and comments of agreement around the table. He continued, "In order to prevent the Rector from engaging in any further desecration of our hallowed ground, I want to make the following motion and have it attached to our cemetery policies. It's short and to the point. Resolved, only the human remains of members in good standing at First Church can be buried in the First Church Cemetery. I so move." There were several seconds around the table.

Stone Clemons' face lit up. He looked like a little boy reeling in his first fish. "Ned, what about ol' Blue?"

Ned looked puzzled. "What do you mean? What about him?"

The devilish grin on the face of Stone Clemons widened. "If I remember correctly, when your Daddy died you had his favorite hunting dog put down, cremated, and buried in the casket with him. Didn't your Daddy call him ol' Blue?"

Ned's long neck began turning red. "That's different."

Stone's eyes twinkled with amusement. "Now, you're not going to tell us that ol' Blue was a baptized member of this church in good standing, are you?"

Stone's question brought forth several chuckles from the members of the Vestry. Ned failed to see any humor in the game. "No, but my Daddy was a member of this church since his birth. And ol' Blue's ashes were put in a proper container and buried with my Daddy in his casket."

Chief Sparks, the local Chief of Police for the last three decades, and another one of Steele's friends and vocal supporters, decided to join in the joust. "Does that mean that you want to amend your motion to allow for animals to be buried in the churchyard so long as their remains are in a proper container and placed inside the casket with a life-long member?"

Ned began to sputter. "No, I just want to put an end to the Rector burying whomever and whatever he wants to bury in our beloved cemetery."

Steele was surprised by the next question, which came from Howard Dexter, "Just how would you propose that we do that, Ned? Do you want the entire Vestry or a committee of the Vestry to pre-approve each and every burial?"

"Yes, that's exactly what I want to have happen. I rescind my previous motion and make a new one. I move that the Executive Committee of the Vestry pre-approve each and every burial that is to take place in the cemetery and that no burial be permitted without the unanimous consent of the Executive Committee."

Again, there were a series of seconds to the motion uttered. "That way," he continued, "we can assure that the Rector is kept under control." Someone called for the question and it passed with only Chief Sparks voting against it. Howard Dexter abstained from voting.

Ned continued, "Now that we have that issue successfully resolved, I want to move that the Vestry go on record as not supporting the opening of a Free Medical Clinic. I'm totally opposed to welfare of any kind. A Free Clinic verges on socialism, which is just one step away from communism. Gentlemen, as Christians and as Americans who believe that every person should earn their own way, we must go on record as being opposed to anything that hints of socialism, or worse, communism. It's our duty to put an end to this Medical Clinic before the Rector brings that demonic movement to our community."

Steele heard himself speaking even before he knew what he was going to say. "Ned, I have a request. You insist on talking about me as though I'm not even in the room. I'm right here. I'm fully present. If you disagree with me or disapprove of my actions, I would prefer that you speak directly to me. Sir, I am your Rector. I'm not a field hand or your employee. I'm your Rector and I insist that you treat me as such. Now Ned, I have a question for you. You're fully aware that I'm going to use the funds from the Chadsworth Alexander Endowment for this Clinic. Since you're opposed to using it for a Clinic, just how would you have me use it?"

Ned smirked, "Any extra funds this Vestry has should be used for the most important work this parish does."

"And just what do you consider the most important work this parish does?" Steele shot back.

"It pains me, Misturh Austin that you have to ask that question." That statement came from Henry Mudd. Henry Mudd had been elected Junior Warden at the parish meeting organized to elect a slate of candidates to the Vestry that promised to unseat Steele as Rector. The Mudds represented an old and prestigious Georgia family. They had been leaders in First Church for four generations. The prayer desks in the nave of the church were given in memory of his great grandfather. Henry was married and had two daughters. At a very young age the girls had learned to emulate their parents' arrogance. Steele didn't like Henry Mudd, but the feeling was returned in spades. Steele's thoughts were interrupted.

"Are you listening to me, Misturh Austin? You must understand that the success of this parish is totally dependent on the success of our parish day school. As goes the school so goes this parish."

That statement took Steele's breath away. "Gentlemen, please understand. I'm not opposed to the school. Please understand that. But I think the school should operate on school funds and the parish funds should be used for the work of the Gospel."

"Sir, that statement makes me angry!" Ned Boone emphasized his statement by slapping his hand on the conference room table. "The work of the school is the work of the Gospel. The students in the day school are the future businessmen in this nation. In order for our system of government to survive and capitalism be allowed to prosper, we must give our future leaders the best education possible."

Chief Sparks interrupted, "Ned, I think you're missing the point. No one here disagrees on the importance of giving our children a superior education, but parochial school isn't the only place in this community that children can receive a great education. I didn't send my children to the day school. You and I both know the parish started that school the same year that the integration order of the public schools came down. Now, we can all swear on a stack of Bibles that's not the reason we started the school, but it was and we all know it. We also know that it's the school of the privileged in our community. You have to have considerable financial resources to send your children to the parish day school."

Ned exploded, "*Surh*, that's just as it should be. Better educated parents will naturally produce better educated children and wealth is best entrusted to the well educated."

Steele spoke cautiously, "Ned, this isn't about the virtues of receiving an excellent education. This is about The Alexander Endowment. That Endowment was set up for ministry to the poor. Jesus taught us that on judgment day we will be held accountable for feeding the hungry, clothing the naked, and visiting the widow, the orphan, and the prisoner." Stone Clemons began tapping Steele on his foot with the toe of his shoe underneath the table. Steele realized that his comments may have done more damage than good.

Colonel Mitchell spoke up, "The Rector is entitled to his interpretation of the Gospel. My hunch is that not many of the faithful sitting at this table agree with him. So, in the interest of moving things forward so that we can all go home, I'll make a motion. I move that the Vestry of First Church go on record as being opposed to the opening of a Free Medical Clinic in Falls City." Again, there were a series of seconds verbalized. Before there could be any discussion, the question was called for and passed with only two familiar dissenting votes. Chief Sparks voted "no" and Howard Dexter abstained from voting yet one more time.

Ned continued, "And now I have but one final concern, but this is of such a positive nature I am overjoyed to bring it to your attention. I would like for this Vestry to go on record commending The Reverend Richard Davis for his exemplary preaching of the Christian Gospel. In particular, we commend him for his courage to openly condemn the homosexual lifestyle. But gentlemen, the sermon that Father Davis preached this past Sunday explaining the reasons that women cannot be ordained to the priesthood was one of the finest, no, it was the finest sermon I've ever heard preached. Richard's faithfulness to Holy Scripture and traditional Anglican teachings is commendable." This time there was a round of spontaneous applause. Richard Davis stood and took a slight bow. Steele shot a look of disgust at Horace Drummond. Horace just began shaking his head.

Colonel Mitchell spoke up. "Obviously, we don't need a vote, the applause speaks for itself. Gentlemen, I agree with Ned. Richard's sermons are the finest I've ever heard from the First Church pulpit. I've taken the liberty of recording his last three sermons and have copies available for each of you. I hope you'll take them and share them with others in the community. I think that this type of preaching will go far in correcting the rapidly growing misunderstanding in Falls City that our church is no longer true to the Gospel and has just become a humanistic organization."

Steele could not contain his anger any further. "Gentlemen, you need to know that I don't agree with Richard's presentation of the Gospel. It's completely without grace and forgiveness. His attempts to give simple answers to complex questions do more to hurt our efforts to bring people into a relationship with Christ than they do to help. Jesus exercised a ministry of compassion and acceptance."

"Don't you think sin should be condemned from the pulpit?" Ned Boone exploded.

"Yes, Ned, I certainly do." Steele fought to regain his own composure. "I believe that the preacher should lead the members of the congregation to examine their own consciences, including his own, and seek forgiveness for our own sins. I also think that the preacher should lead the congregation present to forgive those who have sinned against them. I don't see that anything is gained by using the pulpit to sit in judgment on the sins of people we don't even know."

"Well, I commend Richard for naming sin as sin and defending the Gospel." Ned countered.

Steele took a deep breath. "Is it the Gospel? Pulpit time is precious time. I believe the ministry of Jesus would be better served if we spent less time debating and arguing about the faith and more time sharing the faith. People are hungry to hear about the God that Jesus revealed to us. He revealed to us a Heavenly Father that welcomes his children home with open arms. He doesn't meet us at the door with a pointed finger and a scolding. Now let me make this clear to this Vestry. I've told Richard that unless he ceases to use the pulpit for his own personal agendas he will not be scheduled to preach again."

Colonel Mitchell shook his head, "That, sir, is the wrong thing to do. Richard is preaching the Bible. I suggest that both you and Doctor Drummond could take a lesson or two from Richard."

Steele was furious, but he wasn't about to let them turn this into an opportunity to publicly pit his clergy and himself against each other. He was equally concerned that if he overreacted they would have ammunition to conclude that he was jealous of Richard's popularity. Steele knew that Richard was pulling the rug out from under him at every opportunity. He was moving about the parish telling people that Steele was marginalizing him and that he wasn't being given enough opportunity to preach. He suggested that Steele was, in fact, envious of his preaching ability.

Steele knew further that Richard was telling people that he just didn't know what the Rector did all day. He was raising questions in the congregation about Steele's spirituality, his leadership style, his inability to verbalize a vision, and a host of other things. He made it clear that the rest of the staff agreed with him, but they wouldn't say anything because they were all afraid of Steele Austin. Each of his critiques with the various members of the congregation was designed to discredit Steele as a priest and Rector in the eyes of members. Other clergy and lay people in the Diocese had reported to Steele that Richard was telling them the same things.

"Let's just say that Richard, Horace, and I will continue to have thoughtful conversations about the message that we want to send to the community from the First Church pulpit. I think we can all agree that it would be best if we are sending the same message and not contradicting one another from Sunday to Sunday. The primary message that Jesus preached was love God and love your neighbor. I don't think that we can improve on that message. Everything else is a footnote."

Ned Boone asserted, "It would really be wonderful if you and Doctor Drummond would agree with Richard. Once that word got out, we would have to add services on Sunday morning to accommodate all the people who would want to come and hear the Bible preached."

Steele looked again at Horace. He caught both the eyes of Chief Sparks and Stone Clemons as well. Horace made a cutting gesture across his throat. The other two men nodded. Steele spoke, "Are there any other concerns we need to hear about tonight?"

No one spoke. "Good, then this meeting is adjourned."

As everyone filed out of the room Steele, Chief Sparks, and Stone Clemons walked the opposite direction toward the cemetery. Stone Clemons put his arm around Horace Drummond's shoulder and whispered in his ear. When they were in the churchyard, Stone led them directly to the Boone family plot. "His Daddy and ol' Blue are buried here. There's his mother. This will be his spot." Then he began the ritual that had brought all of them such sweet comfort over the last year. He pulled the flask of brandy out of his pocket and began passing it around. "Come on Horace, don't hold out on us." Horace stood there for a moment with a shocked look on his face. Then he let out a great burst of laughter that started all of them laughing. Horace Drummond was then initiated into the real secret society at First Church. Horace joined in the ritual of brotherhood that now marked the end of each of the Vestry meetings. The location was a moveable feast but was always conducted on the burial site of the person that had been the biggest pain at that evening's Vestry meeting. The ritual in the cemetery after each Vestry meeting included a little brandy and a lot of laughter. It made everything just a little bit more tolerable for Steele.

CHAPTER 10

It just doesn't look good for your boy, Steele." Chief Sparks was sitting behind his desk at the Law Enforcement Center. He was chewing on his signature cigar. It wasn't lit. Steele Austin had incredible respect for Chief Sparks. He had been the Chief of Police in Falls City for over thirty years. He was very progressive for the old south. He was one of the first to integrate his department with African American officers. He brought women onto the force even before it became the fashionable thing to do. And he had developed a *don't ask –don't tell* policy for the gay and lesbian officers before the phrase was even thought of up in Washington D.C. His conclusions regarding Rob McBride, however, stung Steele's ears.

"I just don't believe it, Chief," Steele countered. "I know this man. He's not capable of taking another person's life. I tell you, Chief; your boys have got the wrong man. He didn't do it."

The Chief leaned back in his chair and took a long hard look at Steele. He continued to chew on his cigar. Steele became distracted. "Do you ever light that thing?"

"What, this cigar?" The Chief took the cigar out of his mouth and rolled it in his fingers, studying it like it were a piece of fine art. "Hell, Father, if I lit this thing I'd have to smoke it. Now, we both know that smoking is bad for you."

They both chuckled and then the Chief continued. "Let's just look at the evidence against your Father McBride. First, there's motive. He had spent Sunday afternoon writing letters to the Mission Committee and the Bishop advising them that he was going to divorce his wife. My hunch is that he asked her for a divorce and she refused. They had an argument and a shoving match. He pushed her up against the kitchen cabinet and the fall broke her neck."

"I'm sorry, Chief. I know that they were having marital difficulties, but to me the letters only confirm his intention to handle the situation in a mature manner." Steele paused and looked down at the desk as though he were looking for the answer on the desk itself. "Chief, I just don't believe your scenario. I'm sorry. I really respect you and I value our friendship, but on this one we'll just have to disagree."

The Chief had grown very fond of Steele. He hated the fact that First Church had not given him a very warm welcome. He despised those who had brought so much pain into his life and that of his wife. But when it came to police work he knew his stuff. He rolled the cigar in his fingers. "Steele, he had opportunity. He lied to us about his whereabouts for the weekend. We checked. The Bishop didn't send him to Atlanta to speak to a group of clergy. We don't know where he was just yet, but do we know where he wasn't. One of the very first rules of criminal investigation is that you focus on the person that lies to you first. He became our primary suspect when he lied to us. That gives us reason to believe that he has something to hide. Now, what we do know is that he was in his study typing the letters to the Bishop within an hour of the coroner's estimated time of death. We know that from the time the documents were created on his computer. We also know that there is no evidence of any break-in. The windows and doors were all secure. There was no intruder."

Steele shook his head. "Then she let someone else in the house. Someone she knew."

The Chief took another chew on his cigar. "We have no evidence that anyone else was in the house that afternoon." The Chief studied his cigar. He rolled it back and forth in his fingers. "Steele, if you've been away for the weekend and you get back home, are you satisfied to simply shout your wife's name when you enter the house?"

"No."

"Of course not. Wouldn't you go to the garage to see if her car was there? If it was, wouldn't you continue your search for her?"

Steele nodded.

"Your boy didn't do that. He was alone in that house with his wife's body for approximately one hour. He's trying to tell us that he was in his study typing letters while his wife lay dying or dead just a few feet away on the kitchen floor. And then, when the police did arrive at the house, they found that he had his bags all packed and he was ready to skip town. How would you explain all that to a jury, Parson?"

"What about fingerprints?"

"Steele, it's a Rectory. There are fingerprints all over the house. A Bible Study was held in the house every Sunday night. They entertained parish members, the Altar Guild. Hell, even the teenagers had an ice cream social there a couple of weeks ago. Fingerprints, there are more fingerprints than in a shopping mall." The Chief leaned across the desk to look directly at Steele. "Father, the man – your priest – lied to the police about his whereabouts. The first words out of his mouth were a lie. I don't think I need to give you the statistics on the number of times that a husband or wife is killed by their spouse. Combine those statistics with the lies he continues to tell us and the conclusion is obvious. He is our primary suspect."

"I admit that doesn't sound good and I'll do my best to get him to come clean with you on his weekend. I can't believe he would be so stupid as to lie to you. Why would he do that?"

The Chief shrugged. "Two possibilities come to mind. The one would be that he is protecting someone and the other is that he's simply trying to confuse the situation to buy some time." After a brief pause the Chief continued, "But then again, I'm going with a third possibility. He lied to us because he's guilty."

"Chief, just because he didn't tell you the truth about his whereabouts doesn't mean that he's a murderer."

The Chief opened a file folder and shoved some pictures across the desk at Steele. They were pictures of a shirtless Rob McBride. He was covered with scratches and bruises. Steele looked at the pictures in disbelief. "Obviously," the Chief continued, "they struggled. She must have put up quite a fight. She really left her mark on him."

Steele sat staring at the pictures. He simply could not believe what he was seeing. "There has to be another explanation. How does Rob explain these scratches and bruises?"

"He doesn't", the Chief shot back.

"What about DNA? Surely, the killer would have left his DNA on Esther?" Steele wanted to make sure that every possible explanation was being explored.

The Chief put the cigar on his desk, raised his eyebrows and leaned across the desk toward Steele. "Interesting twist of events, Father, the killer was very careful to scrape underneath the deceased's fingernails. After scraping the woman's nails, he clipped them. Then to make absolutely sure that no DNA would be left, the killer washed the victim's hands, arms, and legs with bleach. They were spotless. He even bleached her face. The killer was meticulous. This murder was intentional and every effort was made to cover it up."

Steele shook his head, "Chief, Rob is a priest. I just don't believe that he did these things."

The Chief stood and walked around the desk. He sat down on the edge of it so that he could look directly at Steele. "Parson, listen to me. We have only one suspect. We have no evidence to suggest that we should even look for another suspect. Steele, no one wants to send a priest to death row, but that's exactly where this guy is headed. He will be found guilty. The prosecutor is ready to file charges against him in the morning. Most likely he'll ask for the death penalty. This is a gruesome crime and the fact that it was committed by a priest will make it even more dramatic. The public will demand the death penalty."

Steele felt sick to his stomach. He knew Rob McBride. He knew he was unhappy in his marriage, but he couldn't see Rob murdering his wife. He simply couldn't visualize a struggle. He couldn't imagine Rob shoving his wife against the cabinets forcefully enough to break her neck. There had to be more to the story. There just had to be a rational explanation for all of this.

"If you could get him to plead guilty to manslaughter, I think the prosecutor would be willing to make a deal. Just get him to admit that it was an accident. Get him to admit that he asked her for a divorce and she refused. Hell, I can imagine that she was so angry with him that she attacked him. He tried to defend himself by pushing her away. She fell against the cabinet and broke her neck. It's all very reasonable and understandable. The judge would probably only give him ten to fifteen years."

"Can I see him?" Steele really wanted to talk to Rob McBride.

"I was hoping you'd say that." The Chief stood and pushed the intercom button on his telephone. A uniformed officer entered. "I want Father Austin to have some time with McBride. Insure their privacy." The officer nodded. Steele shook the Chief's hand and followed the officer down to an interrogation room. He sat for a few minutes waiting on Rob. When Rob entered he was wearing an orange jailhouse jumpsuit. He looked at Steele, made eye contact, and then looked away. Steele sat staring at Rob. Clearly he was a broken man. Rob began to cry.

"Steele, I didn't do this. I didn't kill her." Rob regained his composure. "Yes, I made the decision to divorce her. Yes, I had intended to ask her for a divorce. She wasn't home or at least I thought she wasn't there when I got home. I wrote the letter to the Bishop. I went into the bedroom and packed my bags. I thought that would be better. I figured that when she got home I could simply make my exit after I told her. I went out to the kitchen to get a snack and wait for her to get home. That's when I saw her. Steele, I'm the one that called 9-1-1."

Steele listened intently; he so wanted to believe his friend, but the Chief had planted some questions in his mind. "Where were you, Rob?"

A pained expression crossed Rob's face. "Steele, my friend, please don't ask me that. I don't want to have to lie to you. Just believe me when I tell you that I didn't do this."

Steele tried to be patient. "Rob, this doesn't look good. You have to cooperate with the police. Right now you're their one and only suspect."

"Steele, someone else did this. I don't know who, but I'm telling you it wasn't me."

"You have bruises and the scratches on your neck, chest, back and arms. Where did you get those? Did your wife inflict them on you?"

Rob shook his head. "No, but I can't tell you. Please don't ask me. I'll only have to lie to you."

"Rob, do you realize that you're facing the death penalty? They're talking about putting you to death for this crime. Do you want to die for a crime that you say you didn't commit?"

Rob looked back at Steele, "You don't believe me, do you? You think I did it. Steele, I thought you knew me better than this."

Steele made the decision to be firm. "You're the only person who is in a position to help your case. Lying to the police isn't the answer. Rob, I know Chief Sparks. He will give you the benefit of the doubt, but you cannot lie to him. You have to come clean with him. Rob where were you? Is there anyone who can give you a good alibi?"

Rob was silent. He didn't respond. Steele's questions and doubts had wounded him.

"Do you have an attorney?

"They have assigned me a public defender. I can't afford an attorney."

"What about Bishop Petersen, has he offered to help you find an attorney?"

Rob chuckled. "You haven't heard, have you? The Bishop has relieved me of my congregation. He has placed an inhibition on my priesthood and advised me that, pending the counsel of the Diocesan Standing Committee, he plans to depose me. I'll no longer be a priest."

"I'm so sorry, Rob, but I have to confess that I'm not surprised. Bishop Petersen isn't known for standing by clergy who find themselves in trouble of any kind."

"Who has the Bishop placed in charge of St. Mary's?" Steele asked.

Rob looked back at him, first in shock, and then in amusement. Rob's chuckle flowed into laughter. "Oh my God, you haven't heard. This is too good to be true. I can't believe that you've not been told."

Rob was bent over with laughter. Steele kept asking him what was so funny. "Steele, the Bishop has appointed your Curate to be the Vicar of St. Mary's. Richard Davis is now Vicar. I can't believe the Bishop didn't call you and let you know." Rob could not stop laughing.

Steele was overwhelmed with a cornucopia of emotion. He was embarrassed, but at the same time he was relieved. Richard Davis had been one royal pain in the butt. He had been trying to triangle staff against Steele. He had enamored himself to all of Steele's antagonists. He preached a gospel of hate that would have been an embarrassment to most Anglicans. He had raised questions in the congregation about Steele's spirituality, leadership style, financial management, and his very Christianity. Yes, he was glad to be rid of him, but he didn't like hearing it in this way. If any of the troublemakers from First Church decided to follow Richard Davis to St. Mary's, it would be all the better. In fact, Steele had a list of people he would like to see make the transition.

Steele returned his attention to Rob. "Do you want me to see if Stone Clemons and his firm will take your case pro bono? Stone is a real good guy and his firm is one of the best in the state. Perhaps they'll take your case."

"I need all the help I can get." Rob looked a bit relieved. "If I could get a first rate attorney maybe they could help me find the person who did this. I just know that I didn't do it."

Steele stood and walked around the table to Rob. Rob stood. Steele removed his oil stock from his pocket. He made the sign of the cross in oil on Rob's forehead, "God give you the strength and the patience to go through this ordeal. God give to all of us who want to help you the wisdom and the skill to help you find the truth so that the truth can set you free." Tears streamed down both of their faces.

As Steele Austin drove back to his office from the Law Enforcement Center he was depressed. He could not see a way out for his friend. He really wanted to believe him, but if he wouldn't be honest with him there was little chance that he would come clean with the police. Steele felt that his only recourse was to pray for Rob, for Chief Sparks, and for his detectives.

Back at his office Steele had settled into the routine of checking his voice mails, e-mails, and scheduling appointments for the next day on his personal planner. His secretary interrupted him. "Father Austin, there's a Melanie Mason here. She says that she doesn't have an appointment with you, but she has traveled all the way from Los Angeles to see you. She says she's a friend of Rob McBride."

A smile crossed Steele's face. "Finally, thank you God, finally we are going to get some answers." Steele opened the door leading to his secretary's office. His gaze fell on one of the most beautiful women he had ever seen in his life. With a smile, a glance, and the extension of her hand for Steele to shake, she communicated breeding, education, culture, and wealth. Steele knew the type. She was a lady. He prayed that she would be Rob McBride's lucky lady.

CHAPTER 11

Two hours before the opening of the Free Medical Clinic there was a line of patients that stretched up the block and around the corner. Clearly, they were people in need. There were all ages and a diverse mix of races. There were the elderly leaning against their canes and walkers. Others were in wheelchairs. Mothers held infants in their arms and tried to comfort them. There were people sniffling into handkerchiefs and there were folks who quite clearly were not only in need of medical attention, but a good bath as well.

Colonel Mitchell had valiantly fought the concept of the Medical Clinic. He had tried to rally the doctors in the community against it. When one of the retiring physicians offered his medical building and all of the equipment to Steele for one dollar a year, Colonel Mitchell tried to convince him otherwise. He appealed to the hospital board to intercede. The hospital administrator stunned him by coming out in favor of the Clinic. He reminded Colonel Mitchell and all the trustees of the number of people who use the hospital emergency room as a doctor's office. He supported the concept of the Medical Clinic, stating that it would help them keep the emergency room available for true emergencies.

Steele started receiving telephone calls from the other clergy in town who wanted to help. It was agreed that they would have an ecumenical prayer breakfast near St. Luke's Day, the patron saint of physicians. They would invite all the medical professionals in their various congregations to attend. Steele would present the concept of the Clinic and then the two Senior Ministers in the community would close the sale. It was an amazing sight to watch the Senior Minister of the Methodist Church, who had been in his congregation for eighteen years, and the Senior Minister in the Baptist Church, who had served that congregation for thirty years, use their positions with such grace. They simply told the gathered physicians and nurses that this was a good thing. It was what the Lord would want us to do. And they would be disappointed if every medical professional in each of their congregations didn't sign up to volunteer for at least one evening a month. They then simply began calling out the names of the physicians and nurses present, asking for an individual commitment. They put a positive check by each name.

The professionals from the other congregations followed suit. There were no questions about malpractice insurance. No objections of any kind were raised. In a matter of ninety minutes the Clinic had more than enough volunteer doctors and nurses to be open every night of the month. Colonel Mitchell had threatened to come to the meeting to speak against opening the Clinic, but he was not present.

As word spread throughout south Georgia about the Clinic, pharmaceutical salesmen and physicians in other communities began to open up their sample cabinets to supply needed medications. Another doctor offered his x-ray machine. Others offered lab equipment. Soon the Medical Clinic had most all the equipment that a physician would need to do the basic work-up on the patients who presented themselves for help.

Almeda Alexander surprised Steele by stepping forward to recruit and train the lay volunteers. The volunteers would not only do the initial intake of patient information, but they would also make sure there was a good supply of cookies, coffee, and hot cocoa. It was decided to also seek donations of fresh fruits, vegetables, and fruit juices. Patients standing in line would be escorted into the waiting room as seats became available. The rest would have to remain outside. Each patient would be taken into one of the three volunteer offices so that they could answer the intake questions in complete confidentiality.

Steele and the other clergy insisted that a large cross be placed on the outside of the building and that several classical works of religious art be placed in the waiting room and about the building. They believed that it was important that the patients know that the ministry they were receiving was being done in the name of Jesus.

At five minutes before six o'clock in the evening, Steele gathered all the volunteers, the nurses, and the physicians in the waiting room. He thanked each of them for being present and for giving of their time and talent to the ministry of those less fortunate. He then asked all present to join hands. "Lord Jesus Christ, your heart went out in compassion to those who were sick. You blessed the little children. You opened the eyes of the blind. You made it possible for the crippled to walk. You healed the leper. And you gave hope to the dying. We ask you to bless our ministries through this Medical Clinic. May it be a place of healing and hope for all who walk through these doors."

Everyone then had a group hug. Steele took note that Horace Drummond and Almeda Alexander had been standing next to each other. He also thought their hug was just a bit more lengthy and connected than the other hugs shared by the group members. Then he dismissed the thought, thinking it must be his imagination.

The first group of patients was admitted to the waiting room. Every chair was taken and the three intake room doors were shut. None of the people approached the table in the middle of the room, which was covered with cookies, fruits, vegetables, juices, coffee and cocoa. Almeda twice announced that the food and drinks were for them and encouraged the folks to approach the table. Everyone sat stoically looking at the floor. Almeda decided to take matters into her own hands. She recruited a couple of the other volunteers and they began distributing the food and drinks to the people in their chairs. Each person took the offering and looked up at her. Each graciously thanked her. After a bit, the people began approaching the table to help themselves.

Steele was moving about the Clinic talking with those who were in the waiting room and encouraging the medical staff, in between patients, with words of appreciation. A couple of times one of the doctors asked him to step in the examining room and offer some spiritual guidance to those who were critically ill.

After about an hour and a half, Steele decided to take a break. He walked to the back of the Clinic where there was a small break room for the staff. When he rounded the corner he at first thought his eyes were playing tricks on him. Then he stopped at the door and took a closer look. There, in the corner, leaning up against the wall out of sight of anyone in the hallway, stood Almeda Alexander. Facing her in a most intimate embrace was his associate, Horace Drummond. They were deep in whispered conversation. Almeda had one arm around his waist. The other arm was around his neck and the fingers of her hand were intertwined in his hair.

"Perhaps the two of you should get a room," Steele chuckled. They both jumped and pulled apart. Horace began laughing, as did Almeda.

"I feel like a school girl who has just been caught smooching her beau by her Daddy." Almeda couldn't make eye contact with Steele.

Horace glanced at him and then looked away. Steele continued his torment, "Oh, you mean there was smooching and I missed it?"

"Steele Austin, I'm a grown woman and I'll not be made to feel so foolish by someone twenty years my junior," Almeda scolded.

"Twenty years?" Steele smirked.

"Now, I've just about heard enough from you."

Steele sat down at the table. They sat down opposite him. Horace took Almeda's hand in his and held it on top of the table. "Steele, we're in love."

Steele held up his hand, gesturing for him to stop. "Friends, you don't owe me an explanation. As far as that goes you don't owe anyone an explanation. You're both mature adults. You're both widowed. You both have been around the block. You know better than I do what you're up against in this town. Just let me know what I can do to help you."

Steele stood and started toward the door. Horace and Almeda studied each other. "Steele," it was Almeda. "Just a minute." Steele turned to look at her. This time it was Steele who received a heartfelt embrace from Almeda. She kissed him on the cheek. "I was wrong about you. You really are a darling boy."

The blood rushed to Steele's face. He knew he was blushing. "Shucks, Miss Scarlett, you sure know how to turn a guy's head."

Just then a volunteer tapped Steele on the shoulder. "Father Austin, Doctor Robbins would like for you to come to examining room two."

Steele followed the volunteer into the room. Doctor Robbins shook his hand and introduced him to a man and woman that Steele estimated were in their late thirties or early forties. "This is Mr. and Mrs. Max Weller."

Steele looked at the couple. "I know you. I've seen you at First Church, right?"

Max spoke, "Yes, my wife Sharon and I have been worshipping with you. We really like your church."

"And who is this?" Steele bent over to get a closer look at a little girl who was sitting on her mother's lap. The little girl laid her head back on her mother's breast and gave Steele a side glance.

"This is Mandy," her mother answered.

Steele bent down so that he could come to eye level with the little girl. "Mandy, that sure is a pretty name for such a pretty girl." The little girl gave him a slight smile and then buried her face into her mother even further. "How old are you, Mandy?"

"Can you tell Father Austin how old you are, Mandy?" Her mother coached.

"Show him with your fingers."

The little girl sheepishly looked back at Steele and held up five fingers. "Five years old," he smiled. "That must mean that you're in kindergarten."

She nodded and smiled before leaning her head back again.

Steele studied the parents more closely. It was clear that they had been crying. Steele looked back at Doctor Robbins.

Doctor Robbins suggested that the volunteer take Mandy to the break room and get her one of the ice cream bars that were in the staff freezer. Surprisingly, Mandy went to her at the suggestion that ice cream was just a few steps away. When they were gone, Doctor Robbins began. "Mandy's very ill. She has an inoperable brain tumor. There's nothing that we can do."

"How can you know that, Steve?" I mean, Doctor Robbins, I don't understand how you can draw such a dramatic conclusion based on this one examination." Steele didn't want to believe what he was hearing.

The physician opened a large brown envelope, turned on the lighted panel above the examination table, and placed the x-ray film on it. "These x-rays were taken about two weeks ago at the emergency room here at Falls City Hospital." He then placed another large film next to it. "This is one of the pictures we took tonight. You can see for yourself how much the tumor has grown in just a couple of weeks."

Steele and the parents stood to take a closer look. The parents dissolved into tears. Steele looked at Doctor Robbins. Tears were flooding his eyes. Steele felt his own eyes grow moist. Let me suggest that we all sit down. After the parents regained their composure, Max spoke. "We actually first noticed that something was wrong with Mandy at First Church. She was standing on the kneeler and I noticed she was looking at me funny. Then I realized that she was about to fall. She was having a difficult time keeping her balance. We then began to notice that some of her other movements appeared strange. Her coordination just wasn't right. We took her to the emergency room. The doctors did the x-rays. We got the first diagnosis from them." Tears once again streamed down his cheeks. His voice gave out. He leaned forward and placed his face in his hands.

His wife placed her hand on his back, "We came here tonight, hoping against hope that just perhaps we could get a second opinion. Mandy's our only child. I can't have any more children. In fact, we didn't think that we would ever have any children. Mandy was our little surprise."

Her husband sat up straight again, "We don't have any medical insurance. We moved here so that I could work in the carpet factory. I've not had any luck getting on down there. Sharon works a little waitressing. I'm able to pick up some odd jobs. We're able to get by. I actually have a teaching degree. I used to teach fifth grade, but there are no vacancies in the Falls City system right now."

"What is the prognosis, Steve?" Steele questioned.

The doctor shook his head. Maybe six months, maybe less, maybe more. We'll need to keep her comfortable. She'll most likely lose sight in either one or both eyes before it's all over. Her speech will become difficult, as will her hearing. Her difficulty with balance and movement will worsen." Again, Max and Sharon dissolved in tears. Their bodies shook with pain as they held onto each other.

Steele and the doctor sat in silence with them. When they had once again regained their composure, Doctor Robbins spoke, "I want to be Mandy's physician. I do family practice." He handed them his card, "You bring her to my office. I will work with you to make sure she stays comfortable."

"We don't have any insurance — we really can't afford a private physician. How will we be able to pay you?" Max countered.

"There will be no charge. You'll never get a bill from me. You're to call me or my office at any time — day or night."

Sharon stood and hugged the doctor's neck. Max stood and shook his hand. Steele put his arms around the couple and Steve took his clue from Steele and followed suit. "Let's pray." Steele began, "Lord Jesus Christ, You took little children in Your arms and blessed them. We ask You to bless Mandy. Put Your loving arms around her. Send Your holy angels to minister to her. Give us the faith to trust her to You and to trust You as You walk with us through her illness. Of course, we love her and we want her to be healed. We want to keep her with us. Hear our cries, look on the love and heartbreak of these parents and lead Doctor Robbins and the nurses who care for Mandy to find a way for her to stay with us. And this we ask in Your most precious name. Amen."

Steele led the parents down to the break room where Mandy was sitting on the volunteer's lap, finishing off her ice cream. On seeing her parents she began to reach for them. "Where do you live?"

"Our address and phone number are on the sheet we filled out with the volunteer. We're renting a house on the edge of town."

"I want to come by and visit with you. I want to come over and spend some time with Mandy."

Sharon smiled, "You have the time to do something like that, Father Austin?"

"Nothing is more important to me right now than taking care of the two of you and Mandy. You can count on me."

Steele watched them leave the break room and walk down the hall toward the exit. He sat down opposite the volunteer. Soon Doctor Robbins joined them at the table. They sat in silence for a long time. "Sometimes this job kind of makes it hard for me to believe in your God of love and mercy."

Steele looked at the doctor. His eyes were red and moist. "I know, on occasion this job kind of makes it hard for me to believe in Him as well. But then, we're in pretty good company."

"How's that?" Doctor Robbins questioned.

"Just remember that Jesus also felt forsaken as He was dying." Steele smiled, "I guess if the Son of Man could feel that way, it's okay for a couple of mortals like you and me to have those same feelings."

The doctor stood, slapping Steele on his back. "You're a good man, Charlie Brown. Now let's you and me go see if there aren't some people out there in that waiting room we can help."

Steele stood and followed him down the hall, "Steve."

"Yeah?"

"You know that we're going to help more children tonight than we're going to lose."

Steve Robbins looked back over his shoulder at Steele, "That's the part that keeps me going."

Steele echoed, "It's the part that keeps us all going. Maybe it's the part that reminds us that we are partners with God, but we aren't God."

"Perhaps," Steve muttered.

CHAPTER 12

Steele parked his car in the staff parking lot adjacent to the administration building for First Church. As he eased into his parking place he took note that the name denoting his space had not yet been changed. The other staff members had their names painted on the curbing to mark their spots. His spot was the same as the day he arrived. It was marked simply, "Rector." He had asked the maintenance supervisor months ago to paint over it and inscribe his name, but it still had not been done. He understood from the staff that Henry Mudd had instructed him not to do it.

He took the elevator up to his office on the third floor. He smiled at the receptionist and wished her a good morning. When he entered the Rector's suite he greeted his secretary, Crystal. Crystal had been the receptionist for five years before Steele was called to be Rector of First Church. While she wasn't a member of First Church, her duties as receptionist had allowed her to become very familiar with the members of the parish and them with her. Steele felt that her knowledge and relationships with the key members of the parish would be a valuable asset to him and the parish, so he asked her to be his secretary. "I need you to ask the maintenance supervisor to come to my office.

"Right away, Father Austin." She handed him his telephone messages. "I have marked the most urgent and placed them on the top. Your first appointment isn't for an hour so you might have time to return a few of these calls. After that you have a full day. You have appointments every hour on the hour until 6:00 p.m. Do you want me to order in some lunch for you?"

"I think that might work best." He handed her some money. "Just get me a ham sandwich on wheat bread and a diet soda." Steele walked into the break room and poured himself a cup of coffee. "Now," he thought, "that's the way it's supposed to be. The staff coffee cups were all hanging on the wall in the break room. Each cup had a staff member's name on it. His cup had his name painted on it." He smiled, "In the

Kingdom of Heaven and in the Church on Earth we should be known by our baptismal names and not by our titles."

He went back through his secretary's office to get to his own. "Father Austin, here is one more phone message. It just came in. It's from Doctor Robbins. He said it was really important that you call him on his cell phone right away."

"Thanks." He took the pink telephone slip and continued into his office. He opened his door and to his surprise, there sat Ned Boone. "Ned, you surprised me. I didn't expect anyone to be in here. Did we have an appointment? How did you get in here?"

"Misturh Austin, I had a little visit with the maintenance supervisor this morning about some property issues so I thought I would just have a visit with you as well. I have several things on my mind that I need to discuss with you man to man."

"Ned, I'm sure you'll understand this next question. I pride myself in maintaining the security of these offices, so I'm just curious as to how you got into my office without my secretary letting you in."

"Oh, I borrowed the maintenance supervisor's keys and let myself in through your back door. Your secretary wasn't here yet."

"How long have I kept you waiting?"

"Oh, for about an hour or so."

Steele did a quick survey of his office. When he walked behind his desk he could see that one of his drawers had been left partially open. Clearly, Ned Boone had taken advantage of the time he had available to him.

"Ned, I have to ask you to step out for just a minute. I have an urgent telephone call that I must make. It concerns someone who is gravely ill and I think I should protect their confidentiality."

"Oh, don't mind me. I won't listen. I'll just sit over here in the corner and read a magazine while you make the call."

Steele became all the more determined. "Ned, if this call concerned you or a member of your family, I would insist that anyone sitting in this office step out while I made the call. Now, I feel confidant that you would want to do the same for this person. Steele walked over to his office door and opened it. He asked his secretary to step in. "Will you show Mr. Boone to the staff break room and get him a cup of coffee or whatever he needs while I make this phone call?" He then gave her a determined look.

With a big smile on her face, Crystal walked to where Ned Boone was sitting, "Come with me, Mr. Boone. I'll get you a nice cup of coffee and a fresh donut to go with it."

Clearly Ned Boone was agitated, but in order to save face he stood and took her arm. "Well, how can I turn down such a nice invitation from such a beautiful lady?" At the door he stopped and looked back at Steele. "You'll come get me as soon as you make the call. I have several things to talk to you about."

His secretary came to his rescue. "Father Austin, you have a lot of calls that must be made first thing this morning. Starting at nine o'clock you have appointments every hour on the hour until this evening. Mr. Boone, maybe it would be better if I could make an appointment for you."

"Now don't you go worrying yourself." His voice and demeanor were so patronizing that Crystal literally arched her back. "The things I need to discuss with the Rector are also urgent and I'll not waste his time. I'm sure that what I have to say is every bit as important as the phone calls or appointments he has scheduled."

Steele shrugged his shoulders and gave her a knowing look. He then shut his door behind them and dialed the number. "Doctor Robbins," the voice answered.

"Steve, it's Steele Austin."

"Hey Steele, I hate to bother you so early in the morning, but on my way to the hospital, I decided to stop off and see Mandy Weller. Steele, I'm afraid my prognosis the other night was a bit too optimistic. The tumor is growing much faster than I thought at first. She's going down pretty fast."

"Do I need to go over there right now?"

"No, I just wanted you to know. I don't think it's going to be a matter of months. My best guess is that she won't be here much past Easter, if then."

"Are you going to put her in the hospital?"

"No, right now it's all about pain management and just keeping her comfortable. I called Hospice from the Weller's house. They are sending out a team this morning. I know they would really appreciate it if you would stop by sometime today."

"Sure, I'll be happy to, but I have one of those days with appointments stacked up on top of each other. Unless you tell me to drop everything I'm going to wait until this evening."

"Oh, this evening will be fine. It might even be better then since Max will be home from work. These parents are really fragile, but then I know you realize that. I'll not tell you how to do your job. I fear that caring for the parents in this kind of situation falls on your shoulders."

Steele felt that all too familiar lump return to his throat. "Thanks Steve, but if you have any guidance or suggestions, I'm completely open to them."

"Likewise, my friend. We'll have to work closely on this one."

With that, Doctor Robbins hung up his telephone and Steele followed suit. He sat down at his desk and put his face in his hands. He prayed, "Dear God, give me the strength to minister to this family. Give me the words that I need to say to strengthen them for what they must face and the words to comfort them when the end comes. Give Doctor Robbins and the Hospice team the knowledge and tools they need to make sure that Mandy doesn't suffer. Send Your angels to help us all help her make the transition into Your loving arms." He sat in silence and let the tears run down his cheeks.

"Father Austin, excuse me, Father Austin."

He came back to awareness. It was Crystal on the intercom. He pushed the button, "Yes."

"Pick up."

He picked up the receiver. "Father, Ned Boone is throwing a fit out here. He is making quite a scene with some of the staff and parishioners, complaining that it's so rude of you to keep him waiting. If you're finished with your call I think you should come out."

"I'm on my way."

Ned Boone was standing at the door when he opened it. His long neck was as red as the bowtie he had hanging off it. Clearly, he was angry. "Ned, I apologize for keeping you waiting. My phone call concerned a critically ill patient and I needed to give it my full attention."

"Well, I hope that it justified keeping me waiting. Misturh Austin, my time is just as important as yours or that of anyone else in this parish. And it's certainly just as valuable as whomever you were talking to on the telephone."

"Yes, Ned." Steele tried to keep a calm tone in his voice even though he wanted to name narcissistic behavior for exactly what it was. "Your time is important. That's why I encourage our members to make an appointment with me so that I will be able to give them my full attention."

Ned followed Steele into his office and took a seat opposite the Rector's desk. "I believe that you have kept me waiting long enough to justify all the time that I need."

Steele held up his hand. He wasn't going to let this old bully intimidate him. "Ned, my next appointment is in thirty-five minutes. Until then you have my full attention."

"Well, I don't think we're going to be able to discuss everything that's on my mind in thirty minutes." Ned Boone didn't attempt to hide his disgust. "Fine then, I'll just have to come back, but I'm going to need at least a two-hour appointment and maybe longer."

"That's fine." Steele forced a smile. "My secretary manages my calendar. I'm sure we'll find the time to accommodate you."

Ned Boone sat staring at Steele. His look reminded Steele of an old expression his grandmother had used. She would say, "When you first meet someone that's antagonistic to you, take your time to look them over. Figure them out." She called it "reading their stomach." Ned Boone was reading Steele Austin's stomach.

"I think that you're holding up the wrong kind of people in this parish as an example for the rest of us to follow."

Steele truly was confused by that comment. "I'm afraid you're going to have to give me an example."

"Well, take your sermon last Sunday. You told the story about the man who went to the temple to say his prayers. Do you remember?"

"Yes, go ahead."

"You said that the man was looked on by the general population as a good man. You said that he said his prayers every day, that he was faithful in his attendance at worship, and that he not only tithed, but he double-tithed. Now tell me, Misturh Austin, just what's wrong with those things?"

"Those are all admirable qualities, Ned. Those are good things to do. What's your point?"

"It's not my point that is in error. It was your point that needs to be corrected. Instead of holding up the good things that man was doing, you made the sniffling little sinner the hero. There was the good man that was doing all the right things. And then, there was the evil doer that could only crawl into the church and sink down in some dark corner and beg to be forgiven for all his wrongdoing."

"I'm sorry, Ned. I still don't follow."

"Look, don't you want the members of this congregation to come to church every Sunday, say their prayers several times every day, and tithe? Hell, let's say some of them double-tithe. Now isn't that the type of church member you want?"

Steele nodded, "Those are all good things, but the point of the story is to get us to understand that those things in themselves don't make us better than anyone else. They should be an expression of our love for God. God doesn't want us to use those things to try to justify ourselves in His sight or to try to elevate ourselves in the opinion of others."

"There!" Ned Boone shouted. "There! That's just what I mean. Instead of praising the good man and holding him up as an example for us all to follow, it's like you tried to find fault with all the good things the man was doing. You tore down the good man and made the stinking sinner the hero of the story."

Steele sat studying Ned Boone. He was trying to figure out just what he was saying. "Ned, I tried to tell the story just as Jesus told it. Jesus made the sinner the hero."

"No, Jesus didn't." He was getting red in the face again. "The Bible has to be interpreted. You, Sir, interpreted that story so as to tear down the good works the righteous man was doing. It was you, not Jesus, who elevated the sniffling little sinner."

"But we're all sinners, Ned. We're all in need of God's grace and forgiveness. God only asks that we confess our sins."

"I'm not!" His voice boomed off the walls of Steele's office.

"You're not what, Ned?"

"I'm not a sinner. I have done nothing wrong. I've lived an exemplary life."

Steele literally fell back in his chair. He sat in silence just trying to figure out if he had heard this guy say what his ears had heard him say.

Steele swallowed his disbelief and asked calmly, "Ned, what do you do when you make a mistake?"

Ned slapped his hand on Steele's desk. "Sir, I don't make mistakes!"

"Do you pray the words to the General Confession in the Prayer Book each Sunday?"

"No sir, I do not. That prayer is for the sinners present. They need to pray it. I don't."

"You believe you're without sin."

"I do." He sat staring at Steele. He didn't break eye contact. Then he continued, "I've lived an exemplary life. I follow all the teachings of the Bible. I've never broken any of the commandments. I've never cheated on my wife. I've never stolen so much as one thin dime. I'm a faithful churchman. I've never broken a single one of the Ten Commandments."

"Weren't you in the war?" Steele asked in a voice that was just above a whisper.

"Yes sir, I was in the infantry. I fought the Nazis." Ned paused and then gave Steele a dismissive look. "Oh, I see where you're going. Yes sir, I killed a lot of them, but that's different. I was doing God's work. My only regret is that I didn't get a chance to kill some Japs as well. My greatest regret is that I'm too old to eliminate some of the enemies of America today. I'd gladly pick up my gun and go again. But that's not murder. I broke no commandments."

Ned sat staring at Steele's face. It was as though he was trying to read his thoughts. "You never served our country, did you?"

Steele shook his head. "No, I was never in the military."

"I didn't think so. I figured you for a draft dodger. How does it feel to let others defend the liberties that you appear to take for granted?"

Steele was at a loss as to how to respond. Then a dim light went on in the back of his mind. "Ned, if you had been in the pulpit last Sunday, what would you have said?"

Ned leaned forward toward Steele and rubbed his hands together like a starving person just sitting down to a great feast. "I would have talked about all the virtues of the good man and then I would have said something like… well, like… this story gives us the perfect opportunity to express our gratitude to some of the faithful members of this congregation that are regular in worship, faithful in their prayers, and generous in their tithes and offerings."

The dim light in the back of Steele's mind now glowed more brightly, "For example?"

Ned looked confused. "I beg your pardon."

"For example?" Steele motioned with his hands for Ned to continue. "Who would you have me mention and hold up as an example?"

"Well, I shouldn't have to write your sermons for you, Misturh Austin, but clearly you could hold up Henry Mudd and his wife as a perfect example of a solid Christian family. They should be in the newspaper ad inviting folks who want to be like them to come to our church."

Steele sat stunned. "And?"

"And?"

"Is there anyone else?"

"Well, uhr-uh... yes. You could mention me."

Steele realized the guy was serious so he knew he had to tread lightly. "I want to make sure I understand you correctly. This was the urgent matter that you needed to speak to me about this morning."

"Correct."

"Well, it's certainly something for me to think about. Maybe I haven't done a very good job of commending some of the faithfulness of the members of this congregation."

"Well, I'm relieved to know that we are in agreement."

"You know Ned, you have suggested you and the Mudds, but I can think of some others. Maybe I should hold up Chadsworth Alexander and his Endowment for the Poor? And, you know Chief Sparks was one of the first Chiefs in the south to integrate his police force and admit women and gays."

Ned Boone interrupted, "No, not that kind of thing. I'm talking about church attendance, praying, Bible reading, and tithing. Those are the things that you need to hold up."

"Those are all good things, Ned. We're in agreement on that. They all describe Chadsworth and Chief Sparks as well."

"Yes, but that's where you need to stop." Steele could tell that Ned was on the verge of losing his temper again. "Leave all that good works stuff to the Red Cross and groups like that. Christians need to focus on being faithful members of the church."

"But what would you have me do with Jesus' teachings about the poor?"

"Oh, that's simple enough. Mention them every now and then and encourage people to give to the United Way and so forth. If you'll hold up the good folks in this congregation like the Mudds and me as an example for everyone else to follow, it won't be any time until we have to put an addition on our church to handle the crowds."

"Father Austin, Father Austin." It was his secretary on the intercom.

"Yes."

"The maintenance supervisor is here, as is your nine o'clock appointment."

"I'll be right there." Steele stood and shook Ned's hand. "Ned, I want to thank you for this talk. You have given me a great gift. I now understand you and your view of the church much better. I want to thank you again for giving me this insight."

A big smile crossed Ned Boone's face. "Well, thank you Misturh ... uh ... Steele. I can call you Steele, can't I?"

Steele returned his smile. "Absolutely."

Steele walked Ned to the door and waved at him as he walked down the hall. The maintenance supervisor was waiting at his door. "Step in, Buzz. How are you doing?

"Oh, it's been one of those mornings."

"Anything I can help you with?"

"Well, honestly Father Austin, I don't know how to handle this one."

"What's the problem?"

"Yesterday, Mrs. Howard Dexter told me that I needed to dress up a little more. She said that working around the church in dirty clothes just wouldn't do. She said it was embarrassing. She even thought that I should wear a white jacket and a black bowtie like the waiters do over at the Country Club."

Steele grimaced. "That doesn't sound very practical."

"No, Father Austin, it's not. I get dirty in this job. Sometimes I have to unclog toilets or fix the lawnmower or any number of dirty jobs."

"Did you explain that to her?"

"Yes, but she was determined that I wear nicer clothes to work. I tried to explain to her that I don't worship here, I work here. I wear my work clothes to work and my church clothes to my church. But she said that if I don't start doing as she says, she's going to talk to her husband, the Senior Warden, and get me fired. I can't afford to lose my job. "

"Buzz, let's make one thing clear. You work for me. No one can hire or fire staff but the Rector."

"That's a relief. So anyway, I did put on some nicer clothes to wear to work this morning and I have tried to be really careful not to get them dirty."

"So, what's the problem?"

"You met with Mister Boone?"

"Yes."

"Did I come up in your conversation?"

"No, you didn't."

"Well, when he saw me this morning he chewed me up and down for wearing these clothes to work. He said that he expected to see dirt under my fingernails. The only way that the parishioners would know that I was doing my job was if my clothes were dirty. Father Austin, what am I going to do?"

Steele could not contain himself. The laughter just roared out of him. It felt so good to laugh. "This job just gets better and better. Don't worry about it, Buzz. We'll work something out." Then he laughed some more. "Thank you Jesus, this job just gets better and better."

CHAPTER 13

Have you met her, Steele?" Stone Clemons was pacing back and forth in front of Steele's desk.

"Yeah, I've met her." Steele smiled and winked at his friend. "She's a real looker."

Stone stopped and grinned at Steele, "Yes, and she appears to be rich too."

"Well, she certainly epitomizes the California girl."

"Man to man, Steele, I can understand why she would be such a temptation for Father McBride." Stone started pacing again. "But I don't know if she's going to help our case or hurt us."

"What does his defense team say?"

"Make no mistake about it; I have some of the sharpest defense attorneys in the state working on this." He stopped again to look at Steele. "Do you want the truth?"

"Certainly, what do you need to tell me?" Steele was anxious for his friend Rob McBride.

"Well, let's look at the facts." Stone sat down in the chair opposite Steele. "We now know that he was out of town for the weekend. He was shacking up with his girlfriend. He met her at a church conference in California a couple of months ago." Stone paused as if to let that sink in. "He lied to the police about that. That really hurts his defense. Father McBride's wife is dead. He spent the weekend in Atlanta with his mistress. And he lies about his whereabouts. That's even more incriminating. Motive is easily established. He wanted his wife dead so that he could marry his mistress and not have to sacrifice his priesthood."

"I'm sorry, Stone; I just don't believe that he did it."

"Father, it isn't important right now what you and I believe. It's a jury of his peers that we're going to have to convince. I think the prosecutor will nail us to the wall on motive." Stone shrugged his shoulders.

"But he wanted to do the right thing. He had written his letter of resignation. He had written the Bishop asking for a leave of absence from his priesthood. He had the number of a divorce attorney in his possession."

Stone shot back, "Opportunity." He held up a finger and continued to pace before an imaginary jury. "We know that he was in the house with his wife. We know that from the liver temperature indicating the time of death. That corresponds, give or take a few minutes, with the recorded time that he was writing the letters on his computer. It looks like he was in the house with his wife's body for almost an hour." Stone was now holding up a second finger. "And then there's the physical evidence."

"What physical evidence? I didn't think there was any."

"True, true enough. This is where his girlfriend has been able to help us. We were able to match her teeth marks to the teeth marks on Rob's shoulders and chest. Clearly they were made by her and not his wife. They were marks of passion, but when you're in front of a jury, is that going to help you or hurt you? A good prosecutor can make much of the sensuous love affair with a California beauty versus the monotony of relations with your wife of a couple of decades. The prosecutor will argue the new and the exciting versus the familiar. And, to top it all off, she's loaded. She's filthy rich. Let's see, a poverty-ridden priest married for twenty years to a librarian falls in love with a wealthy California beauty. The poor librarian wife ends up being murdered the very weekend he meets his mistress for passionate sex in an Atlanta hotel. Now, just how do you think that will play with the married women on his jury?"

"What about the scratches?"

"Oh, that is even more incriminating. He and Miss Mason both claim the scratches on his body were also marks of passion. That would be a good defense just as the teeth marks could be a good defense except for one thing."

"What's that?" The killer clipped Mrs. McBride's fingernails and then soaked her fingers in bleach. That takes us back to Rob McBride, the only suspect, and the only person with motive to insure that no transfer of physical evidence to his wife could survive."

Stone sat down. "Steele, I know you believe your boy is innocent, but it just doesn't look good. My men are going to keep working on it, but frankly, unless we can locate another suspect, I just don't know..."

"He's out on bail, right?"

"Miss Mason posted his bail. It was a big one."

"What's next?"

"She has brought in some high-powered private investigators from Atlanta and has made them available to our legal team. They're going to focus on trying to find another suspect. We could have overlooked something, but I just don't know what it could've been. Are you still in touch with both of them?"

"I've talked to her a couple of times and I saw him in jail a few times, but I wasn't aware that he was out. Where's he staying?"

"She has rented an apartment for them over off Maple, but that doesn't help his case either. It doesn't look good for the grieving widower to continue sleeping with his mistress. His priestly credibility isn't helped by that behavior. We've tried to talk to him about it. If you have any influence on him I wish you would remedy that situation."

"How would it be if one of them stayed in our guest room?"

Stone clapped his hands together. "Perfect. That would certainly help the appearance of things before a jury."

"I'll talk to them."

"Have you talked to the Chief?"

Steele nodded, "Yes, I fear that I may have challenged our friendship. As far as he's concerned, the case work is done. They have all they need. To use his words, he has no intention of spending the taxpayer's money chasing after some one-armed man."

Stone chuckled, "I'd just about forgotten that television show. What was it called? Oh yeah, *The Fugitive*... Richard Kimball, right?"

"Stone, I saw the movie. I'm too young to remember the television series. As far as the Chief is concerned he has the guilty party. I believe he has turned everything over to the prosecutor's office. Unless they ask him to do something else he's finished."

"Well, that's that." Stone shrugged again and lifted his arms. "Just one final word, Parson."

"Yes."

"It may be that my defense team will need you to help them to get Rob to accept a plea bargain if it's offered."

"What would the deal be?"

Stone placed his hands on Steele's desk and looked him in the eye. "Manslaughter may be offered. It could mean the difference between ten to twenty and your friend Rob going to death row."

Steele stood, "Let's just hope it doesn't come to that. I believe him. I believe that he didn't do it and I'm going to organize some prayer warriors to help these private investigators find the elusive one-armed man."

"I'd suggest that you not stop with a few warriors, Father. If I were you I'd call out the entire tribe."

"Well then, Mister Clemons, if that's what I need to do, consider it done."

CHAPTER 14

It was Holy Week and Steele Austin was tired of death. Palm Sunday was always an emotional drain. The Sunday worship begins with the Blessing of the Palms and music marking the triumphant entry of Jesus into Jerusalem. And then, the joy turns quickly to sorrow as the congregation relives the trial and crucifixion of the innocent Christ in the Gospel reading. The service always left Steele exhausted and filled with sorrow.

There were services appointed for every day of Holy Week. That, in itself, would normally be more than enough for him to plan and conduct, but this particular Holy Week Steele was also called on to conduct two funerals. The first was for a woman who had lived eighty-seven wonderful years. She had died peacefully in her sleep. Her children, grandchildren and great grandchildren filled the church to celebrate her life. She had been a faithful member of First Church from the time she was baptized as an infant. Most everyone thought she still had several more years to enjoy, but her housekeeper found her sleeping her final rest in the comfort of her bed.

The service celebrating her life was attended by a host of friends in the community. Steele recognized well over fifty percent of the mourners as members of First Church. While he really didn't need an additional service of any kind during Holy Week, Steele found this particular funeral easier to conduct than most. Long life, love, service, and friendship all characterized this gentle woman of faith.

The other funeral that week had not been so easy. It too was for an elderly woman, but one basically unknown to Steele. In fact, he could not remember ever laying eyes on the woman. The family reported that she was a member of the church and the parish register did in fact record her as such, but there was no evidence of any membership activity. This woman had also lived into her eighties, but it was difficult to find a theme for her service. She was alienated from her two daughters. Her husband had died thirty years before her. There appeared to be no record of service or volunteerism. She had basically been a recluse. The family gathered for the service. There were just a few neighbors. One of the daughters asked to speak at the service, but even she had a difficult time finding words that could celebrate her mother's life. Steele could not help but notice the contrast. It was this type of funeral that he found most tiring.

The altar flowers for Thursday in Holy Week are white. The veils on the crosses and crucifixes had been changed from purple to white. On this night, the liturgy was designed to remember Christ and the Disciples in the Upper Room. At this particular service the faithful would remember that Jesus commanded us to make Him present in the sacred bread and wine. Steele and the assisting clergy, along with the Altar Guild, would end the service by reverently removing all the sacred vessels, flowers, and altar cloths from the sanctuary. The candles would be removed and the lights in the church would be turned out. The faithful would leave the church lit only by the exterior lights reflecting on the stained glass windows. They would go out into the dark night in silence. Just as Jesus and the disciples had gone to the Garden of Gethsemane to watch and pray.

The Good Friday Liturgy was equally dramatic. The readings, the hymns, and the anthems were all intended to take the worshippers back to the death of Jesus on a cross so long ago. This particular Holy Week, which included two funerals and his ongoing anxiety for his friend Rob McBride, had been particularly difficult for Steele.

On Holy Saturday the Altar Guild took charge of the church once again. All of the veils were removed from the crosses and the statues. Easter lilies were literally stacked behind and around the altar. The lilies were placed in the windows and around the Baptismal Font. The smell of these fresh flowers filled the vast building. Outside the church and throughout Falls City, God was also preparing for the celebration of new life. The dogwood trees and the azalea bushes were in full bloom. The purple wisteria intertwined in the trees, forming floral sprays dripping from the branches. It was Steele's favorite time of the year in south Georgia. It reminded him of spring back home in the hills of Oklahoma. Holy Week, with its dark shadow of suffering and death, was behind him. He felt himself being renewed as he prepared for the celebration of Easter.

Sleep eluded The Reverend Steele Austin most of Saturday night. He rehearsed his Easter sermon over and over again in his mind. He tossed and turned. Randi woke and started rubbing his chest as the moonlight streamed into their bedroom through the windows. "Anything I can do to help you go to sleep?" Steele smiled and pulled her closer to him. "Just having you at my side is all that I need."

They lay together whispering like children up past their curfew. "Did we put everything out for the Easter Bunny?" Steele whispered.

"Our little boy is so excited." She smiled. "I just hate it that you won't be here when he wakes up."

"I know. It's one of the things I hate the most about being a priest. I have to be at the church by 5:00 a.m. I don't guess I'll ever get to be here when the Easter Bunny comes. Please help him understand." Steele Austin loved Randi, but since their son Travis had come into their lives, he loved her even more than he thought possible.

"I will. I'll tell him that Daddy talked to the Easter Bunny with me and wanted to make sure that he would come to our house. I'll tell him that the little stuffed rabbit was what you asked the Easter Bunny to bring him. Can't you sleep at all?"

Steele rolled toward his wife so that he could look at her beautiful face in the moonlight. "I think I have an idea of what football players must feel like the night before the Super Bowl. I guess, in a very real way, Easter is the Super Bowl for clergy. I don't want to let our regular folks down. I know they want to have a great Easter celebration. I also know that God is going to bring a lot of people to First Church tomorrow who are filled with questions and doubts about Jesus. I especially don't want to let them down."

Randi reached up and put her hand on Steele's cheek. "Honey, aren't you forgetting one thing?"

"What's that?"

"God's not going to let you fail. God will give you the words to say. You know that, don't you?"

Steele smiled, "Yes, but I need a really smart wife to remind me." He kissed her on the cheek. "Thanks, I don't think I could do this job without you."

Randi jabbed him in the side with her elbow, "Oh, you could do it, just not as well." Then they giggled. Sleep finally came for Steele just minutes before the alarm went off.

The church was packed to overflowing. The children led the procession down the center aisle. They were carrying flowers to be placed on a cross which had been specifically designed for that purpose. The thurifer then followed and the clouds of incense lifted toward the heavens. The brass and timpani led the organ, choir, and congregation in the hymn proclaiming that Jesus Christ has risen. All the people in attendance at First Church were dressed in their finest spring clothing. Steele thought that all the children were adorable, the women all beautiful, and every man was handsome. On this Sunday, Steele Austin loved being a priest. He loved being the Rector of First Church. After he had taken the incense thurible from the acolyte and walked around the altar, blessing it with the holy smoke, he turned to look out at the smiling congregation lost in the joyful hymn. There on the front row stood Randi. In her arms she carried their son, Travis. He was cuddling a little stuffed bunny that his Daddy had made sure the Easter Bunny brought him. Travis waved at Steele with the toy. A smile sprang from Steele Austin's soul and spread across his face. Christ is risen. Christ is risen indeed.

CHAPTER 15

Steele Austin was sitting at the desk in his office. He had turned his chair to look out the window. From this vantage point he could see the church parking lot, a partial view of the cemetery, and the walk leading through the cemetery up to the front door of the church. Even though the service wasn't supposed to start for another hour, mourners were already arriving. Steele was struck by the number of children coming to the funeral with their parents. He knew he was going to have to say something to help the parents help their children through the death of one of their own.

He had just finished all the services on Easter Sunday. He was both elated and exhausted. Steele and Randi had planned to leave Easter Sunday afternoon and drive down to Destin, Florida for Easter Week. After all the services, funerals, his concern for Rob McBride and all his other parish responsibilities, they had agreed that he needed a week on the beach. His cell phone rang just as he was pulling out of the parking lot. His plan had been to go home and load the car for their Easter vacation. It was Doctor Steve Robbins. "Steele, I just got a telephone call from the Hospice nurse. The time has come. I'm on my way over to the Weller's house right now."

"I'll meet you there."

When he arrived, there were several neighbors standing in the yard and on the front porch. The front door was standing open. He walked into the living room to see a few older folks sitting in tears and whispered silence. He assumed they were the grandparents. The Hospice nurse was standing at the door leading off the living room to Mandy's room. Steele could hear Doctor Robbins talking. He walked toward the familiar voice. Mandy's mother and father were sitting on her little twin bed. They were holding Mandy. Mandy's head was in her mother's arms and lying on her breast. Her legs and feet were stretched across her Daddy's lap. Mandy was already unconscious. Clearly she was leaving. There was a Barbie tape recorder sitting on the side table. It was softly playing some children's songs. They were being sung by a female soloist and what Steele surmised was a children's choir.

Doctor Robbins looked over at Steele and shook his head. Steele walked up to Mandy's mother, leaned down and kissed her on the cheek. She managed a brief smile. He then put his hand on her dad's shoulder. While they both had been crying, at that moment they were surprisingly calm. Sharon Weller was gently rocking her daughter back and forth. Max was lightly rubbing Mandy's legs and holding her bare feet in his hands. Max spoke first. "She's not suffering. Thank God, no more suffering. No more pills. No more needles. No more pain. I just don't think we could have handled another night of torment. Now she's peaceful."

Mandy was still receiving oxygen. She appeared to be sleeping. Her breathing was very light. The movement of her chest was just barely perceptible. Steele knelt down on the floor in front of Mandy and her parents. He reached into his pocket and pulled out his oil stock. He first anointed Mandy with the sign of the cross on her forehead and then he reached up and anointed each of her parents in the same way. "Lord Jesus Christ, receive this Your child Mandy into Your loving arms." Steele felt his voice break. He had to stop for just a moment to regain his composure. A tear dropped down his cheek. He looked up to see that Doctor Robbins was wiping away a tear as well. Steele took a deep breath. Then with a quiver in his voice he continued, "Fill this room and this house with Your holy angels. Comfort Max and Sharon, Mandy's grandparents, and all who love her. Give us all the strength to release her into your eternal presence. While we all love her and have wanted with all our hearts to keep her with us, give us comfort in the knowledge that You loved her first and that our love cannot possibly measure up to the love that You have for her."

Again, Steele had to stop and compose himself. Then a strange calm came over him. He looked at Sharon and Max. They too were calm and they each gave him a gentle smile. Steele then leaned up so that he could whisper directly into Mandy's ear. "Mandy, your Mommy and Daddy are here with you. They love you. They're holding you right now. We all love you, but Jesus loves you even more. Mandy, Jesus is waiting for you. It's okay. You don't have to stay here. Your Mommy and Daddy want you to run to Jesus." Steele looked up at Sharon. She nodded and smiled. Then she leaned down and kissed her daughter on her forehead. "It's okay, baby.

You do what Jesus wants you to do." Tears now rolled down the cheeks of all in the room.

Steele sat back on the floor and took Mandy's hand in his. He rubbed it gently. And then, like a feather caught in a gentle breeze, she was gone. Peacefully and without any pain or struggle, she left.

Steele and Doctor Robbins stayed with the parents and the grandparents until after Mandy's body had been removed. That was the most difficult part for Sharon. It was then that her grief was released in great screams. Her husband and Steele held on to her, attempting to comfort her, but for several moments she was beyond comfort.

"Father Austin... Father Austin," it was his secretary, Crystal. "Are you all right?"

Steele turned his chair to see that she was standing at his desk. "Father Austin, you look exhausted. Are you sure you're going to be able to do this funeral?"

"Do I really look that bad?"

"Father Austin, you look like a ghost. I've never seen you look so bad. After this service, you've just got to get some rest." It was now Wednesday of Easter Week. He and Randi had canceled their trip to the beach so that he could be able to take care of the Weller family and do Mandy's funeral. He nodded his head.

"Father Austin, we've got to talk to you." It was a well-dressed couple standing at the door. Crystal turned to look at them. "I'm sorry. Do you have an appointment with Father Austin? I'm his secretary, Crystal. I don't remember scheduling any appointments for him. He does have a very full afternoon."

"No, we don't have an appointment. Why would we need an appointment to talk to a priest? We're here now. We need to speak with you right now." The man led his wife into Steele's office and they seated themselves opposite his desk. Crystal gave Steele a troubling look. "It's all right, Crystal. I'll do what I can for these folks." Crystal gave the couple a long hard stare, shook her head at Steele and then closed the door as she left the office.

"What can I do for you?"

"I'm Tom Barnhardt and this is my wife, Sara. You probably don't know us. We don't come to your church, but we have a daughter in your school." Steele did recognize the couple from several school events he had attended. Sara did a lot of volunteer work for the school and he had learned that Tom was a C.E.O. or C.O.O. of some big company headquartered over in Jacksonville. The town gossip was that they had lots of money and they didn't mind making that fact known.

"Tom, Sara, I really don't involve myself in school affairs. I leave the running of the school to the Head of School. Have you discussed your concerns with her?"

"Yes," Tom thundered back. "That was a big waste of time."

"Well, if she can't help you, what makes you think that I can?"

"Listen, aren't you the Rector of this parish?"

"Yes."

"Then you're also Rector of the school, right?"

"Legally, I suppose that's true."

"Then you're the C.E.O of this corporation and the school is one of your companies."

Steele was getting frustrated. "Yes, but...."

"No buts. We have a problem and we want you to resolve it."

Steele decided to relent. "And your problem is?"

"Our daughter tried out for cheerleader, but she wasn't chosen."

Steele shrugged, "I believe a committee of the faculty and the current cheerleaders make that decision."

"Yes, and they decided wrong." Sara's voice was shaking with anger. "Our daughter has been destroyed. She has cried for a week."

"I'm really sorry that your daughter is so disappointed, but Tom, Sara, I'll not overturn the decision of a duly appointed school committee. Now, I'm sorry that your daughter is disappointed, but my hands are tied. There isn't a thing that I can do. You're going to have to excuse me, but I have a funeral that I must conduct."

"Oh, so that's why all those people are going into the church." Then Tom spewed, "I guess it's for one of your aristocrats here at First Church."

Steele responded calmly, "No, it's for a little five year old girl that died of a brain tumor."

They were indifferent to Steele's statement. "Well, what are we supposed to tell our daughter?" Sara now adopted her husband's bitter tone.

Steele leaned forward across his desk so he could look directly at them. "Unlike those poor parents waiting for me over at the church, you still have your daughter. I suggest that you go home, take her in your arms, and tell her how much you love her and that you're terribly proud of her. Then help her understand that she will have a lot of disappointments in life, but that you'll always be there for her, loving her through them."

Tom shouted, "We didn't come here for a sermon. Now, I demand that you overturn that decision."

Steele stood, "I'm sorry. You're going to have to excuse me. I need to go over to the church."

Tom shrank back in the chair. "We're not going anywhere. You go do your funeral, but we'll be sitting right here when you get back. We're not leaving until you do as we've asked."

Steele punched the intercom to Crystal's office. "Crystal, Mr. and Mrs. Barnhardt are leaving. Would you please come and show them out?" It was a prearranged signal that he had with Crystal when he needed to be rescued. He and all the staff also had panic buttons connected to the alarm service if needed, but he didn't think removing these bullies would require that.

Soon his office door opened and Crystal entered, "This way, Mr. and Mrs. Barnhardt." Standing behind Crystal was one of the uniformed motorcycle officers that had come to escort the funeral procession to the cemetery. Crystal had asked him to come stand with her at the door.

When the Barnhardts saw the officer they stood and started walking toward the door. Clearly, they were not happy. Tom Barnhardt turned at the door to look back at Steele, "You know, Misturh Austin, I'd heard that you were a jerk. Now, I know that you are!" Steele didn't respond.

"Everything okay, Crystal?" the officer asked.

"Yes, thank you." She shook his hand. "Father Austin, you need to go over to the church, but I'm worried about you. You didn't get your week off so I'm canceling your appointments for next week."

"Crystal, you can't do that. I have so much to do."

"Father Austin, consider them canceled. Now, if you don't do something to take care of yourself, I will personally call the Vestry."

"Okay, okay. Just let me look at everything before you start making phone calls."

Steele walked into the Altar Guild Sacristy. Mrs. Gordon Smythe turned and looked at him. She then walked toward him and wrapped her arms around his neck and gave him a very motherly hug. "You dear man, you've got to take care of yourself. If you don't take care of yourself you can't take care of us." Steele nodded. And this from a woman that just over a year ago was one of his primary antagonists.

Just as quickly as she had hugged him, Mrs. Gordon Smythe was back to business. "The church was still filled with Easter lilies from Sunday. I told the florist to take all the lilies that people had sent over here for the funeral to the Weller's house. There must have been a couple of dozen plants. I just don't know what they're going to do with them. I hope that is acceptable to you, Misturh Austin?"

Steele nodded and then began vesting. When he was dressed in his robes he walked out of the Sacristy into the nave of the church. The crucifer, acolyte bearing the Resurrection Candle, and a verger were waiting on him. He followed them down the side aisle to the back of the nave and onto the front steps of the church. There he saw Mandy's casket covered with a white pall. Around the pall were embroidered colorful flowers of every kind. On the top of the pall an angel had been embroidered. Steele had never seen such a beautiful pall for a child's casket. He hoped he would never have to see one again.

Standing with Max and Sharon Weller were Mandy's grandparents. There were other family members, the Hospice workers that had cared for Mandy, and Doctor Robbins. Steele walked past the little casket and up to Max and Sharon. He put his arms around both of them and brought them close for a hug. At that, they started to sob. Max and Sharon let out great heaves. It was just too much for Steele. He too let out his own grief. The three of them stood there in an embrace, sobbing until the hurt became manageable – at least for a short time. Wiping his eyes and face, Steele whispered, "Max, Sharon, you're living every parent's nightmare. I really don't know what to say to you and I'm at a loss as to what to do for you. The only thing that God is allowing me to do is to cry with you."

Sharon hugged Steele's neck again. Max did the same. Steele then walked to the head of the casket. He made the sign of the cross over Mandy's body. "We receive the body of Mandy, a child of God, for burial." He offered the prayer appointed in the Book of Common Prayer for receiving a body at the church doors for burial. He looked at Max and Sharon, "Are you ready to proceed?" They nodded.

The crucifer led the procession down the aisle of the church. He was followed by an acolyte carrying the Resurrection Candle which had been blessed at the parish baptisms on the Saturday before Easter, just four days ago. Normally, Steele would follow the verger in front of the casket, but this time he walked in between Max and Sharon. He held each of their hands as they followed Mandy's body down the center aisle to the front of the church. He had decided not to do the opening sentences appointed in the Prayer Book until the procession had ended and the family had been seated. He had instructed the organist to play the hymn, "All Things Bright and Beautiful" as they entered the church. When all were in place he would ask the congregation to join in singing the hymn.

The scriptures were read by Mandy's grandfathers. Each managed to keep their composure and read the comforting words as though they were reading them to Mandy herself. During the scripture readings Steele was able to look over the congregation. The church was full and there were even more children present than he had anticipated. He knew that he would need to speak to the parents through the children. At the time appointed for the sermon he walked down to stand next to Mandy's casket.

"Mandy isn't here." He paused to look at the children. "This box contains Mandy's body, but Mandy isn't here. In fact, do you know that about a month before Mandy died, she told her parents that Jesus had come to visit her? She did. She said that Jesus came to visit her and that he had a white pony with him. She said that Jesus took her to a beautiful place where she could ride her pony. She told her parents that she was so happy and that there were lots of happy people in that place. Jesus told her that he had to leave, but he would come back and get her and take her to that beautiful place and she could ride her pony all she wanted."

Again, Steele stopped to study the faces of the children. "It's confusing isn't it? How can Mandy be in heaven with Jesus while her body is still with us?" Steele looked out at the children. They were all listening. "Let me explain. I have a son. He is three years old. His name is Travis. Travis and I have a game that we like to play. I put Travis on my knees and we play *The Really, Really Me Game.* I hold some of Travis's hair in my hand." With that Steele reached out and took the hair of a little red headed boy sitting near the front of the church. He looked at the little boy. "Is this hair the really, really you?" The little boy shook his head. "Of course not, this is your hair." Then he put his thumb and finger on his nose. "Is this nose the really, really you?" Again, the little boy shook his head. "No, this isn't the really, really you. This is your nose."

Some of the children were now standing up on the kneelers and the pews so that they could better see what Steele was doing with the little boy. "If I touch your stomach, or your mouth, or your arm or your leg, are any of those things the really, really you?" Now several of the children shook their heads and said, "No."

Steele walked back to the casket and placed his hand on it. "Then where is the really, really you?" The little red headed boy pointed at his heart, "In here, the really, really me is in here."

"In this casket is Mandy's body. It's her hair, her nose, her arms, her legs, but her really, really me isn't here. Her really, really me has gone to that beautiful place that Jesus showed her."

The procession to the cemetery took almost an hour. Max and Sharon had asked Steele to keep the service at the cemetery short. He was more than happy to oblige. Doctor Robbins stayed with Steele until after Mandy's casket had been lowered into its final resting place. "Steele, my friend, I'm worried about you. You've simply got to go home, take the phone off the hook and get some rest. I've called in a prescription to the pharmacy for you. It's going to be delivered and should be at your house when you get home."

"I don't need a prescription."

"And I think you do, as does your wife, your secretary, and Mrs. Gordon Smythe. Now, do you really want to argue with that team? You'll lose. Take one pill and go to bed. Doctor's orders."

Randi was waiting for Steele when he got home. She had the pill and a glass of water waiting. "I've disconnected all the phones from the wall. Your bed is ready. Now go, Cowboy, and don't let me see you again until you're caught up on your sleep." It really didn't take much before Steele was sleeping. He woke for just a few minutes. It was dark outside. He could hear Randi and Melanie Mason playing with Travis in the nursery. He was glad that Melanie had accepted their offer to live with them in their guest room until this mess with Rob McBride was resolved. Randi and Melanie had become great friends. He liked that. Then sleep washed over him again. He finally awoke with the morning light pouring into his bedroom window. He stretched and smiled. He felt wonderful. He looked at his watch on the side table. It showed the day and the date. He shook his watch. It must be broken. His watch recorded that it was a Saturday.

CHAPTER 16

"You've just got to talk to her, Misturh Austin. She's the talk of the town. Now, you have just got to put an end to this nonsense." Steele had been cornered in the Rectory living room by Mrs. Gordon Smythe and Mrs. Howard Dexter. He and Randi had decided to have a Mother's Day Tea for the Altar Guild. Randi had gone all the way to prepare the dining room. She had a beautiful flower arrangement in the center of the table. There were two large silver candelabra on either side of the flowers. She had rented two silver services and had one service at either end of the table. Randi had asked the clergy spouses to take turns pouring the tea for her guests.

Almeda Alexander arrived at the Rectory on the arm of Doctor Drummond. When they entered the crowded living room every eye turned to look at them. Eyebrows were raised and looks were given. These were not hard to miss. To both Steele and Randi's surprise, Almeda positioned herself as one of the clergy spouses at the end of the dining room table and started pouring tea for the members of the Altar Guild.

"Just look at her over there. Do you see her, Misturh Austin?" Mrs. Dexter had a disgusting tone in her voice. "We warned you about what would happen if you brought that African American priest, as you call him, to this parish. She's making a complete fool out of herself. She's an embarrassment to her dear husband's memory. Chadsworth would literally be turning in his grave if he could see her. Now, what are you going to do to stop this nonsense?" Mrs. Smythe and Mrs. Dexter had determined looks on their faces.

Steele shrugged, "Ladies, just what do you think I can do? They are a grown man and woman. They're not children. My goodness, they're both old enough to be my parents."

"He works for you. You tell him you're going to fire him if he doesn't break it off with her," snorted Mrs. Dexter.

"Ladies, ladies, I can't do that. Have either of you considered the possibility that they really are in love?"

"Don't be silly, Misturh Austin. That just isn't possible."

"Well, I don't feel like I have a right to interfere."

"Who's that?" Mrs. Gordon Smythe was looking at Melanie Mason, who had just walked into the living room.

Steele followed her gaze. "That's Melanie Mason. She's a friend of Rob McBride's. She's staying in our guest room until we can get his case resolved."

The two women stared at Melanie with disgusted looks on their faces. Something about *if looks could kill* crossed Steele's mind. "Don't you mean his mistress?" Mrs. Howard Dexter chuckled. "Shameful, Misturh Austin, just shameful that you would house an adulteress on church property. I know you won't agree with me, but I think women like that should be stoned. Not only are they the worst kind of predators chasing after other women's husbands, but the men that get involved with women like her are double liars. They break both their marriage vows to their wives and to God. In your friend's case, I guess that makes him a triple liar since he also took ordination vows. Any man or woman that will break their vow both to God and their spouse can never be trusted."

Steele interrupted, "Gosh, those seem like awfully harsh words."

"Oh," she lifted her eyebrows. "Let's say your friend does get proven innocent. How will he ever be able to trust that woman? If she'll cheat with him, then she'll cheat with anyone. Or vice versa, how can she ever trust him? He's just as guilty as she is if not more so. Adultery is one of the most disgusting of all sins. Just read your Bible and see what Jesus had to say about it. I tell you she's disgusting. She's despicable and I can't believe that she's staying in our Rectory."

Steele held his hand up, "Please stop, ladies. Rob is a friend of mine. You need also to know that Melanie is becoming a close friend of mine and Randi's. I believe with all my heart that he's innocent. I don't believe for one minute that he's capable of murdering anyone. And, yes, he and Melanie are in love and hope to be married just as soon as his name is cleared. As to their current marital status, Rob is a widower and she's a single woman."

"I suppose that's one way to tell the story." Mrs. Dexter winked at Mrs. Smythe. She then continued talking to Mrs. Smythe, completely ignoring Steele. "My husband tells me that he's guilty as sin. The evidence is incontrovertible. He was having an affair with that woman over there. He wanted to divorce his wife to marry her and she refused. So he murdered her."

"Then why did he call 9-1-1?" Steele interrupted.

"What?"

"He called 9-1-1. If he simply wanted her dead, then why did he stay? Why did he try to get help for his wife?"

Mrs. Dexter shrugged and looked again at Mrs. Smythe, "I only know what I hear. And what I hear is that man is headed for death row."

"Misturh Austin, you've just got to consider our counsel." Mrs. Gordon Smythe was whispering.

"What counsel?"

She continued, "Things have been going so well for you at First Church the last few months. You have won the hearts of a lot of us in this congregation. But Misturh Austin, we don't like being the center of gossip in Falls City. First Church and First Church people are a proud lot. But right now, every onion farmer in the county is making fun of us and we don't like it. Between Almeda's love affair with your *Negara* priest and you housing a murderer's mistress in the church Rectory, things are beginning to deteriorate pretty fast. You're our Rector. Our good name rests in your hands. Now, do something or we will."

With that the two ladies walked away, leaving Steele standing in the corner. He caught Horace Drummond's eye. Horace walked toward him. "Now just why do I think that I was the topic of that whispered conversation?"

Steele smiled, "Oh, you were certainly included, but the new bruises I'm wearing aren't all due to you."

"Hmm," he smiled. "I saw the look on their faces when Almeda sat down at the table and began pouring tea. Those looks were exceeded only by the ones on their faces when Melanie walked into the room."

"You're a most observant and astute priest, my friend." Steele smiled.

"What are you going to do?"

"Well, I can't do what they want me to do." Steele took a sip of his tea and a bite out of the cookie that had been on his saucer for the past half hour. His tea was cold. "They want me to turn my back on my friends. I'm not going to do that. Let's go to the table. I need a fresh cup of tea."

He and Horace walked into the dining room. Almeda was still pouring tea. Horace bent down and kissed her on the cheek. She glowed like a co-ed. Almeda took Steele's cup from him. She then handed him a new cup and filled it with tea. "One lump or two?"

"One."

Horace and Steele walked back into the living room. It was empty. There were just a handful of ladies in the dining room and entry hall taking their leave from Randi. "What are you guys going to do, Horace?"

"I love her, Steele. I want to marry her. After my wife died, I didn't think I would ever have these feelings again for another woman. But Almeda is different. She's special. What we have is special. I don't want to live my life without her. I think we can have a wonderful life together. At our age, we're living on borrowed time anyway, so every day counts."

Steele was silent for several minutes. "You've only known each other, what, six months?" Steele stood looking at Horace. He sipped his tea. "Have you asked her?"

"You mean, down on my knee, diamond in hand ask her? No, but we have talked about it and we know what we want. We know that we might have to leave Falls City. I don't know if there's another black man married to a white woman in this entire county. But if we have to leave here in order to love each other in peace, then that's just what we're going to do."

"I would hate to think that it would come to that."

"It may not, but we're ready to move if need be." Horace sat down on the sofa. He put his tea cup and saucer on the coffee table. He studied Steele Austin's face. "We want you to preside at our wedding. Will you do it?"

Steele was caught off guard. He hadn't expected that question. "When? Where?"

"Oh, not for several months yet. Maybe in November around Thanksgiving. We aren't planning anything big. There will just be the two of us, her boys, and my daughter and sister, in the Chapel. Of course, we want Randi to be there."

Steele sat down in the rocker by the fireplace. "Of course, of course, I'd be honored. Thanks for asking me."

"But?"

Steele glanced back at Horace, "But?"

"Steele, I sense that you have some reservations."

"Horace, you and Almeda are mature adults. No one knows better than the two of you the difficulties that are before you if you decide to do this. But, my friend, please, please think this through."

Horace nodded, "We have, Father. And we will. I just regret that I came here to help you and I fear that I am creating problems for you."

Randi, Almeda, and Melanie walked into the living room. Rob had come into the Rectory through the back door and was with them. Randi was holding a bottle of white wine in each hand. She held them out. "Everyone is gone so we decided that it was time for the real party to begin." Almeda, Melanie, and Rob were carrying the glasses. Steele and Horace laughed.

When the wine glasses were filled, Steele stood. "I would like to propose a toast to my beautiful wife and incredible hostess. And a toast to you, Almeda and Horace, and to you, Melanie and Rob; may God bless you, open doors for you, and grant you the futures filled with love and happiness that we all desire. Here's to love, happiness and a long life to enjoy both."

CHAPTER 17

Steele had learned to listen to the jungle drums before the Vestry meetings at First Church. There were certain things that he could watch. Who on the Vestry was talking to him? Who on the Vestry was unusually silent? He knew also to keep an eye on the wives of the Vestrymen. Which ones made eye contact with him? Who smiled at him? Who had been spending more than the usual amount of time in the church office visiting with the staff? He also knew to watch the staff. Sometimes the staff would pick up on an impending confrontation before he did. Before this month's meeting, all the signs pointed to a conflict. Steele hated these episodes with the Vestry.

He knew the usual pattern. First, his antagonists would choose a meeting when any supporters he had on the Vestry would be absent. On this particular Vestry, Steele didn't have a lot of supporters. His strongest advocate, Stone Clemons, ended his term at the last annual meeting. He wasn't eligible for re-election to the Vestry for at least one more year. So Steele had appointed him as Chancellor to the Vestry with voice, but no vote. Most of those antagonistic to Steele could easily see just what he was attempting to do and had been somewhat dismissive of Stone. Normally, Steele was just happy to have him sitting at the table and his supportive voice helped relieve Steele's anxiety. However, Stone would not be at this particular Vestry meeting. He was on a fishing trip in the Gulf of Mexico.

Howard Dexter, the Senior Warden, had been neutralized. He really didn't know the particulars, but he knew it had something to do with the financial arrangements Chadsworth Alexander had made with Howard's bank before he committed suicide. There were five Vestrymen elected at the last annual meeting. All of them were openly antagonistic to Steele. They were led by Henry Mudd, the Junior Warden, and Ned Boone. The remaining members of the Vestry, with the exception of Chief Sparks, were neutral, but they were not supportive. Chief Sparks had not hidden his friendship and support for Steele.

Steele examined the Vestry roster. Howard Dexter would not be present. This left Henry Mudd as the primary Warden. Chief Sparks was with Stone Clemons in the Gulf. Of the five neutral Vestrymen, only two would be present. Steele felt an uneasy feeling in his stomach. They had chosen their time and their meeting. He knew that Henry Mudd and Ned Boone would be orchestrating the meeting. They would have a meeting before the meeting at the Magnolia Club. It would probably be over drinks and dinner. They would script every motion, every second, and every vote. They would know that they had the votes to pass each motion before Steele could even call for one.

Steele prepared for the Vestry meeting in his usual method. He would spend some time on his knees in the Chapel. He would try to anticipate the confrontation. He would practice some relaxation exercises. He would try to calm himself and stay focused on the real business of the church. On this particular occasion he was uncertain as to just what the confrontation would be about, but he knew one was coming.

Steele led the Vestry through the published agenda with relative ease. He was beginning to relax. There was some good humor at the table. As far as the particulars that needed Vestry action, all were in accord. It was actually a very good meeting. Having worked the agenda, Steele called for a motion to adjourn. Henry Mudd made a motion, but it wasn't the one Steele wanted. "Misturh Austin, I move that the Vestry go into Executive Session. I'm going to ask the staff and visitors to leave the room. Only the Rector and the elected members of the Vestry are to remain." Steele felt his stomach do a flip.

When the room was cleared of staff and visitors, Henry Mudd shut the conference room door. "Misturh Austin, I have a petition signed by forty families in this church that I need to present to you in the presence of this Vestry."

This one really caught Steele off guard. "A petition? What kind of petition?"

Ned Boone answered, "Misturh Austin, I have tried to reason with you. Several members of this Vestry have tried to reason with you. We have tried to give you the benefit of the doubt, but you just won't listen. Is this not true, gentlemen?"

Most all the men at the table nodded and murmured their agreement.

"I don't understand."

Henry Mudd was standing at the end of the conference room table. "After you hear this petition you'll understand."

"Go on."

Henry Mudd distributed copies of the petition to the other members of the Vestry. He handed Steele the last copy. He then read, "Resolved, we the undersigned have great reservations about the leadership style of the Rector of First Church, The Reverend Steele Austin. We are gravely concerned about the direction he is leading our parish. We find his inability to take a stand against the cultural popularization of the Gospel to be inexcusable. In particular, we find that he is unable to uphold the Bible's teachings regarding homosexuality, divorce, and the traditional role of women in the family. Until such time as Misturh Austin returns to the Biblical foundation of the Episcopal Church or is removed from office, we the undersigned have reduced our financial commitments to First Church. We will send the major portion of our stewardship to support the ministry of The Reverend Richard Davis, the Vicar at St. Mary's Episcopal Mission. And further, we will actively encourage the other members of First Church to join us in this endeavor."

Steele quickly looked down at the names on the petition. It appeared that at least half of the Vestry had signed the petition. Mr. and Mrs. Henry Mudd and Mr. and Mrs. Ned Boone led the list. The queasiness in Steele's stomach was turning into a full case of nausea. "Henry, Ned, what is it you want me to do that I'm not doing?"

Ned Boone's neck stretched up over his oversized red bow tie. "We anticipated that question." Steele could see them sitting around the table at the Magnolia Club, rehearsing his every question and their agreed upon response. "Misturh Austin, you can begin by preaching a series of sermons upholding the Bible's teachings on the matters we listed in the petition."

Steele studied Ned and Henry. He then looked around the table at the faces of the members of the Vestry. Most avoided eye contact with him. A couple of them glanced at him and then quickly resumed staring at the conference table. He concluded that this petition wasn't being enthusiastically presented by all present and that maybe a few of them had reservations about it. After a period of silence, Steele leaned forward to look directly at Ned Boone, who met his stare. "Ned, I have hunch that just preaching a couple of sermons won't satisfy you. What else do you want me to do?"

Ned reached into his sports coat breast pocket and brought out a sheet of paper. He opened it and began to read, "First, you'll give up plans to start a halfway house for the homosexuals. Second, you'll work with our Bishop to help Horace Drummond find employment in another parish. On this particular demand we believe the sooner the better. Third, you'll no longer house an adulteress in the guest room of our Rectory. And fourth, you'll cease being seen in public in this city with the accused murderer, Rob McBride."

Steele sat back in his chair. Again, he looked around the conference room table. He could not make eye contact with any of the Vestry present except Henry and Ned, who continued to give Steele piercing stares. "Are you making that a motion for Vestry vote?"

"Of course not, Misturh Austin. This is counsel. Your Vestry here present and the Junior Warden are offering this to you as Godly counsel. And..."

"And?"

"Misturh Austin, we're not against you. We don't want you to take all of this personally. We just want to do what is best for our church. Our primary concern is for our beloved parish."

"And withdrawing your financial support is the best thing you can do for your parish?"

"Misturh Austin, if that is what we have to do to get your attention, then so be it."

Steele was quiet. He really didn't know how to respond. Ned Boone handed him the sheet of paper he had pulled from his pocket. Steele studied the paper. He read it over and over again. The room was filled with an uncomfortable silence. Steele didn't know if he was angry, tired, fed up, or apathetic. He really couldn't get in touch with his own feelings.

"Well?" Henry broke the silence.

"Gentlemen, let me try to clarify some of your demands. First, I'm not planning to start a halfway house for homosexuals. My intention is to start a halfway house for homeless men living with AIDS. These men are very ill. They will die on the streets with no one to care for them."

"God's just punishment," shouted Ned Boone.

Steele just looked at him. He chose not to respond. "Horace Drummond is a valuable member of this staff. He is coordinating all of our outreach ministries. He doesn't cost this parish a single dime. His salary and his ministry are covered by the Chadsworth Alexander Endowment for the Poor."

Henry Mudd interrupted, "This isn't about his ministry and you know it. The ladies of this church are embarrassed by his relationship with Almeda Alexander. She, and by association, this parish, has become the gossip of Falls City. The quickest way to end that nonsense is to get rid of that *Negara* priest."

Again, Steele chose not to respond. "My friend Rob McBride hasn't been found guilty of anything. He is innocent until he is found guilty by a jury of his peers. Once he is found innocent, he and Miss Mason planned to be married."

Ned Boone chuckled, "Semantics, Misturh Austin. Semantics. I swear, gentlemen, I think the Rector missed his calling. He should have been a trial lawyer." There were a few chuckles around the table. "Gentlemen, I believe that we have accomplished our purpose. We have delivered the message the Rector needed to hear. Now, let's all go home." Everyone began to stand and walk toward the door.

Henry Mudd walked over to where Steele was still sitting and leaned down so he could look Steele directly in the face. Then through gritted teeth he smirked in a voice that only Steele could hear, "Listen to me and you listen good. I've run out of patience with you. Do as we say or you'll discover that this is only the beginning of the end for you. Comprende, Padre?"

Again, Steele chose not to respond. When the room was empty, he spread the two sheets of paper on the table in front of him. He stared at them, but didn't read them. He simply could not find an emotion. He was numb. "You all right, Steele?" It was his Business Manager, Ted Holmes. "I figured something big was up. What gives?" He sat down at the table with Steele.

Steele handed him the papers. "They gave me these."

Ted read the two sheets of paper and then pursed his lips to give a gentle whistle. "You realize that some folks on this list of canceled pledges have never made a pledge?"

Steele smiled, "What?"

"I need to double check, but I think there are four or five non-pledging households on this list." He shrugged and chuckled, "How can you cancel a pledge that you've never made? In fact, I'm pretty sure these…" He circled a half dozen names, "… these have no record of giving anything to First Church for at least a decade."

"Some of the people on that list are significant donors though, aren't they?"

He raised his eyebrows and nodded, "Yeah, there are some big bucks represented on this sheet."

"Do you have any idea as to just what the total might be?"

"Well, it could be forty or fifty thousand… maybe more."

Steele sank down in his chair. "Wow!" The two men sat in silence. "I guess the first thing we need to do is get a total. After you have done that, let's get together tomorrow morning and look at the ministry budget. Obviously, we're going to have to make some cutbacks. I just hope we don't have to lay off any staff."

"You do have the operating reserve. I think you also have around twenty grand in gifts that have been given for you to use at your discretion. I carry those in the Rector's Funds on the balance sheet.

"Well, let's put it all together in the morning and make a budget plan."

Ted opened a manila folder that he had brought with him. "Have you seen this?" He handed Steele a letter. "I think it was mailed to every member of First Church."

Steele took the letter and began reading.

Dear Christian Friend,

As you know, I have become increasingly concerned about the direction of the Church. I know that you share my concern. The Church in America has lost its moorings. It has become more concerned with popular culture than Biblical teachings. It appears that despite the protests of many Bible believing clergy and lay people, the Church continues to stray away from the scriptural understanding of human sexuality, marriage, and the family.

As a member of the largest and most prestigious Episcopal Church in our city, if not the Diocese, I know that you're discovering that the frailties of the larger Church are being mirrored in your own parish.

Our entire nation is being controlled by liberal politicians, press and clergy who are more concerned with secular popularity than holiness. I fear that the clergy of First Church prefer to give priority to the bottom line of the financial statement while ignoring the spiritual needs of their members.

If you share my concerns, I would like to invite you to become an affiliate member of St. Mary's Mission. You may retain your membership in First Church while directing your financial support to St. Mary's. Please feel free to worship with us instead of or in addition to your worship attendance at First Church. We welcome the opportunity to contrast the Gospel being preached from this pulpit with the bleeding heart liberalism being poured from what was once a great pulpit for Jesus Christ in the Episcopal Church.

I look forward to discussing an affiliate membership with you.

Your Servant in Christ,

Fr. Richard Davis +

"This is unbelievable." Steele read through the letter one more time. "And you believe this was mailed to every member of First Church?"

"I haven't called every member, but all indications are that it was. Should you call the Bishop and report him?"

Steele let the laughter roll out of him. Finally, he was in touch with his emotions. The Business Manager stared at him in amazement as Steele continued to laugh. As he wiped the laughing tears that had welled up in his eyes and were beginning to stream down his cheeks, Steele stood and slapped Ted Holmes on the back. "Call the Bishop? That's a good one. Just who do you think dictated this letter?" And he laughed some more as he walked toward the door. He lifted his hand in a backward wave. "See you tomorrow, Ted." Steele laughed all the way home. He laughed himself to sleep that night. The next morning he awoke, but he didn't feel like laughing.

CHAPTER 18

The Society Pages in the *Falls City Gazette* might have reported it this way. *"There was a most unusual dinner party held in the Rectory of Historic First Church this past Wednesday evening. The Rector and Mrs. Steele Austin hosted an intimate party attended by only two other couples. Mrs. Almeda Alexander, the widow of the late Chadsworth Alexander the Third, a well known businessman and philanthropist in our community, looked resplendent in her bright red silk dress. Of course, the glow on her face was pale in comparison to the multi-carat diamond engagement ring on her finger. One wonders if her intended, The Reverend Doctor Horace Drummond, has hidden assets that would allow a parish priest to purchase such a token of his love and devotion.*

Also in attendance were Miss Melanie Mason of Beverly Hills, California and her escort.

They were all seated at the dining room table. Rob and Melanie were on one side. Almeda and Horace were seated on the other. Steele and Randi sat opposite each other in the captain's chairs. "I propose a toast to the newly engaged couple. Almeda, Horace, may you always be as happy as you think you are this night."

"Now Steele," Randi chided, "that sounds more like a joke than a toast. It lacks a bit of sincerity."

"Oh, I don't know, Honey. Can you remember a happier night than the night we got engaged?"

She blushed, "Oh, that was a great night, but there have been many wonderful nights since."

"Oh, please give us details." Horace whistled.

"Randi, I believe you're embarrassing yourself and us in the process." Almeda was chuckling like a school girl.

Steele lifted his glass to clink it with the others. All followed suit and took a sip of their wine. Steele spoke as Randi began serving the plates, "I wish this evening were not clouded by what I need to tell you good folks, but I want you all to hear about last night's Vestry meeting from me. So let's get this bit of unpleasantness over with first."

"Steele, my friend," Horace interrupted. "The fact that the meeting last night was contentious is pretty common knowledge among the staff and a large portion of the congregation. What we don't know are the specifics."

Steele took another sip of his wine. "Then let me show you. Steele handed each of them copies of the two pieces of paper that had been given him at last night's Vestry meeting. They each took the papers and started reading.

"I've never liked Henry Mudd." Almeda began. "Just who does he think he is? He and that pseudo snob of a wife and those two prissy little daughters are just too much."

"Now, now darling, we've got to decide how to best help Steele resolve this." Horace patted Almeda on the hand.

"I don't have to stay in your guest room," Melanie offered. "I can get a suite at the hotel or as far as that goes, I can move into the apartment that Rob has been using. The authorities have released his house and he is going to move back home."

"Steele, I can escalate my search for a new position. Almeda and I have known all along that we might have to leave Falls City after we get married." Horace put his arm around Almeda. "I'll do whatever I have to do to make sure that this beautiful lady and I have a peaceful and a happy marriage."

Rob McBride spoke, "Steele, I really value our friendship. In fact, the people sitting at this table are the only friends I have left, but if it'll make life easier for you, we can put our friendship on hold until my name is cleared."

Steele looked at Randi. She looked as though she was on the verge of tears. He held up his hand. "You misunderstand my purpose this evening. I have no intention of doing any of the things on this list. Randi and I have absolutely no intention of turning our backs on our friends, putting our friendships on hold, or anything that even resembles one of these preposterous demands. We're in this together. Is that understood?"

All at the table nodded. Horace raised his glass. "Then let's toast friendship." And they did.

"One final clarification and then we're going to happier conversation. The only reason I showed you those sheets of paper is that I wanted you to hear their contents from me and not through the gossip mill." Again, Steele asked, "Understood?" They all smiled.

"Tell us about your wedding plans, Almeda." Randi gushed.

"Well, we're thinking of the Saturday before Thanksgiving." Almeda could not contain the excitement in her voice. "We want the people at this table present, as well as Horace's sister, his daughter, and my two sons."

"How are your families receiving your news?" Steele asked.

"Actually," Horace chuckled, "Almeda's two boys are doing a better job of accepting things than my daughter and sister."

"Well, now, Horace," Almeda took his arm and gave it a squeeze. "That's because you have taken the time to get to know the boys and they have gotten to know you." Then, she glanced around the table and gave a squeamish look. "The first time they saw us together, both boys threw an absolute fit. They accused me of being a disgrace, an old fool, and bringing shame on their father. We weathered that storm, but not easily. Horace took the initiative. He went to see each boy one on one. But, I think the real turn in their attitudes came when Horace went dove hunting with them. They all camped out together and really got to know each other."

"Let's just say that during the drive to the hunt I needed to keep the car heater at its maximum temperature or I would have gotten frost bite. By bedtime, however, after some Jim Beam and conversation around the campfire, things were beginning to thaw."

"You said your sister and daughter are having a more difficult time. How's that going?" Steele inquired.

Horace and Almeda began laughing, "Oh, they think Almeda is a gold digger. They're convinced she's only after my money. They're demanding that I get a pre-nup."

"Horace, have you been holding out on us?"

Almeda and Horace laughed all the harder. "The only things I have of any value are my IRA and the house my wife and I lived in up in D.C. I've leased out the house all these years thinking that eventually I would retire and I could move back there."

"So what are you going to do?"

"Oh, we're getting a pre-nup." Now everyone at the table was laughing. "It's only right. That way Almeda's fortune is preserved for her sons and my little house will eventually go to my daughter."

"But while we are both alive, Horace, what is mine also belongs to you. I insist." Almeda gave him a stern look. "Agreed?"

"Yes, dear, whatever you say," Horace hummed.

Randi sat wide-eyed. Steele loved that look on her face. He knew that the wheels were spinning and she had a question that she wanted to ask, but wasn't sure whether or not she should. "Go ahead, Randi. You've got something on your mind. Out with it."

Randi looked at Almeda and Horace. The curiosity in her voice could not be disguised, "Almeda, Horace's daughter and his sister... do they have any idea just how much money you do have?"

Horace let out a big roar of laughter. Almeda joined in. "They've not got a clue. Once they find out they're going to feel so silly."

Randi looked at Melanie and Rob in an effort to bring them into the conversation, "Rob, you've lost quite a bit of weight, but I have to say that you look great."

"I've now lost close to thirty pounds. For awhile I just didn't feel like eating, but now I'm going to the YMCA, exercising, lifting weights. It really helps me keep the stress down. Lately, I've started putting just a few pounds back on."

Melanie grabbed his bicep. "Look at this, my man's got muscles." Rob blushed and she giggled.

"You do look good, Rob." Steele added. "Do you have any updates on the investigation that you care to share with us?"

He shook his head, "Regrettably, no. There isn't anything new. Just more dead-end streets."

Melanie joined in, "I have a team of private investigators working on it, but so far they aren't finding anything either. They have interviewed every neighbor for blocks to see if anyone saw anything. They've literally gone through the roster of St. Mary's, talking to every parishioner. No one knows anyone who would have wanted to murder Rob's wife. Oh, a couple of the women in his congregation complained that she flirted with their husbands, but nothing. Right now, the investigators are working the community college where she was the assistant librarian. They're talking with students, faculty, anyone they can find to see if they can get any leads. We're hopeful that something will turn up."

"Rob, you told me the other day that they still haven't set a trial date."

"No, Steele, I just know that they think it will be sometime shortly after the first of the year."

This time it was Melanie who took Rob's arm and gave it a squeeze, "There's not going to be a trial. My investigators are going to find the person that did this so that Rob and I can get married and grow old together."

Steele quipped, "Is that another announcement I hear?"

Rob shook his head, "No ring and no announcement, but the day that I'm cleared I'm going to go to the jewelry store and by this gorgeous woman an engagement ring that will make that one you're wearing, Almeda, look pale in comparison."

Almeda reached across the table. She held out her hand for Rob to hold. She squeezed his hand, "Rob, you do that very thing. And once you do, we'll all have dinner at my house to celebrate. I insist."

Rob squeezed Almeda's hand in return. "Father Austin, you have thrown a most interesting dinner party this evening. Your dinner guests are of a most unusual nature. And, Mrs. Austin, you're the perfect hostess."

All present lifted their glasses yet one more time to toast Randi. Steele sat back to watch his guests as the small talk began over coffee. He reasoned that one of the greatest joys in life was watching God perform His miracles. Prejudice is broken down by love. Hope rails against the darkest night. Antagonists become friends. And the Almighty continues to prepare a table for all of us.

CHAPTER 19

Gentlemen, I asked you to meet with us today so that we could begin the process of revising the parish budget." Steele indicated with his hands for the Senior Warden Howard Dexter, the Junior Warden Henry Mudd, and the Business Manager Ted Holmes to be seated.

"Well, Misturh Austin, I think it's a little premature to be working on next year's budget." Howard Dexter shifted in his chair.

"That's true, Howard, but this meeting isn't about next year's budget. Because of the information that Mr. Mudd shared with us at the Vestry meeting last week and the canceled pledges that have come into the finance office since last week, we are faced with quite a budget challenge for the balance of this year." Steele nodded to Ted.

"As of this morning, we now have right at seventy thousand dollars in reduced or canceled pledges to First Church. These members have indicated that they are redirecting their pledges to St. Mary's Mission."

"As you can imagine, Gentlemen, this puts our current budget in jeopardy." Steele opened a manila folder and handed out copies of a revised budget. "My first priority was to maintain job security for the current staff. At the same time I wanted to protect all of our ministry programs and not do anything to weaken our ministry efforts."

"I trust that you aren't proposing a cutback on our support of the Diocese!" Henry Mudd's tone was vitriolic. "The mission churches and the Diocesan program don't need to be punished for your lack of judgment, Misturh Austin."

A not very Christian response crossed Steele's mind, but he chose not to verbalize it. "You'll see that I propose that we budget the full Diocesan asking."

Henry Mudd nodded his approval. "I notice that you have increased the anticipated amount in the Other Income column. Just where is that money going to come from?"

Steele lifted his finger, signaling his Business Manager to answer. "We are moving twenty-three thousand dollars from the Rector's Funds into that budget column."

Henry Mudd was perplexed. "Rector's Funds? Just what are Rector's Funds? Where did that money come from?"

Ted continued, "From time to time, members of the parish give the Rector donations with the instructions that their gifts be used for projects or ministries that the budget doesn't provide for. These gifts are to be under the Rector's sole control and discretion."

Henry Mudd threw his hands up in the air. "I've never heard of Rector's Funds. I think this is a ruse. Did you know about these Funds, Howard?"

Howard nodded, "Henry, they're right there on the balance sheet that you receive at every Vestry meeting. They're carried as an off-budget asset."

"Balance sheet? Who pays attention to the balance sheet?" Henry was really frustrated. "I'm an attorney. I'm not an accountant. I think these funds need to be investigated. I want to know just who has been donating this money and I want to know just how the Rector has been expending it."

Howard interrupted, "Henry, these funds are audited each year by our external auditors, along with all the parish funds. I don't think it would be appropriate for us to delve into the donor detail."

Steele was pleasantly surprised by Howard's response. He sat silent so that the two men could continue to examine the budget detail.

"Misturh Austin, if you haven't cut back on the Diocese or the parish programs, just where have you cut back?" Henry Mudd was talking to Steele like he was a hostile witness that Henry was cross examining.

"The staff and I have all agreed to take a fifteen percent decrease in our salaries for the balance of this year."

"And the staff is in agreement?"

"They're not happy about it, Henry, but they all agree with me that it's preferable for all of us to be paid less versus putting one of our own in the unemployment line."

Again, Howard surprised Steele. "Misturh Austin, we've just got to find another way. I don't think that this parish should be built on the backs of the staff."

Clearly, Howard's comments were rubbing Henry the wrong way. "Ted, didn't you tell us that the reduction in pledges totals seventy thousand dollars?"

"Well, actually they are just shy of sixty thousand dollars, but the Rector has asked me to allow for the possibility that another twelve thousand dollars in pledges could be reduced or canceled."

Henry Mudd took a ballpoint pen from his pocket. He started doing some calculations on the sheet. "If my math is correct, Misturh Austin, you have only reduced the anticipated pledge income by forty thousand dollars against a projected seventy thousand dollar decrease. I believe, sir that you still need to trim thirty thousand dollars out of this budget."

Steele had been anticipating that question. He was relishing the moment it would come, but even more he was relishing the look that would surely come to Henry Mudd's face when he heard his answer. "Yes, the math would indicate that you're correct except for one thing."

"Oh, what's that?"

Steele was struggling to contain himself. Ted Holmes was looking down at the table and doodling on his folder with his pencil. He could not contain the smile on his face. "Well, Henry, over the past week I have been telephoning some of the members of our congregation advising them of our current financial circumstances. I have asked each of them to join with me and the staff by increasing their pledges for the balance of the year to offset those that have been reduced or canceled. So far, I have received thirty thousand dollars in increased pledges. I plan to continue to make those phone calls right up to the time I need to present a revised budget to the Vestry."

"Make that thirty-five thousand dollars." Steele's head jerked involuntarily to look at Howard Dexter.

"Excuse me?"

"I'll say." Henry Mudd was angry. "Howard, you're not endorsing what this man is doing?"

"Just calm down, Henry." Howard was making calming motions with his hands. "I agree with everything that you and the others object to, but I don't agree with your method. Nothing is gained by hurting the staff and our ministry program. This is my church and it has been my church since the day I was born. I want it to be the best church that it can be. I voted for the budget that Misturh Austin presented us last

January. There isn't one cent in that budget that I can argue with. It's a good budget and a good program. The things that you object to have nothing to do with this congregation's ministry plan for this year. I can only hope that you and the others will reconsider before our beloved parish is irreparably harmed."

"Well, Sir, you and I are just going to have to disagree on that one." Henry Mudd was smoldering. "I'll not support anything this man does until he comes to his senses. And I can damn guarantee you that none of the others will change their minds either."

Steele stood, "Well, Gentlemen, that being said, my next step is to take this budget to the Finance Committee. It will be their responsibility to bring it to the Vestry for a vote." Howard and Henry didn't stand. "Come on Ted, we have some other things to discuss."

When they were in the hallway Ted asked, "How do you think that went?"

"Howard Dexter continues to surprise me. I know that he's against what I'm trying to do, yet, well, you heard him."

"How do you explain it?"

"I can't, but one day in eternity The Boss and I have just got to have a long talk.

"CHAPTER 20

THE FALLS CITY GAZETTE

EXTRAORDINARY GROWTH AT ST. MARY'S

The Mission Church of St. Mary's has been idle for the past two decades. The little Episcopal congregation was begun by a handful of members from historic First Church. It was believed that another parish was needed to serve the Episcopalians who were moving into the south side of our city.

The tiny congregation has been served by only one priest. Rob McBride was assigned to the congregation soon after he was ordained. The anticipated growth of the congregation never occurred. Now, Mr. McBride is awaiting trial for the murder of his wife and has been removed as a priest.

But his dark cloud hasn't cast a shadow over this vital congregation. The Bishop of the Diocese, The Right Reverend Rufus Petersen, assigned The Reverend Richard Davis to serve as Vicar. "He is a rising star in the Episcopal Church", so stated Bishop Petersen in a telephone interview from his office in Savannah. I'm just delighted that he is at St. Mary's. I'm so proud of him. I just know that great things for the Lord will continue to happen in Falls City and they all will be Father Davis's doing."

Father Davis is an articulate man who leaves little room to question his understanding of the Gospel. "Some people have called me a fundamentalist. I am not a fundamentalist, but I do believe that we should adhere to Biblical teachings. The Bible isn't up for discussion. The words of Holy Writ mean exactly what they say."

Father Davis has preached some blistering sermons from the pulpit at St. Mary's, condemning what he calls the "bleeding heart liberals" who have adopted a revisionist view of the Bible. "They take the words of scripture and revise their intent to serve their own liberal causes. It's not the Bible they are being faithful to, but their own agendas."

When pressed for specifics, the young priest began a menu that few in Falls City would find offensive. "This isn't just about homosexuality, although I believe that the teachings of Scripture are quite clear on that one. It's an abomination. It's the responsibility of every faithful person to call the people who have chosen that perversion to repentance."

While homosexuality isn't his primary preaching topic, it certainly finds its way into most every sermon being preached at St. Mary's. Other hot buttons for the young priest's oratory are the issues surrounding divorce, the family, and the traditional role of women in the home.

The average Sunday attendance at St. Mary's has grown in just a few short weeks from seventy worshippers to close to three hundred. The annual giving is projected to quadruple.

St. Mary's has become the flagship in Falls City for evangelical and conservative Christians. "We now have people worshiping with us who formerly attended services in the Methodist, Baptist, and Presbyterian congregations. Close to one hundred families from First Church have become affiliate members of our congregation," so stated Father Davis.

This reporter asked Father Davis for an explanation of his sudden and explosive success at St. Mary's. The priest responded, "God is blessing our work. I think He has put us here as an example for the other congregations in this city. As the ministers of these other churches watch their numbers dwindle, perhaps they should take a closer look at the Gospel as it's preached at St. Mary's. God only blesses that which pleases Him."

CHAPTER 21

Hey Preacher, are you about to call it a day?"

It was Chief Sparks. He was standing at the door to Steele's office. "I called Crystal and she said that it looked like you were about to wrap things up."

"Chief, how was your fishing trip?"

"We had a great time. I would've caught more fish if Stone hadn't insisted on talking all the time. I swear he scared off all the good ones."

"Who caught the most?

"Me, of course."

"And the largest catch was landed by...?"

"Me, again."

"And Stone would verify this information?"

"Now you and I both know that man doesn't know how to tell the truth."

"And you're our Chief Law Enforcement Officer?"

"Just who are you going to believe? You gonna believe the Chief of Police or some part-time lawyer-slash-entrepreneur who spends most of his time on hunting and fishing trips?"

Steele laughed, "I plan to believe the one who has the power to arrest me."

"You, Parson, are a smart man."

"Oh, I don't know. You guys missed the latest round of fireworks."

"I got an update, but it sounds like to me you're holding your own." He reached into his coat pocket and brought out a check. "It's not much, but it will help make up the money that Mudd is trying to steal from his own parish. I've lived in this town my entire life and sometimes I think the biggest crooks are the ones that I can't arrest."

"Thanks, Chief. Slowly we're making up for the lost funds, but as of today for every dollar I raise Ted tells me about another dollar being diverted to St. Mary's. It's tough."

"Hang in there, Parson; we're not going to let a bunch of malcontents bring this parish down."

Steele closed his briefcase. He had some correspondence that needed to be answered. He planned on taking care of it on his computer at home after Travis had gone to bed. "Buy you a drink, Chief?"

"No, actually I need you to take a ride with me."

"Now that sounds ominous."

"I need you to go with me over to the Coroner's office. There's a body over there that I think you might be able to identify for us."

"What makes you think that?"

"My bicycle patrol found the body of a transient under the Falls River Bridge last night. It seems that he had one of your calling cards in his pocket. You got time to take a ride with me?"

"Sure, if you think I can help. Just let me call Randi and let her know that I'm going to be a little late getting home."

At the Coroner's office the Chief and the Coroner led Steele into the embalming room. There were four embalming tables in the room. There were bodies on two of them. They were covered with sheets. The Coroner stopped at the first. "You ready?"

Steele nodded. The Coroner pulled the sheet back that was covering the man's face. Steele studied the face for a few seconds. He just wasn't sure... and then he nodded, "Yeah, I know this man. I only know his first name. He's been a regular at our Soup Kitchen, although... you know, he's not been there for a few weeks. His name is Duke." Steele looked at the Coroner. "You're aware that he had AIDS?"

"We haven't gotten all our tests back yet, but..." He pulled the sheet down to reveal Duke's naked chest. "These lesions were a pretty good indicator."

"What do you know about him?" the Chief asked.

"He told me his story one day at the Soup Kitchen. I know he was married and that his only son drowned in the family swimming pool as a small boy. His wife could not handle the grief. He said she went out to the boy's grave and took her own life there. It was all just too much for Duke here. He started with booze and graduated to the hard stuff. He lost his job. He lost everything. He ended up on the streets. That's about all I know. I don't even know where he's from. I asked him a couple of times, but he wouldn't tell me."

"We can help you with that." The Coroner covered Duke's face with the sheet. He then reached for a folder that was lying at the bottom of the embalming table. "We ran his fingerprints through the national data base. Seems our boy was arrested a couple of times up in Atlanta for trying to buy drugs from undercover officers." He opened the folder. "His name is Edward Mark Young. His last known address was on Barrington Drive in Marietta, Georgia."

"Anything else?" the Chief asked.

"No, that's as far as we could take it. I'm afraid that the rest is up to your office, Chief."

"Give me a copy of what you have there and I'll get some guys on it tomorrow."

"Can you think of anything that might help us, Steele?"

"No, Chief, I wish that I could."

"One more thing, is there any evidence of foul play?"

The Coroner shook his head, "No, Chief, at least not from our preliminaries. It looks to us like Duke, or Edward here, died with all the usual complications associated with AIDS. If I find otherwise, I'll call your office."

The Chief thanked the Coroner and led Steele back out to the squad car. He and Steele got in the back seat. The uniformed officer behind the wheel asked, "Where to, Chief?"

"You got time for a cool one before you go home, Steele?"

"Always."

"Can you drop me at my house after we have one beer together?"

"No problem."

"Take us back up to the church."

When they were in Steele's car the Chief asked, "You ever been to O'Henry's?"

"No, I've never been there."

"It's just off Main around the corner from the station house. It's a favorite hang-out for my officers when they're off duty. Let's go give them a thrill."

When they walked into the bar the Chief immediately became the target of some good natured ribbing. "Hey Father, you brought him to the right place to try to save his soul, but take it from every guy in this room, he doesn't have one!" About a half dozen guys at the bar got a great laugh at the Chief's expense.

"Don't pay any attention to these guys. We really should've gone some place with a higher class of clientele."

One of the young officers rebutted, "You know they keep turning you down for membership at the Magnolia Club. Now just why do you think that is, Chief?"

"Guilt by association with you guys. Come on, Parson, there's a table in that far corner. Let's get as far away from these discount store security guards as we can get."

"You can run, but you can't hide. We know where you live." More laughter followed.

After they had gotten their beers the Chief asked, "Just where are you in your plans to open that shelter for men like Duke?"

"Horace Drummond and the committee are in the process of trying to find a location right now. When I met with him this morning he told me that they had a couple of places for me to look at later this week."

The Chief wiped his lips after taking a sip from his beer mug. "Good, the sooner the better."

"I'm glad that I have your support. I wasn't sure."

"Listen Padre, you have my complete support. The thing that people like Ned Boone and Henry Mudd refuse to acknowledge is that there is a direct relationship between drugs, poverty and crime. Oh, not all crime for sure, but the crime that takes up most of my time and that of these officers is poverty-driven. It's the poor and the homeless just trying to get a drug fix, or in some extreme cases, get something to eat. The more that the churches and service agencies can do to help us get these people off the street the better off we'll all be." He took another sip of his beer. "What about those that are mentally ill?"

"My heart just goes out to those poor folks that live with all those voices in their heads. Our plan right now is to use the doctors at the Free Medical Clinic to get them on their medications and use our resident counselors to make sure they stay on them. We'll do the same with the AIDS medications. With the advances that have been made medically, most of the men that will live in the house can have normal and productive lives. AIDS doesn't have to be a death sentence."

"Well, I hope that it all comes together. It sounds like the house you're planning to open will help keep guys like Duke off the embalming table in the Coroner's office."

"I don't know, Chief. I feel a bit like a failure. I wasn't able to help Duke. In fact, he wouldn't let me help him. I don't think he even wanted help. My hunch is that he would not have met the conditions we're going to require of those that will want to live in our AIDS house."

"I understand, but Steele, for every Duke who refuses help I think there are two who will let you help them. You've got to focus on the people who want to be helped."

Steele nodded, "I know that you're right. It's just that seeing him on that table, and then thinking about him dying under that bridge last night all by himself with no one to comfort him... I don't know."

"Do you have any idea the number of corpses my officers find every month in this town? And we're not even a big city by Atlanta standards. Can you imagine the number of homeless the large cities must deal with?"

"I've read the statistics, but I guess the numbers become more meaningful when you've actually known one of them."

"Then that's where you begin, Padre."

"What do you mean?"

"Begin by helping the Ned Boones, the Henry Mudds, and all of us realize that these poor souls aren't statistics. They are people just like you and me. How do you preachers put it? They're our brothers and sisters in Christ."

"Chief, have I told you just how lucky I am to have you as a friend?"

The Chief lifted his glass to Steele. "Right back at you, Preacher."

CHAPTER 22

Steele stepped out of the hearse. He had chosen to ride to the cemetery in Atlanta with the funeral director. Standing at the grave was an elderly gentleman leaning on a cane. He was well-groomed in a suit and bowtie. Standing next to him, being supported by an aluminum walker, was a woman that Steele guessed to be well into her eighties. There was a nurse in a white uniform standing behind them. There were only about a half dozen other people standing behind the nurse. Steele assumed that they were all friends of Duke's parents.

While the funeral director and the cemetery attendants proceeded to unload the casket from the hearse, Steele walked over to the elderly couple. "Mr. and Mrs. Young, I'm Steele Austin. We spoke on the telephone."

He shook both their hands. Mrs. Young looked up at Steele, "You're a lot younger than I thought you would be."

"Thank you, Ma'am. Again, let me tell you just how sorry I am about your son."

Mr. Young offered Steele the portrait that he was holding in his hand. "This is a picture of Edward."

Mrs. Young smiled. "Wasn't he handsome?"

Steele took the picture from him. Clearly, it was a professional portrait. The man sitting on the edge of a desk was dressed in a dark blue suit, white shirt, and crimson tie. He was surrounded by all the symbols of success. There was a big smile on his face. "Yes, Mrs. Young, he is very handsome. He looks so happy here."

"This was taken just a couple of weeks before..." Her lips and chin trembled as she wiped at the tears rolling down her cheeks.

Mr. Young spoke in a soft voice with a pleasant southern accent, "We had all but given up. We didn't think we would ever hear from Edward again. In fact, we assumed that he had died long ago."

"That must have been very difficult for you."

"Not knowing was the most difficult part."

The men carried Duke's casket to the metal frame around the open grave and slid it onto the rollers on the frame and pushed it into place. "Please," Mrs. Young pointed to a floral wreath on the folding chairs. "Put these flowers on top of the casket." The funeral director did as she requested.

Steele leaned over so that he could speak more softly to the couple. "Mr. and Mrs. Young, do you want to see Duke's, I mean, Edward's remains?"

He looked at his wife. "It's up to you, Honey. I don't think I want to. I have some happy pictures of him in my heart. I want to remember him before his world caved in on him."

She wiped a tear from her cheek and nodded. "I don't think we need to do that. We know that he's at peace now. That's really all we need. May I ask you something, Father Austin?"

"Sure, whatever you want."

"Why do you keep calling Edward, Duke?"

"That's how he introduced himself to me. I never knew his real name until just a few days ago. Now, may I ask you something?"

"Sure."

"Why do you think he chose to call himself Duke?"

Mister Young grinned, "He was a graduate of Duke University. He was so proud of his alma mater. He loved that school. He was so happy while he was there. That's where he met the young lady that was later to become his wife. They were so much in love. They were living their dream until... well, you know the rest."

Steele nodded, "You ready to begin?"

They took their seats. "Before I start, I'm going to be using the Burial Service from the Book of Common Prayer. It's brief and to the point."

"Edward never told you?" Mr. Young asked.

"I beg your pardon?"

"Edward was raised in the Episcopal Church. Our entire family has been Episcopalians for generations. Edward was an acolyte when he was a boy. He even served on the Vestry at our parish here in Atlanta."

"Then you're familiar with the Burial Service."

Mrs. Young nodded. "Please proceed, Father. We find great comfort in the words of the Prayer Book."

Steele took his place at the head of the casket. "In a certain place there was a garden and in that garden there was a sepulcher that had never been used. In that sepulcher they buried the body of Jesus. Lord, bless this grave that he whose body is to be buried here may rest in peace and be raised to life eternal on the Day of the General Resurrection."

When the service was over, Steele asked the funeral director to lower the casket into the grave. He then took the shovel from one of the attendants, filled it with dirt from the edge of the grave, and tossed the dirt onto the casket. He then handed the shovel to Mr. Young, who did likewise. He handed it to his wife. Each of the people present did the same.

After the Youngs and the other mourners had departed, the cemetery attendants began rolling up the artificial grass that had been placed around the grave. It was then that Steele was able to see the headstones. There was one for Duke's wife. Next to it and in between the one that was already in place for Duke was a tiny marker with two cherubs on it. Duke had made arrangements to insure that their child would be buried in between the two of them.

While the funeral director and the attendants finished filling the grave, Steele took a walk around the cemetery. There were markers denoting the graves of entire families. From the dates on the tombstones he could discern which graves belonged to the parents and which belonged to the children that had been laid to rest in the family plots.

He wandered into a section that had a beautiful statue of Jesus blessing the children. All around the statue were tiny little headstones. There were hundreds of them. Steele walked among them. The sign at the entrance to this section designated it as The Garden of the Innocents. He could only think of it as a Garden of Pain. It was almost unbearable to consider the heartache and grief that each of these little stones in the ground represented. For every stone, there were young parents, perhaps brothers and sisters, grandparents who had literally had their hearts torn from their chests. Every stone marked a nightmare from which those who loved these little ones could not wake.

Just beyond The Garden of the Innocents there was a section of the cemetery with a statue of four soldiers at its entrance. One soldier represented each branch of the military. Here were single white headstones. They were marked with the names preceded by titles - Private, Corporal, and Colonel. The dates on the markers were like a history lesson. They each denoted young men, some still in their teens, who had made the ultimate sacrifice for their country. One in particular caught Steele's eye. It was a fresh grave. It was for a PFC. He had just died a few weeks ago. From the dates on the monument Steele figured he was but twenty-four years old. On the grave was a little red toy fire truck. It had a gift tag tied to it. The writing on the gift tag was in a child's handwriting. Steele knelt down so he could read it. *"To: Daddy. Love, Ben."*

As Steele walked back to the hearse, the words that he had just recited over Duke's grave came back to mind. "In a certain place there was a garden. A garden...It was in that garden that the women came on the First Day of the week. It was there that they encountered Jesus. Oh God," Steele prayed, "Let Jesus be in this place and in all the gardens filled with grief throughout the world."

Back at Duke's grave, Steele stood to offer one final prayer. "You ready to go back to Falls City, Father Austin?" The funeral director startled him. "Yeah, I've got something I need to make sure gets done before Christmas."

"Oh, mind if I ask what?"

"I'm going to make sure that some of the men like Duke here will celebrate this Christmas in a warm house with a Christmas tree, presents, and a big feast."

"Just how do you plan to do that?"

"We're going to open a house in Falls City for homeless men living with AIDS."

"What are you going to call it?"

Steele opened the door on the passenger side of the hearse. He looked back at the cemetery. In the distance he could see The Garden of the Innocents, the graves of the fallen soldiers, and the little fire truck that was a gift from Ben to his Daddy. And then his eyes fell on the grave of Edward Young, the grave he had just blessed. Today, a heartbroken man was reunited with his family for all of eternity. He held up the portrait of Edward Young that Steele had borrowed from his mother with the promise to return it once he had made a copy. Then he smiled and turned to look at the funeral director. "We're going to call it Duke's House."

CHAPTER 23

"Misturh Austin, you can't be serious." The two women gave each other confused looks. They were torn between disbelief and laughter.

"Knock, knock." It was Steele's secretary, Crystal. "Mrs. Smythe, I believe you wanted coffee with cream." Putting it down in front of her she continued, "And Mrs. Dexter, you wanted some tea. Do you want one lump or two?"

"Two, please."

"Can I get you ladies anything else?"

They shook their heads.

"Father Austin?"

"No, I'm fine. Will you close the door on your way out? Thanks, Crystal."

"Yes, thank you." The two ladies spoke at the same time.

"Mrs. Smythe, Mrs. Dexter, if I could just get you to think about it."

Putting her tea cup down on Steele's desk, Mrs. Smythe responded, "Misturh Austin, it hasn't been five months since we pleaded with you to do something about this. Do you remember our conversation at the Altar Guild Tea?"

"Yes, I remember."

"And you've done nothing. This foolishness has continued and now you want us to join in the nonsense."

"Please."

"I'm just beside myself," Mrs. Dexter interrupted. "I don't know whether to be angry with you or simply dismiss this entire conversation as a request coming from a desperate man."

"Ladies, please don't be angry. I can assure you that I'm not desperate. I'm quite serious about what I'm asking you to do."

"Does she know that you're asking us to do this?"

"No one knows. I've not even discussed this request with my wife. I'm coming directly to you because I believe that you're the best people to do this."

"But why, Misturh Austin?" Mrs. Dexter was pleading. There was a childlike whine in her voice. "Can't you do something to stop this? What about the Bishop? Can't he refuse the marriage?"

"No, they're both widowers. They don't have to get the Bishop's permission."

The two ladies shuffled in their seats. In silence they sipped their tea.

"Look, let's approach it this way. First, they're going to get married. There's nothing that we can do to stop them. Their marriage is a done deal. Now, First Church has a choice. We can ignore the entire event or we can join in their celebration."

"They're already the gossip of the town. They're out all the time going to restaurants, concerts, and the theatre. So far she hasn't tried to take him to the Magnolia Club or the Country Club. At least she's had the good sense to respect the club policies."

Mrs. Dexter joined in, "I've been told that people have seen his car over at her house all night long. Now just what do you think of that, Misturh Austin?"

Steele chose to ignore that question and pretend to pick up on the last thing that he heard Mrs. Smythe say. "Ladies, I'm not really concerned about club policies. My primary concern is for two people that I've learned to love and admire. My loyalty is to my friends. They've made the decision to go against all the odds and build a life with each other. You do consider Almeda a friend, don't you?"

"Well, since Doctor Drummond has come on the scene, she hasn't had much time for us or any of her female friends. I'm not sure, but I don't think she's even been to an Altar Guild meeting in months. Do you recall?"

Mrs. Dexter shook her head. "No, I really haven't seen her at any of our women's group activities. She just sits on the front row of the church staring up at him. It's all so pathetic."

Steele studied the two women. "We all know that there's a lot of gossip right now. Which of our alternatives is going to change the tone of the conversation? If we do nothing for Horace and Almeda, we will only add fuel to the flame. On the other hand, if we join in their celebration, the gossips have nothing to talk about."

"Oh, they'll have plenty to talk about," Mrs. Dexter spewed. "A mixed marriage in Falls City, it's just not done. A mixed marriage between a Neg..." Steele held up his hand. "Oh, all right. A mixed marriage between a black priest and a white woman, oh it's just too much."

"Ladies, let's get back to reality." Steele spoke calmly. "First, Jim Crow is dead. As America grows and changes, there're going to be more and more marriages between blacks and whites. It's the future and we need to accept it."

"Well, it may be the future, but I don't have to like it." Mrs. Dexter pushed her tea cup toward Steele.

"And you, Mrs. Smythe, how do you feel?"

She nodded. "I know that you're correct. I'm embarrassed to tell you that my niece is attending the University of Chicago and my sister told me the other day that my niece has been dating a Mexican boy."

"And, if she were to marry that young man?"

"Oh, my," Mrs. Smythe started fanning herself with her napkin. "I just can't even think about that."

"For the purposes of our conversation, let's do." Steele leaned forward on his desk. "How would you respond to that marriage? Would you attend the wedding if invited? Would you invite the couple to stay with you in your home when they visit Falls City?"

"Of course I would. It would be difficult, but I would do it. I love my sister and I love my niece."

Steele stood and walked to the front of his desk. He sat down on the edge. "Maybe I've been approaching this request in the wrong way. Ladies, how do you feel about Almeda Alexander?"

"She's been my friend for over forty years. We've worked together on most every important endeavor the women in this community have ever undertaken." Mrs. Smythe looked reflective.

"And you want her to be happy?"

"I do." Mrs. Smythe nodded while looking at Mrs. Dexter, who also nodded. "Of course, we both do. We just think she's making a big mistake."

"And ladies, she may very well be. But it's her mistake to make. It's not up to us. Then again, she could just be making the best decision of her life." Steele turned and walked back to his chair behind the desk. He sat down. "Now what do you say, ladies? Can we plan a wedding reception for a friend?"

"Well," Mrs. Smythe looked at Mrs. Dexter. She nodded her agreement. Mrs. Smythe reached into her purse and brought out a notebook and a pen. "Just what did you have in mind?"

"Great," Steele smiled. "This is just marvelous. I'm grateful to both of you." He pulled a calendar out of his desk drawer and placed it on the desk so that they could see it. "They're getting married in the Chapel on the Saturday before Thanksgiving. They're leaving that evening for Jamaica. They'll be there for one week. My thought is that we could have a reception for them after the late service on the Sunday they return. What do you think?"

"I suppose we could put it all together." Mrs. Dexter was now smiling. "We could divide up the duties among our members and we can have the food catered."

"I want to leave the details to you and the other ladies on the Altar Guild." Steele sat back in his chair. "This is just wonderful."

"Are you going to tell them?" Mrs. Smythe asked Steele.

"I think it would be best if the two of you did it. I think it should be a gift from Almeda's friends on the Altar Guild. The two of you should advise her of the wedding gift you all want to give her. And, I would prefer that you tell her that it's your idea. Please don't mention me or our meeting this morning."

"Yes, yes. You're so right. May I use your telephone? If she's at home, we're going to go advise her right now."

Steele looked over at Mrs. Dexter. "Are you in agreement?"

"Yes, I suppose I am, but Misturh Austin. I just have to let you know how disappointed I am that you could not stop this."

"I can appreciate your feelings, but I fear you greatly overestimate my influence over Cupid. We all know that when Cupid's arrow hits its mark, temporary insanity sets in. We call that love. I really, truly believe that Horace and Almeda are in love. We just have to trust their hearts and choose to be happy for them." Steele stood, "You've pointed out that they're going to have a very difficult time. The odds are against them. They're going to encounter obstacles that you and I can only imagine. For all those reasons, my dear ladies, they need all the help they can get. I want to be one of the people pulling for them. They're going to need all their friends pulling for them. My prayer is that this church will go on record as pulling for them."

The two women stood. Mrs. Dexter continued, "I can already think of some women on the Altar Guild who will have nothing to do with this."

"Like who?"

"Well, Virginia Mudd for one."

Mrs. Smythe shook her head, "Oh, she has an opinion about everything and everyone. We'll have more fun without her. Let's go see Almeda. I think this is going to make her very happy."

Mrs. Smythe turned and hugged Steele's neck. "Thanks for asking us to do this. It's not often that we get the chance to give someone a surprise gift that's going to please them so much."

To Steele's total amazement, Mrs. Howard Dexter hugged him as well.

CHAPTER 24

His heart was racing. He wiped his sweaty palms on his jeans one at a time. He was careful to keep one hand on the steering wheel of the car. Reaching for the box on the passenger seat, he withdrew a tissue. He wiped the sweat from his forehead first and then dried his sweat from the steering wheel. He glanced in the rearview mirror and slowed so that the car behind him could pass. He wanted to make sure that no one was following him.

He took the frontage road to the freeway. He would take the by-pass around Falls City. Once again, he glanced into the rearview mirror. There was no one behind him. He relaxed a little. He knew that he had to be careful. He must not get caught. Still, he felt compelled to do this. The drive and desire that he was feeling was overwhelming. He knew he had to give in to it. It had been weeks since he had felt any satisfaction. All of his efforts to resolve his needs had only proven to be temporary. He needed more than the fruits of his imagination. He longed to touch and be touched.

There was only one semi-truck in the parking lot when he pulled into the roadside rest area. The running lights were on. The interior cab lights were off. The driver could be sleeping. Then, he saw the driver hitting his tires with a rubber mallet. He pulled into a parking space immediately in front of the rest stop bathrooms. He stared at the truck driver. He wanted to make sure that he was the only person in the area. Turning off his engine and headlights, he cracked his window to let the cool winter air into the car. He also wanted to be able to hear if any other cars were approaching.

The truck driver finished his task and seemed satisfied that all was well. He then climbed into the cab of his semi, turned on the headlights, and pulled forward onto the freeway.

He reached for his door handle and started to step out of the car when he saw the headlights of another car coming up behind him. He sat back in his seat, pretending to be sleeping. The car pulled up immediately next to him. A man and a little boy got out. They made shivering motions as they ran into the men's restroom. He waited. In a few minutes, the scene was repeated as they returned to their car. Once the little boy had his seat belt on, the man returned to the driver's side. The man started his car. He turned on his headlights and backed out of the space. The red lights on the rear of the car glowed in the night as the car resumed its journey on the freeway.

Looking around, he could see no one. He decided to just sit back and wait. He buried his face in his hands. Once again he prayed for God to cleanse him of these sinful desires. He pounded the steering wheel with his fists. He begged God to deliver him from Satan. "Jesus, through the power of Your cross drive this demon from me." There was no answer. There was nothing but the sound of the passing traffic on the freeway. He laid his head back against the headrest on his car seat and closed his eyes.

He remembered the night that the boy next door had slept over. He was fourteen at the time. His friend was a year older. The boy had encouraged them to experiment with each other. He remembered just how excited they both had become. He recalled the feelings. He was enjoying what the older boy was doing to him. He liked watching and touching his friend in his private places. But then, the door to his bedroom swung open. The light came on. His mother started screaming. She made his friend get dressed. She called his mother and sent him home.

His mother came back into the bedroom with a tray of ice. She put the ice in a towel and then placed it in his shorts and held it there. She started praying that God would chase Satan out of him. She read from the Bible. She sang some hymns. The pain of the ice on his private parts was almost unbearable. He protested, but his mother was firm in her resolve and physically stronger than he realized. He begged her to remove the ice. She was unmoved by his tears. Soon he became numb. He cried himself to sleep. When he awoke the next morning, his mother had breakfast waiting for him. They never discussed that night again. He had known the desire the older boy had brought out in him many times since, but he tried to chase it from his spirit with cold showers, prayer, and Bible reading.

His thoughts were interrupted by the sound of a motorcycle pulling up beside him. The rider removed his helmet and stood for a moment staring at him. He stared back. The motorcycle rider smiled at him. He returned the smile. He sat back in his seat so that he could further observe the man. He needed to be sure. To make a mistake would be disastrous. The rider was dressed in a black leather jacket and was wearing black leather pants. He watched him as he walked up to the men's room door. He didn't go in. Instead, he stood under the light outside the restroom door and lit a cigarette. The rider stood staring back at the car.

Once again, he looked around. The highway appeared to be practically deserted. He could not see anyone else in the area. He knew what he had to do. He wiped his hands on his jeans. He thought his heart was going to leap out of his chest. He was torn between desire and fear. He reached for the car handle, opened the door, stepped out, and walked toward the rider.

He stopped directly in front of him. He stood staring into the rider's eyes. The man returned his stare. The man took one last drag on his cigarette, tossed it onto the sidewalk and stepped on it. The rider was wearing heavy black boots with silver chains on them. On seeing the boots, his heart jumped once again. He hated this dance. He hated himself for needing the dance. He started to turn and run back to his car, but just as he was turning around he felt a hand on his shoulder. He sensed the muscular strength of the man behind him through his grip. He turned back to look at him. The rider wet his lips and then ran his tongue over them. He mimicked the gesture. The dance would now become more intimate.

The rider began walking away from the restrooms and toward the picnic tables. He followed him. He walked past the tables into the woods behind the rest stop. He continued to follow. When they came to a clearing, the leather clad rider turned to face him. Excitement and desire now overcame fear. He walked up to the rider for one last look at his face. He could tell that the rider was preparing himself. He had just finished kneeling in front of the man when he heard rapid footsteps coming toward him. He looked up at the rider. Then bright lights were in both of their faces. A hand grabbed him by the hair and pulled him to his feet. He let out a yell, but it was too late. His hands were pulled behind him and he felt the metal cuffs being locked. He glanced back over his shoulder to see that two officers were cuffing the motorcycle rider. One of the officers shouted, "Gentlemen, you're under arrest. You have the right…."

CHAPTER 25

Travis was sick. He had been ill for several days now. His nose was running. He had a cough. He was pulling at his ear. Randi took him to the pediatrician. The doctor prescribed a couple of medications. Still, he didn't feel good and each time he woke up he would start crying. It was Saturday evening and Randi had tried to keep Travis quiet so that Steele could put the final touches on his sermon. Travis woke up reaching for his Daddy. Steele laid his sermon aside and took Travis in his arms. He rocked him in the rocking chair in the nursery. Travis would drop off to sleep, but each time Steele tried to put him in his bed he awoke and started crying again.

Randi was exhausted. Steele suggested that she go take a nap. He would take care of Travis so she could get some rest. "But Steele, what about your sermon?"

"Oh, I've got a basic outline. If we can get Travis to settle down, I only need a couple more hours to finish it up."

Travis would have nothing to do with sleeping in his own bed. Steele carried him into the living room and reclined on the couch. He held Travis on his chest. This appeared to be an agreeable arrangement. Steele patted Travis until he once again went to sleep. Steele reached for the sermon outline that he had taken into the living room with him and attempted to work on it while Travis slept on his chest. Time slipped away. It was 1:00 a.m. Travis was sleeping soundly so Steele put him in his bed in the nursery. Steele then went back into his study to try to put the final touches on his sermon.

At 2:30 a.m. he quietly entered the master bedroom and slid into the bed next to Randi. She was sleeping soundly. It took only a few minutes for Steele to drop off as well. Their sleep was short lived. They both woke to the screams coming from the nursery. Travis was sitting up in his bed and was once again rubbing his ear. They both tried to comfort him, but Travis wanted his Daddy. Randi gave Travis some more of the medicine and put the ear drops in his ear. She took Travis from

Steele and sat down in the rocker in an effort to comfort him. "Steele, it's almost 3:00 a.m., you've got to preach three services in the morning. Please try to get some rest; I'll take care of Travis." Steele kissed them both on the forehead and went back to the master bedroom. He was exhausted, but he couldn't sleep. He was awake when Randi came into the bedroom. "Is he asleep?"

"For now," she answered. "Can't you sleep?"

"No, I'm worn out, but I can't go to sleep."

"Steele, it's almost five o'clock. The alarm is going to go off in one hour."

"I know."

"Do you have a sermon?"

"Sort of."

"I know you'll do a good job. You always do." She snuggled up to him and rubbed his chest with her hand. "I don't guess I'll be there to hear it though."

He nodded his head. Sleep rolled over him. Steele didn't hear the alarm go off. Randi woke him. "Steele, aren't you doing the 7:30 service?"

"Yes, oh my gosh, what time is it?"

"You only have fifteen minutes to get to the church."

Steele hurried as fast as he could, but he had to start the 7:30 service fifteen minutes late. He tried to explain to the congregation that there had not been much sleep in the Rectory the night before. He attempted to preach his sermon, but his mind was cloudy and he had a difficult time focusing on the subject matter at hand. He knew his sermon wasn't very good. In fact, it could hardly have been called a sermon at all.

He endured what he chose to believe was some good natured kidding at the door. He also realized that there were some who were clearly put out with him. "I'm certainly thankful that you're not a surgeon or an airline pilot. And thank God, you're not my surgeon or pilot."

Another grumpy man complained, "I worked for my company thirty-two years and I was never late to work one single time. You need to get your priorities straight, Mister Austin. I think it's inexcusable that you kept this congregation sitting here for close to half an hour."

Steele went over to the parish hall and swallowed several cups of coffee. He then hid in his office to do some further work on his sermon.

He was exhausted. He still had a difficult time focusing. The words on the sermon outline lacked life. They lacked passion. Steele preached it for the second time. He feared it didn't preach much better the second time than it did the first. He caught several couples giving each other questioning looks. Other folks started thumbing through the hymnal and prayer book or re-reading the parish bulletin.

The comments at the door were just a repeat of those that he endured after the earlier service. "Rough night, Father? Saturday might not be the best night for you to tie one on."

"I understand that you almost slept through the early service. Wish my boss would let me sleep in."

"It must have been a good party last night. Next time make sure they invite me."

Some of the comments lacked charity. It was as though those that Steele knew were opposed to his ministry caught the scent of blood and decided to close in for a kill. "I counted at least eight dangling participles. Really, Father, don't they teach English grammar in the Oklahoma schools?"

"Well, it wasn't your best sermon, was it? But then again, your sermons have all gotten rather formulaic. We know what you're going to say even before you say it. So why don't you just print them up and hand them out for us to read over lunch?"

The later service was but a duplicate of the first two. The comments at the door after the late service were the most brutal of all. In fact, Steele thought that there were people in church at that service that he hadn't seen since that awful annual meeting when they tried to unseat him as Rector. It was as though someone had gotten on the telephone and summoned all his antagonists to attack the wounded victim.

When Steele got home, Randi met him at the door. "Travis is sleeping. I think he is breathing easier. The pediatrician stopped by the house on his way home from his church. He thinks Travis is now on the mend."

Steele kissed Randi and then walked into the living room and stretched out on the couch. She followed him into the living room. "Are you okay?"

He shook his head. "Honey, it was as though I couldn't do anything right this morning. Everything went wrong that could go wrong. My sermon was the worst I have ever preached in my life."

"Oh, Steele, you're just tired. Everything will look better after you have a nap."

"No, Randi, I don't think so." Steele was surprised to realize that his voice was quivering and his eyes began to grow moist. "Randi, I explained to them that Travis had been sick and that we had not been able to get any sleep for several days. It just didn't matter to them. It was as though they saw that I was down and decided to start kicking me."

Randi sat down beside him and took his hand. "Was it really that bad?"

He looked into her beautiful black eyes. "Randi, if I didn't know better I would think that someone was out there orchestrating the attack. There were people in church today that I have never seen in church except Christmas and Easter. It was as though they came for only one purpose and that was to take a punch at me. I can handle a criticism every now and then, but this was just one right after another. It was like running a gauntlet."

"I'm sorry, Steele. What do you want to do?"

"Randi, I really do think I've had enough. They don't want us here. And I've grown tired of trying to get them to love us. We deserve better treatment. Jesus doesn't call us to be anyone's punching bag. I'm ready to start looking for another position. If these people can't have a little compassion for us when we have a sick child, then it's time for us to move on."

"But Steele, not everyone here is like that. We have some good friends in this congregation. There are people in this church that love us. They will be devastated if we leave."

Steele nodded. "I know, but I just don't think I can take any more."

Randi sat quietly rubbing his forehead and then running her fingers through his hair. He closed his eyes and soon Steele Austin was finally able to sleep. Randi watched the love of her life. Her heart was breaking for this kindhearted man. She wanted to do something to help him, but what? She needed to call someone and get them to help him, but who? And then, in an instant, Randi knew exactly who she needed to call.

CHAPTER 26

Just what's it going to take for this Vestry to get through to you, Misturh Austin?" Ned Boone was furious. It was approaching midnight. The formal agenda had taken ninety minutes. This particular executive session called for by Henry Mudd and Ned Boone was now into its third hour. Coats had long since been removed and ties loosened. "I'm just beside myself. I've tried everything that a reasonable man could possibly do to penetrate your thick skull, but Preacher, you just won't listen."

Henry Mudd was on his feet and had been staring out the conference room window. His face was flushed. Steele feared that both men were on the verge of having strokes. The remainder of the Vestry sat around the table like whipped school boys who were being forced to remain after school. Some slumped down in their seats. Others were leaning forward on the table staring absently at the papers in front of them. Steele's one ally on the Vestry, Chief Sparks, was on his annual hunting trip with Stone Clemons.

"Okay, let's take the issues one at a time." Henry Mudd returned to his seat at the head of the table. "We're going to present the issue and then we want your response for the record. Once we have your response we are going to take a Vestry vote on whether or not we support your position. Do you understand, Misturh Austin?"

Steele nodded. "Let's get started."

"Out of consideration for the hour we're going to keep our description of each issue brief. I would appreciate it if you would keep your response equally brief. We have already discussed each of these problems for hours. Are you in agreement?"

Again, Steele nodded.

"I'm going to instruct the clerk to take down our description of each issue and your response word for word. I want this for the record. Are you in agreement?"

Steele nodded yet one more time.

"Do you understand that a vote of non-support on each of these issues by this Vestry most likely will be interpreted by the members of this congregation as a vote of no confidence in your leadership?"

Steele was tempted to rebut his assumption, but he was exhausted. "Let's not prejudge how the members of this parish might interpret any vote of this Vestry."

Ned and Henry shot each other a shocked look. Ned spoke first, "I think the boy has a death wish." He and Henry then had a chuckle at Steele's expense.

Henry lifted the sheet of paper that he had earlier distributed to each member of the Vestry. "Gentlemen, if you'll refer to the sheet of paper that I gave you when we began our Executive Session." There was a shuffling of paper on the table as the Vestry members found the particular page.

"Issue One," Henry's voice was hoarse. "This Vestry goes on record as objecting to your performing a marriage between your associate Horace Drummond and a white woman in this parish. Sir, how do you respond?"

"Horace and Almeda Alexander, the person you describe as a white woman, are mature adults. They're in love. They have asked me to preside at their wedding. There's no moral impediment, scriptural, or canonical reason that I should not perform that marriage. There is no law against my doing so."

"There was until a few years ago." Henry Mudd exploded.

Steele responded, "The Supreme Court of the United States revoked the laws forbidding interracial marriages."

"A bunch of communist liberals got their way, but we'll get that law reinstated. It's just a matter of time."

"Well, that may be, but for now I intend to preside at a wedding for Almeda and Horace on the Saturday before Thanksgiving in our Chapel."

Again, Ned and Henry shot each other looks. "Then, I ask for a second to my motion."

Ned Boone quickly seconded the motion.

"Before we vote on this one, guys, I think we need to reconsider." Howard Dexter stood up and placed his finger tips on the conference table. "I believe that this motion could ultimately prove to be a great embarrassment to this Vestry and to some of us personally."

Steele was shocked. He could not believe that Howard Dexter was coming to his defense. Howard was standing and his voice was strong, firm, and clear. He was taking charge. Up to now, he had been neutral on most every issue. He had not said much of anything to support Steele, but by the same token, he had not said anything to oppose him. Steele figured that Howard was simply honoring his agreement with Almeda. But this Howard, the one standing before him right now, was a different Howard. It was as though he had decided to really be the Senior Warden. He would be the Rector's Warden. He would support and defend the Rector. Steele wondered if Almeda had issued a new set of instructions to Howard. Steele's thoughts were interrupted by Howard's response to Ned's statement opposing the marriage of Almeda and Horace.

"Surely you're not condoning this marriage, Howard?" Ned Boone shot the words at Howard.

"I'm not sure it's up to me to tell Horace and Almeda just who they can and cannot marry. Now, if you ask me if I'm happy about it, the answer is 'no'. But frankly, gentlemen, I think their wedding is beyond the prevue of this Vestry. Further, you need to know that the Altar Guild is going to host a wedding reception for the bride and groom when they return to the parish from their honeymoon."

"I know about that." Henry didn't attempt to hide his disgust. "Your wife asked my wife to help with it. I'll not repeat her response for you, but needless to say, she won't be helping."

"Howard, are you trying to tell me that the Vestry can't inhibit the Rector from presiding at marriages in this church?" The disbelief in Ned Boone's voice was difficult to disguise.

Howard continued, "Ned, that's exactly what I'm telling you. As long as all canonical requirements are met, the Rector or any of the parish clergy are free to marry anyone they want. The Vestry has no say over the weddings the clergy choose to perform."

"Well, that being said, I still want a vote." Ned Boone was determined.

"Ned, I can appreciate what you're trying to do, but I really don't think you want to bring this to a vote."

"Oh, why not?"

"Well," Howard had a sheepish grin on his face. "Ned, I've been sitting here doing some math and I don't believe the motion will pass."

"Math? What kind of math? What are you talking about?

The sheepish grin on Howard's face returned. "My wife is one of the co-chairs of the committee to put on the wedding reception that I mentioned to you earlier. So, I can't vote for your resolution. It would not be supportive of the woman that fixes my breakfast."

His comment brought some uncomfortable chuckles from the other members of the Vestry. "Gentlemen, will those of you who have wives on the Altar Guild that have agreed to assist with this reception hold up your hands?"

Over half of those present held up their hands. Again, there were some uncomfortable chuckles around the table. "You see, I just don't think your motion will pass."

Henry Mudd threw his hands up in the air. He looked over at Ned Boone. "In light of this revelation, I don't think I have any choice but to withdraw the motion."

"No," Ned Boone shouted. "Let's just move to table the motion so that it will remain a matter of written record."

Howard smiled sheepishly, "Ned, if memory serves me correctly, a motion to table also requires a vote. It will be defeated. My counsel is that you allow Henry to withdraw his motion."

Ned sat back in his chair and nodded. He then gave Steele a defiant look. "Let's move on to the second resolution."

"In the matter of the accused murderer, Rob McBride, this Vestry formally instructs the Rector not to provide shelter for the mistress of Rob McBride in the home owned by this congregation. Sir, do you want to respond?"

Steele was really growing weary, emotionally and physically. "Your resolution contains only one truth. Rob McBride is accused. In America, he is to be treated as innocent until proven guilty. The woman you call his mistress is actually his girlfriend and soon to become his fiancé."

"Semantics, Misturh Austin, semantics!" Henry Mudd's voice was almost completely gone. It was now not much more than a whisper, but if he could have been yelling he would have been shouting at the top of his voice. "Are you going to remove her from our house?"

"No, Henry, I'm not."

The total look of exasperation returned to Ned Boone's face. "On this one you don't have any say. That house belongs to this parish and we will say who lives there and who doesn't."

"No, Ned, I don't think you have that authority legally or canonically. That house is a part of my Letter of Agreement with the Vestry. In no portion of my Letter of Agreement are there any conditions on whom I might entertain in the house that is my home while I'm the Rector."

He shot back. "Then we'll amend the Letter of Agreement."

"Not without my consent." Steele replied calmly, "The Letter of Agreement clearly states that it cannot be amended without my consent."

Howard Dexter smiled, "I fear that he has us on that one, Ned."

"You mean that he could take our house and run it as a house of ill repute or worse and we can't stop him?"

"Well," Howard chuckled. "Criminal activity isn't protected by his Letter of Agreement." Again, the entire table chuckled. Steele felt some relief in joining in the laughter.

"Are you trying to tell me, Howard, that this motion won't pass either?"

"I'm just telling you that it's without merit. It's not enforceable. I'll not vote for it."

"Well then, let's try the third one," Henry Mudd whispered. "Ned, will you read it? My voice is all but gone."

"That this Vestry goes on record as being opposed to the opening of the halfway house for homosexuals. Further, this Vestry instructs the Rector to preach a series of sermons during the month of December, the Advent Season, condemning homosexual behavior as being sinful. Now, how do you respond to that one, Misturh Austin?"

Steele thought this meeting was never going to end. "We are going to call it Duke's House. It isn't a halfway house for homosexuals. It's to be a home for men living with HIV and AIDS who have no other place to live."

"Same thing!" Ned shouted. "AIDS, homosexuals, they're all the same. Will you please stop playing word games with us?"

Steele took a deep breath, "I'm too tired to give you a lesson on just who the victims of that terrible disease are. Let's just get to the point. The money for that project is coming out of the Chadsworth Alexander Endowment for the Poor. This Vestry has no control over the expenditure of that money and the trust document strictly forbids the Vestry to interfere."

Again, Howard Dexter spoke up, "I fear that once again he's correct. Further, the trust document states that any attempt on a Vestry's part to interfere with the Rector's free administration of this Endowment could lead to the loss of the Endowment itself. While I may not approve of the Rector's use of the funds, I really don't want to risk that. And I don't think anyone at this table does." Howard looked around the table and saw that several of the Vestry members were nodding their heads in agreement.

"You mean the Rector has no accountability on the use of these funds?"

"To the contrary, they are audited by an independent auditing firm up in Atlanta and their report is filed with this Vestry. He must expend the funds in accordance with the provisions of the trust. This House he plans to open meets the terms of that trust."

Steele was beginning to feel some relief and was just about to ask if the meeting could be adjourned when Ned caught his attention. "And, the series of sermons? Are you in agreement? Will you preach those sermons?"

"No, Ned, I will not."

"Well sir, just how would you respond to a resolution that this Vestry will review all your sermons before you preach them?"

Steele shot back, "Church law forbids it."

Again Howard Dexter joined in. "The Vestry has no authority over the content of a priest's sermons."

Ned sat back in his seat in disbelief. "Misturh Austin, Father Davis makes reference to the sinful nature of homosexual behavior in most every sermon he preaches at St. Mary's. We have lost a lot of people from First Church to St. Mary's. We have an even larger number who have become affiliate members of his congregation and have taken their pledges with them. Because of the lack of scriptural preaching here at First Church, St. Mary's is packed every Sunday by people hungry to hear the word of God. It wouldn't hurt you to go on record as being opposed to the queers. Why not follow Father Davis's example?"

"Because I don't agree with him."

"Surely you don't condone the homosexual perversion?"

Steele was tired beyond exhaustion. "Ned, we've had this conversation before and we can have it again, but I'm just too tired to do it tonight.

A Vestry doesn't have the authority to instruct a Rector on what he can or cannot preach from the pulpit. Your only recourse is to file charges against me with the Bishop and Standing Committee if you believe I'm preaching heresy."

"Pabulum, sentimentality, secularism, these are the things coming from the First Church pulpit." Ned mocked Steele's pulpit voice.

"I'm really sorry that's what you hear, Ned." Steele remained calm. He kept a gentle tone in his voice. "I hope that you hear the teachings of Jesus that are dominated not by condemnation and judgment, but by love, forgiveness, understanding, and acceptance. Ned, if you'll read the words of Jesus in the Gospels you'll discover that His harshest words were for those consumed with pointing out and condemning the sins of their neighbors. I'll not do that. I want the worshippers at First Church to leave our services filled with hope. I want them to leave knowing that God loves them just as they are. God will never turn His back on them no matter who they are or what they have done."

"And you call that preaching?" Ned stood and started walking toward the door. "I don't want anything else to do with this man. I've had enough." He turned and looked back at the Vestry. "You'll have my formal resignation from this Vestry in the morning mail. And you sir, will have my request to transfer my letter of membership to St. Mary's. If the rest of you want to hear the Bible preached and have your children raised in the faith, you'll follow my example. And now, I'm going to do what Christ told his disciples to do when they went into a place and the people refused to hear the truth." To everyone's surprise, Ned Boone stood at the door and stomped his feet. "I'm shaking the dust of this place off my feet." He turned, walked through the door, and slammed it behind him.

The entire room sat in silence. Henry Mudd whispered, "Well, Preacher, how does it feel to lose one of your most valuable members? Just how many more good people are you going to run out of this church before you come to your senses?"

Steele sat in silence for a minute. "Do you have any more resolutions to present?"

Henry shook his head, closed his folder, stood and started for the door.

"The Chair will entertain a motion that the Executive Session of the Vestry be adjourned at 12:38 a.m."

"Second," Howard Dexter stated.

The motion passed. The Vestry left the room without saying a word to Steele or each other. When he walked into the parking lot he had expected to see several after- meeting conversations taking place, but the parking lot was empty.

Steele walked quietly into the Rectory and into the master bedroom. He didn't turn on a light until he was in the master bath where he could undress, brush his teeth, and prepare for bed. He slid quietly between the sheets next to Randi. "Sneaking in here after midnight, uh Cowboy? I want an explanation and I want it now. Just where have you been? What's the little floozy's name?"

Steele knew that she was teasing him. "I thought the Vestry meeting would never end. Ned and Henry had a bunch of resolutions designed to turn me into their puppet."

"And?"

"Well, let's just say that the resolutions failed, but the performance ended with a real stimulating encore."

"Oh?"

"Ned Boone literally stood at the conference room door and stomped his feet."

"He did what?"

Steele snickered, "He said he was shaking the dust of First Church off his feet, resigned his office, and requested that his membership be transferred to St. Mary's."

"So that's why you're smiling. Don't deny it. I can see you smiling even in the dark."

He pulled her close so that he could cuddle with her. "Well, let's just say that I believe in the principle that sometimes you have to lose a few in order to gain the many."

"Are you going to be able to sleep?"

"I think I'm going to sleep like a baby." And he did.

CHAPTER 27

Eight people were gathered around the conference room table at the law offices of Stone Clemons and Associates. There was the accused, Rob McBride. Sitting next to him was Melanie Mason. Their hands were intertwined as though they were hanging on to each other for life itself. The two detectives that Melanie had employed to help find Esther McBride's murderer were sitting on either side of them. Rob's two defense attorneys were sitting on the opposite side of the table. Stone Clemons and Steele Austin were sitting on either side of them.

"Rob, we have to level with you," one of the attorneys began. "The detectives that Miss Mason employed haven't found any new evidence to implicate anyone else in the death of your wife. We have read their reports and we have shared them with Mr. Clemons here. Their investigation has been extensive, but they are at a dead-end."

"So, what are you telling me?" Rob's voice was shaking.

"First, let me assure you that we're not going to give up and as long as Miss Mason keeps these investigators on the payroll, they will continue to look for the person that murdered your wife."

Rob appeared to relax. "That's good. Can we do that, Honey?"

"Of course, Rob, we're not giving up."

The second attorney spoke, "Having said that, Rob, you need to realize that the police and the prosecutor consider this to be an open and shut case. The police long ago put an end to any further investigation."

"I know they consider me to be guilty beyond any reasonable doubt."

Stone shifted in his chair and then leaned across the table toward Rob. "If we go to trial, your defense team here has a monumental task ahead of them. And Rob, I have to be honest with you. The odds are against us."

"But I didn't do it. I'm innocent, damn it. You do believe me, don't you?"

Stone motioned with both of his hands for Rob to calm down. "Every person in this room is convinced of your innocence or we wouldn't be sitting here."

The lead defense attorney cleared his throat, "It's just that we don't have any evidence to implicate another person. There's no DNA, no finger prints, no suspicious activity in your neighborhood, no enemy, no evidence of a spurned lover, no unnamed stranger seen with your wife or around your house the day of the murder. While we believe that you didn't take your wife's life, we simply haven't been able to find one shred of evidence that we can use to point to someone else."

"Oh, God, I think I'm going to be sick. Please..." Rob put his hand over his mouth and ran into the bathroom adjacent to the conference room. Everyone sat in silence as the sounds of a very ill Rob McBride came through the closed door. Soon Rob returned, wiping his face with a wet cloth.

"Are you going to be all right, Honey?" Melanie patted his arm.

One of the attorneys handed Rob a glass filled with ice and a soda.

Rob took it and nodded, "Guys, what am I going to do? If I understand what you're telling me, well, to use the vernacular, I'm screwed."

One of the attorneys started to speak, but Stone motioned for him to hold his thoughts. "Rob, we're having this meeting with you not to tell you that we're giving up, but to bring you current with our findings. We would be less than honest with you if we didn't tell you that it just doesn't look good."

"So, what you're really telling me is that I'm going to lose. You think I will be found guilty."

Stone's voice was soothing, ever fatherly, but he knew the message the team had to deliver. "Rob, no lawyer worth his salt is going to try to second-guess a jury. And we certainly aren't going into that courtroom resolved to lose. We'll put together the best defense strategy we know how to do on your behalf. We just wish there was some evidence pointing to another person. Have you been able to think of anyone that would want your wife dead?"

Rob shook his head. "No one."

Everyone sat in silence for several minutes. Finally Stone spoke again, "Rob, there is something else that you need to consider."

"Oh?"

"The prosecutor is offering you a deal."

"What kind of deal?"

"Well, in the interest of saving you and the State of Georgia a prolonged trial, they will accept a guilty plea on your part to involuntary manslaughter."

"But I didn't do it. Please, do you understand? I didn't do it."

"Rob, we're not suggesting that you accept the plea, we're just advising you that it's being offered. To accept it could mean five to ten years in the penitentiary. Not to accept and to go to trial, well, if you're found guilty of murder, it could mean the death penalty."

"Oh, God, this is a nightmare. This is an absolute nightmare."

Melanie began crying. "Isn't there something else we can do? Are there other experts or investigators that we can bring in to help you? There just has to be something else."

The attorneys looked at each other. "In all honesty, unless there's a miracle, Rob, we think you should accept the deal. That's our best counsel to you."

"Are you telling me that you're giving up? Don't you think you can win?"

"Rob, if you choose to go to trial we're going to give it our best effort, but please consider everything we have said to you this morning."

"How long do I have to...?"

Melanie interrupted him, "Rob, you're not thinking about accepting the plea?"

He looked at her and then looked across the table, "Steele, you're my best friend. What do you think I should do?"

Steele shook his head. "I can't tell you what to do. I'm not an attorney. I'm a friend. I don't believe you did it. I think there is some DNA evidence. It's just not in your DNA to take anyone's life."

"Thanks, thanks Steele." Rob looked back at Stone. "How long will the deal be on the table?"

"Well, they know we're having this meeting with you. They would like an answer today, but I believe I can get them to give us a few more days for you to think about it."

"Some time to think about it would be nice, but it goes against everything I believe to plead guilty to anything that implicates me in my wife's death. Gentlemen, I'm an innocent man. I need you to continue to believe in my innocence. I'm going to think about it, but as of right now I want you to continue to prepare for trial. I didn't do it and I want to clear my name."

The two attorneys looked at each other. "You're the boss, Rob." The lead attorney looked over at the investigators. "Well boys, until we are advised otherwise we need you to continue looking for Esther McBride's murderer. He or she is out there. Let's see if we can't find them."

Everyone stood and began shaking hands with each other. Steele walked Rob and Melanie to their car. "I wish there were something I could do, guys. I'm just out of my element. I wouldn't even know where to begin."

Rob hugged his friend, "Father, I've pretty much given up on God, so I need you to do my praying for me. I just hope God hasn't given up on me."

Steele put his hands on Rob's shoulders so that he could look him in the eye. "Rob, I don't blame you for feeling like God has forsaken you. I certainly understand your feelings, but hang on to your faith. God never gives up on us. Deep down, I believe that you know that."

As Steele drove back to his office, he prayed for Rob, the investigators, and the defense team. He prayed for those who would serve on Rob's jury. He prayed for the judge that would preside at the trial. He prayed for the repose of Esther McBride. He prayed for their son. And he prayed for the person that was responsible for Esther's death. He really didn't remember pulling into the staff parking lot. He didn't realize just how long he had been sitting in his car lost in his prayers. A knocking on his car window got his attention. It was his secretary, Crystal. "Father McBride, Chief Sparks is waiting for you in your office. He says it's urgent."

As Steele got out of his car his heart skipped a beat, "Oh God, You've heard our prayers." Steele ran up the interior staircase two stairs at a time. He was so excited. He just knew that the Chief had some good news about Rob McBride's case. As he rounded the corner he saw the Chief standing at his door with a big grin on his face.

"You have some good news about Rob McBride's case?"

The Chief's demeanor immediately changed. "No, I don't know anything new there. That case is closed as far as we're concerned."

The disappointment washed over Steele. The Chief sensed it as he followed Steele into his office. "I'm sorry, Parson. I don't think they're going to find a one-armed man. I fear you're just going to have to accept that your friend is guilty."

"No, Chief, I'll not accept it. Even if he is found guilty by a jury I'll still not believe it."

"Rob's lucky to have a friend like you, Father. I'm sorry that I can't be of more help."

Steele sat down in his chair and the Chief sat opposite him. The grin returned to the Chief's face.

"O.K., if you're not here to bring me some good news about Rob then just what has put that Cheshire cat grin on your face?"

"Have you seen the morning paper?"

"No, I had to preside at the early service this morning and then I had a meeting over at Stone Clemons' office. I just got back. I've not had a chance to read the paper."

The Chief pulled a newspaper out of his inside coat pocket. "I think this might put a smile on your face. What is it I've heard you say, oh yes, that which we find most unacceptable in others just may be the very thing that we detest in ourselves?" The Chief tossed the paper across the desk and then pointed to one article in particular. He thumped the article several times with his finger tips. "I've got to get back down to the station house. I'll leave this for you to read." The Chief then walked out of Steele's office, closing the door behind him. Steele stared at the newspaper article, trying to absorb the headline. Then he picked it up and began reading.

POLICE RAID ROADSIDE PARK

Falls City Police, in cooperation with the Georgia State Highway Patrol, raided the rest area and adjacent park on the bypass around Falls City. The stakeout and raid came after several complaints by citizens that the park had become a favorite meeting place for men to meet for the purpose of engaging in lewd and illegal sexual activity.

The late night raid resulted in the arrest of ten men. Among those arrested was The Reverend Richard Davis, Vicar of St. Mary's Episcopal Mission in Falls City. The Reverend Mister Davis was released on bail after being held overnight in the County Jail. Efforts to get a comment from him were unsuccessful. The telephone at the church office is being answered by an answering machine and our requests for a return call have been unsuccessful. The office itself appears to be closed.

The Bishop's Office for the Diocese in Savannah released a statement that simply reads, "We are conducting our own investigation into the circumstances surrounding the arrest of Father Davis. We are hopeful that he will be vindicated. In the interim, he has been relieved of his position as Vicar of St. Mary's Mission. He is currently in a spiritual retreat house where he can receive the appropriate pastoral care."

Steele placed the newspaper on his desk. He leaned back in his chair and closed his eyes. The Chief was wrong. This didn't make him happy. The article didn't make his day. To the contrary, he felt a profound sadness. Steele leaned forward and opened his desk drawer. He removed one of his correspondence cards and picked up a pen. He stared at the blank note card for several minutes and then he wrote...

Dear Richard,

I'm probably the last person on earth that you want to receive a note from right now. Please indulge me for just a minute. I just wanted you to know that you're in my thoughts and prayers. It's difficult for me to imagine the pain and fear that you must have lived with for most of your life. I pray that God will grant you peace at this most crucial time. If there is anything that I can do for you, please don't hesitate to call upon me.

Faithfully,

Steele+

CHAPTER 28

D id you walk through the church?" Mrs. Gordon Smythe was
carrying the chalice and paten from the Altar Guild Sacristy
out to the church altar.

"I sure did," Steele smiled. "It's absolutely packed this morning. It's
a great beginning for the Advent Season."

"What did you think?"

"I think we're going to have a great service."

"No," Mrs. Smythe wiped her hands on the towel hanging by the
Altar Guild Sacristy sink. "Did you really look at the congregation?"

"No, is there something in particular you want me to see?"

"Follow me." She made a motion with her hand for him to follow
her. She opened the Sacristy door just a bit. "Now, look out there and tell
me what you see."

Steele was really confused. "Like I said, I see a full church."

"Look at the faces of the people. Now, what do you see?"

"Okay, I see Almeda and she's absolutely glowing. She's sitting next
to Horace's daughter and his sister. On the other side of her is her oldest
son and his wife and next to her is her other son. Is that what you wanted
me to see?"

"Men." Mrs. Smythe sounded disgusted. "I swear you would all be
blind if you didn't have women to point out the obvious to you. Now,
look in the transept. Look five rows back behind Almeda. Look in the
balcony on the first row. Look on the end of the pew third row from the
back. What do you see?"

"Mrs. Smythe, I just see people waiting for church to begin."

"Misturh Austin, honestly, look again. Don't you see all those black
faces?"

"Oh." Steele shut the door and started laughing at himself. "I'm
sorry. I guess I missed your point. I think those are all people that Horace
works with on the various outreach boards in the city. I'm sure they're
here for the wedding reception."

"That may be, but Misturh Austin this is a first for First Church. We've never had that many Neg..."

"African Americans," Steele interrupted.

"Oh, all right. We've never had that many African Americans at a service here at First Church."

"And how do you feel about that, Mrs. Smythe?" Steele started vesting in his robes. She brought him a blue stole to put on.

"Actually, I've surprised myself. I think it's just fine. I know some of those folks and they are fine people. A couple of them are real leaders among their people in this community. They do a lot of good." She turned to walk away. "But I'm not about to walk past my parents' graves out there in your cemetery."

"Oh," Steele smiled. "And why's that?"

"Because I know that there will be a breeze coming from their resting place."

"What sort of breeze?"

"Misturh Austin, my parents, along with most of our ancestors buried out there in that cemetery, are spinning in their graves." She chuckled, "But you know, things are changing in Falls City, and I guess I've accepted that it's just about time."

The organist made the transition from the prelude into the opening hymn. Steele opened the Sacristy door to find that the crucifer and two torch bearers were waiting on him. He fell in behind them and began walking up the side aisle. He caught a glimpse of Almeda smiling at him. He smiled back.

It was during the reading of the scripture lessons appointed for the First Sunday in Advent that it hit him. He realized that the Advent sermon he had prepared for this morning wasn't the sermon that he needed to deliver. He decided to forget that sermon and share the thoughts that he felt God was placing on his heart. When it came time for the sermon he chose not to walk into the pulpit, but to stand at the steps of the choir.

"I had a sermon prepared for you this morning based on the Gospel appointed for today. As I listened to the lessons being read, I realized that while they are appropriate for this First Sunday in the Advent Season, they aren't compatible with our life together on this particular Sunday at First Church. So I want to remind you of another story from the Gospels. Do you remember when a blind man came to Jesus and asked Him to heal him? Jesus touched the man and then asked him, 'Can you see?' The blind man responded that he could see men, but they appeared to him as trees. So Jesus touched the blind man a second time. He asked him again, 'Now can you see?' And the man responded, 'Yes, I can see men as God sees them.'"

Steele paused and looked over the congregation. "After our service this morning, the Altar Guild of First Church is hosting a wedding reception in the parish hall for The Reverend Doctor and Mrs. Horace Drummond. We have several visitors with us this morning that have come specifically to celebrate their marriage with them. I fear that the obvious escaped me about some of our visitors' presence with us this morning. A good friend of mine helped me see this particular congregation more clearly. I want you to see that which I almost missed. Horace and Almeda are now husband and wife. I know, because one week ago my sweet wife, Randi, Horace's daughter and sister, Almeda's two sons and daughter-in-law, Rob McBride, and Melanie Mason and I, all gathered in the Chapel to witness their exchange of vows.

It's important for us to remember our history. Just a few short years ago it would have been against the law in nineteen states for me to have presided at a wedding for Almeda and Horace. I'm not talking about ancient history. The laws forbidding interracial marriage remained on the books until the Supreme Court ruled them unconstitutional not in 1867, but in 1967.

My own uncle, who is a Cherokee Indian, fell in love with a ravishing redhead from Sicily. They had to cross several state lines in order to be legally married. Or can we forget that just before Thurgood Marshall was appointed to the Supreme Court of the United States, he could not lawfully live with his wife in a Virginia suburb of Washington D.C.? He was black and she was East Asian.

This morning this church is integrated. There are a few black faces sprinkled among a sea of white. It's that way for this Sunday. Next Sunday, I fear that this church will once again mirror every church in America. The Church of Jesus Christ remains the most segregated community on the face of the earth."

Steele feared that he just might have gone too far in his challenge to the congregation. He stopped to study the faces of those sitting closest to him. There was no shaking of heads. There were no arms across the chests.

No whisperings or rolling of eyeballs could be seen. He felt encouraged so he continued. "Almeda and Horace are showing us another way. In fact, they are reminding us of something that was at the very heart of the ministry of Jesus. Almeda and Horace are profound evidence of the fact that love... let me repeat that..." Steele paused again. "Almeda and Horace are irrefutable evidence of the fact that love is blind!" There were some uncomfortable chuckles in the congregation.

"And aren't we glad?" There were more chuckles. "Seriously, isn't every person within the sound of my voice this morning absolutely thrilled with the message that love is blind? Jesus touched the man a second time, 'Now, can you see?' 'Yes,' he replied. 'I can see men as God sees them.' When we see one another as God sees us, we look through the eyes of love. When a parent looks at their child they don't see the child's imperfections. Love is blind. Thankfully, when children look at their parents they don't see our shortcomings. No, love is blind. When a husband and wife look at each other they only see their beloved in all their beauty or strength. Love is blind."

Steele paused once again to study the faces in the congregation. "So my brothers and sisters, as you glance around this church this morning, as you look at one another, can you look through the eyes of love? If you do your love will be blind. It will be blind to the pigmentation in our skin. It will be blind to old hurts, prejudices, and pains. If we look at one another through the eyes of love, we will discover that we are blind to the things that separate us. And we will see one another as God sees us. Now, I ask you again, aren't you glad that love is blind?"

Steele turned to look at Doctor Drummond who was sitting with the other clergy in the sanctuary. "Horace, thank you." He then looked down at Almeda sitting on the front row. "Almeda, Mrs. Drummond..." Steele smiled at her. "Thank you. Thank you for giving us the opportunity to learn one of the most valuable lessons in life. Thank you for giving God the opportunity to reinforce a truth that we all carry deep in our souls. Thank you for allowing us to celebrate the truth that is at the very heart of the Gospel. Love is blind.

Jesus touched the blind man and then asked him, 'can you see?' The blind man answered, 'Yes, I can see men but they look like trees.' So Jesus touched him a second time. 'Now, can you see?' And the man born blind answered, 'Yes, now I see men as God sees them.'"

Steele stopped to look back out over the congregation. To his surprise, he didn't sense that unseen emotional wall that any audience of people can toss up against a speaker when they don't want to hear what they have to say. To the contrary, there were some nods of the heads here and there. A few couples glanced at each other and smiled. No, to his amazement his message had been heard and received.

The parish hall was decorated beautifully. There were large floral arrangements everywhere. Almeda, Horace and their families formed a receiving line at the entrance to the parish hall. Virtually every person that had been in worship waited patiently in line to wish them well. There were waiters moving through the parish hall with glasses of champagne and hors d'oeuvres.

Steele caught the eye of Mrs. Dexter. She came toward him. "Mrs. Dexter, I could not be happier. You and Mrs. Smythe have outdone yourselves. This is a wonderful reception."

"You're welcome, Misturh Austin. I agree, everything is just the way we planned it."

"I will be writing you, Mrs. Smythe, and the Altar Guild a thank-you note."

"I'm sure that would be appreciated. Now, may I ask a favor of you?"

"Sure, I hope I can help."

"I hear that you're going to start letting girls acolyte here at First Church."

"Yes, that's true." Steele felt a knot in his stomach. He wondered if he was going to have to argue with her about that too.

"I understand that you're going to unveil these new acolytes at the Christmas Eve services."

"That's also true."

"Well, why haven't you asked my granddaughter to be one of the acolytes?"

"I'm sorry, but I don't ever remember seeing your granddaughter or her parents in church. Do you think she would want to acolyte?"

"I think it might be a way to get the whole family back in church. Will you call her and ask her?"

"Consider it done."

"Thank you, Misturh Austin. Howard and I would really appreciate it."

"Again, I want to thank you for this reception."

She stood next to him looking around the parish hall at all the people. "You know, Misturh Austin, I've had a really hard time with a lot of the things that you've done and wanted to do here at First Church."

"I know. My intention wasn't to upset you, but simply to be faithful to the Gospel."

"Well, that may be, but...." She paused and looked around again. "Black faces worshiping at First Church, girl acolytes, a Soup Kitchen, Free Medical Clinic..." She shook her head. "I just don't know, but Misturh Austin, I've decided I can't miss a single Sunday here."

"Why's that?"

"Oh, I'm not going to miss a single Sunday because I just can't wait to see what you're going to try to do next." Then, to Steele's surprise, her short little body shook with laughter.

CHAPTER 29

Duke's House was a great old plantation style home in a wonderful neighborhood in Falls City. It had ten bedrooms, a maid's quarters where the manager could stay, and a garage apartment with two more bedrooms. The volunteers had beautifully decorated the house for Christmas. There was a large Christmas tree in the living room. The house was filled with poinsettias. Pine garland was strung over the doorways and the fireplace mantle. There was a roaring fire in the fireplace. Almeda, Randi, and Melanie Mason had gone shopping to make sure that each resident would have a few presents wrapped and ready to open on Christmas morning. The presents were gracefully displayed under the Christmas tree.

The house was filled with invited guests who had come for the dedication of Duke's House. The local newspaper had sent a reporter. There was also a television crew from the local station moving about the house, interviewing both the residents and guests. It was impossible at first glance to discern the residents from the guests. On closer examination, Steele realized that the residents' nametags were permanent. The guests had temporary nametags.

Almeda and Horace were busy carrying food from the kitchen to the dining room table. After the House Blessing, the guests would enjoy an evening of carols and the buffet. The television reporter spotted Steele and approached him for an interview. "Father Austin, can you tell us just why you and First Church would want to start a house for homosexual men?"

Steele smiled into the camera. "Please allow me to clarify our mission for your television audience. Duke's House is a house for homeless men who are living with HIV or AIDS. While some of the men may be homosexual, the ministry of this House is dedicated first and foremost to those who are seriously ill and have no place to live."

"But does this mean that you and First Church endorse homosexuality?"

Steele paused and smiled again into the camera. "Let me repeat. Duke's House is first and foremost for homeless men who are seriously ill. Their sexuality is a non-issue."

The reporter was insistent. "How can you say that?"

Steele felt himself getting irritated, but he knew he was on camera. "Jesus didn't ask a person's sexual orientation before he healed them. In fact, if you're looking for a Biblical parallel, you might consider the lepers of New Testament times who were not only homeless, but had to ring a bell when they came near anyone else. Often, those who saw the lepers responded by throwing rocks at them. Jesus ministered to these ill people. Would He have us do less for the people that so many in our society simply pretend don't exist?"

"So you're saying this house is an appropriate ministry for the Church?"

"I think any ministry that fulfills the admonitions of Jesus to visit and care for the ill, or any that we might consider the least of those among us, should be the Church's first priority. It isn't to be relegated to an afterthought."

"How long can these men live in this house?"

"This house is now their home. They are here for life."

"Can they be removed?"

"I hope that doesn't happen, but we do have policies and rules that must be respected. We want them to consider this their home. We want them to think of us and the other residents as family. Now, if you'll excuse me. It's time for the House Blessing to begin."

Horace Drummond summoned all the guests and residents to the living room. He and Steele stood in front of the fireplace. When all were gathered, Steele began. "Before we bless the house, I want to call your attention to the portraits of the two men that are hanging here above the mantle. The one on your right is a portrait of Chadsworth Alexander. Chadsworth was a friend of mine. He and his family have lived here in Falls City for generations. Chadsworth became very ill last year. It was an illness that led him to take his own life. He is greatly missed at First Church and in Falls City. Before he died he set up an Endowment to be administered by the Rector of First Church. That Endowment has made possible the purchase and the annual operations of this House. I want you to always remember the Christian charity and generosity of

Chadsworth Alexander." Steele looked over at Almeda. She smiled back at him. Horace put his arm around Almeda and gave her a squeeze.

"The portrait on your left is of a man by the name of Edward Young. I first met him at our Soup Kitchen. He called himself Duke."

"That's Duke?" One of the residents interrupted him. "Some of you guys remember Duke, don't you?" Several men in the room nodded their heads.

"It pleases me to know that some of you remember Duke." Steele continued. "You may also recall that Duke died of complications from AIDS. He died all alone underneath the Falls River Bridge. It was Duke's death that motivated me to make sure that all of you would have a home by Christmas this year. This house is named for Duke and for all the men in this community who are without a home. Note that we don't refer to the people without a home as houseless. No, we describe them as homeless. Our Lord Jesus said of Himself, *the foxes have holes, the birds of the air have nests, but the Son of Man has no place to lay His head.* We want to make sure that you who now call this place home, and men in your same circumstances, will always have a home."

With that there was a general round of applause. Horace asked all the residents to go to their rooms and wait for the priests and the guests to come by each room to bless it. Steele, Horace and the guests then began processing through the house with the holy water, blessing each room. When they arrived at each resident's room, the resident was asked to share his story and how he had been led to the streets and then ultimately to this house. Then Horace and Steele would bless their room.

When Steele and Randi drove into the staff parking lot at First Church, they were disappointed to see that there was a group of demonstrators gathered in front of the church. As they approached the front entrance to the church some of the people carrying signs spotted them and began shouting, "You should be ashamed of yourself, Reverend Austin. Shame, shame on you. God condemns homosexuals. They are going to burn in hell. Church funds should not be used to build houses for queers."

Steele glanced up at the signs they were carrying. All the signs carried the same sentiment. Some had Bible verses on them. Steele and Randi stood looking at the scene. Just then, he spotted a couple of police officers. They were moving the demonstrators off the church grounds to the sidewalk across the street. Steele glanced one more time at their signs. Then he turned to walk up the front steps of the church. As he did, his eyes fell on the familiar red, white, and blue sign of The Episcopal Church. It read simply, *"The Episcopal Church Welcomes You."* He put his arm around Randi and pointed at the sign. "Quite a contrast, huh?"

As they walked into the narthex they spotted Chief Sparks talking with one of the officers. "Hey, Parson, you just keep stirring things up around here, don't you? I'm going to have to assign one squad full time to you."

"Are we safe? Is it safe to have our Christmas Eve services?" Steele was worried.

"Oh, I think they're harmless enough, but I'll keep some officers on assignment here to make sure they don't disturb your worshippers."

"Who are those people? Is it the Klan?"

The Chief chuckled, "No, I don't see any Klan members out there. They're all members of Creekside Church for the Full Gospel."

"Who?"

"Oh, it's a tiny little church out in the country, but it appears you have riled them up real good."

"My hunch is that they represent quite a few others."

The Chief shook his head, "Now, we got church people picketing church people. I can't help but wonder what the Lord would think about that?"

Steele nodded, "I think it's pretty sad when people can't look beyond their prejudices to have compassion on folks that are sick and dying. Personally, I think the Lord would not be happy."

The Chief walked over to Steele and Randi. He put one arm around each of them. "Listen, you need to take Randi back to the Sacristy with you. Stone is waiting for you there. He has something he needs to tell you."

Steele felt his heart skip a beat. He looked over at Randi and saw that she had that deer caught in the headlights look on her face. The Chief patted them and smiled. "It's not like that. You don't have anything to worry about. Stone has some good news for you. Now go on. He's going to tell you something that will make you very happy. It just may be the best Christmas present that you get this year."

Steele took Randi's hand. As they walked into the nave of the church, the smell of fresh evergreen filled the air. The Altar Guild had put garlands and wreaths over all the arches in the church. It was hanging from the balcony and over the altar. Poinsettias were stacked up behind the altar itself. Two large Christmas trees were standing on either side of the altar. The church was beautifully prepared for the celebration of the birth of Christ.

Steele and Randi walked to the middle of the nave so that they could look at all the decorations. Steele let go of Randi's hand and put his arm around her and hugged her. "This is just great. I don't think First Church has ever looked prettier." Randi nodded and smiled.

As they opened the door to the Sacristy, Steele saw Stone standing in the doorway with a big smile on his face. "Merry Christmas, Father and Mrs. Father." He shook Steele's hand and hugged Randi. "We've been waiting on you."

"We?"

Stone moved out of the doorway so that Steele and Randi could see a glowing Rob McBride and Melanie Mason standing behind him. Rob shouted, "They found the one-armed man!"

"Huh?" Steele looked at Stone. "What one-armed man?"

"Steele, they found the guy that murdered Esther." Rob was bouncing up and down as he spoke. Tears of joy were running down Melanie's cheeks.

Steele and Randi were still trying to understand what they were saying. "How? I mean who?"

Stone chuckled, "Seems that Rob here got a call from the bank over in Cedarville."

"Cedarville? Where's Cedarville?" Steele was still perplexed.

"It's a wide spot in the road just over the Alabama state line. Not much there, just a general store, a gas station, and a bank."

"Why would that bank be calling Rob?"

"Well," Stone's smile had turned into a full grin. "It seems that Esther had rented a safe deposit box in their little bank. The rent on it was past due and they needed to know if she wanted to keep it."

"Did you know she had a safe deposit box over there, Rob?"

"No, but that's when the case broke open."

Stone continued, "We got a warrant and got the box opened. It was filled with love letters, photographs, and cards from one of Esther's co-workers in the library at the college. So we sent the Chief and a couple of his boys to talk with the man."

"And?" Steele could not hide his anxious curiosity.

"And he melted like butter on a hot stove." It was the voice of Chief Sparks. He was standing behind them in the door leading into the Sacristy. Steele and Randi turned to look at him. "We brought him into the interrogation room and within minutes he was confessing everything. He and Esther had been having an affair. He went over to her house to break it off, but she didn't want to end it. She grabbed him and was pleading for him to run away with her. He pushed her. She fell back and hit her head on the edge of the kitchen counter. He admitted to trying to cover his tracks, but honestly, I think he was relieved to just get it all out in the open."

Steele grabbed Rob and gave him a hug. "So, you're free!" They were patting each other on the back and laughing. "This is just great. This is wonderful."

The Chief and Stone just stood smiling as they watched the entire scene. "Steele, Rob, I owe you both an apology." The Chief's voice was contrite.

"No you don't, Chief." Steele smiled back at him. "You were doing your job and you believed what the evidence was telling you. I'm Rob's friend. I believed in what that evidence was telling me." Suddenly the sound of the organ, accompanied by the brass and timpani in the church, caught Steele's attention. "Folks, that's my cue to get out there. We have a Christmas service to celebrate. And my friends, other than the first Christmas, this just may be the best Christmas ever. I'll see you all in the church. We have so much to celebrate." He kissed Randi on the lips, Melanie on the cheek, hugged Rob, and gave a very uncomfortable hug to Stone and the Chief.

Stone reacted, "Come on, Chief; let's get away from this love fest. The Preacher's gone from shaking our hands to trying to hug us. I don't want to see what he might try to do next. After all, we both know the type of company he keeps." Laughing, the two men locked arms and danced out of the Sacristy.

CHAPTER 30

The service began with a roll of the timpani and then a trumpet fanfare. The great organ blended into the processional music. The congregation rose to their feet as the thurifer carrying the incense thurible entered the church and began moving down the aisle. The congregation turned so that they could view the procession. The thurifer swung the incense pot in circles over his head and then to each side. Immediately behind the thurifer came the large processional cross. The Mudd girls carried the candles on either side of the processional cross. Steele smiled at the first girl acolytes to ever process down the aisle of First Church.

"Ironic," he whispered to the verger. "The Mudds have opposed every progressive movement I've tried to make in this church but this one."

The verger smiled, "They do look awfully cute."

Steele remembered that the Mudds had not easily accepted every aspect of girl acolytes. "But no one will be able to see the Christmas dresses that the girls will be wearing." Virginia Mudd was resolute in her appeal that the acolytes not have to wear vestments. Steele was equally resolved to help her understand that those who wore vestments down the aisle of the church did so to insure that the focus was on the worship of the Almighty and not the latest fashions. She was disappointed, but she really wanted her girls to be acolytes.

Howard Dexter's granddaughter walked immediately behind the processional cross. She was carrying a banner with an image of the Blessed Mother on it. Steele could see that the Dexters were proud. They looked happier at that moment than he had ever seen them. Sure enough, sitting next to them was their daughter and son-in-law. The son-in-law snapped a photo of his daughter as she approached them.

The choir processed behind the banners. The clergy cross and torches led the servers and the assisting clergy. The verger stepped in front of Steele. He followed the verger. The congregation began singing the hymn, *O Come All Ye Faithful*. Steele spotted Max and Sharon Weller.

As he approached them he reached out and grabbed each of their hands. It pleased him to see that Doctor Steve Robbins and his wife were sitting with them. When Steele touched each of their hands they forced a smile. Steele sensed their pain. He knew just how difficult this Christmas and every Christmas would be for them.

Steele approached the altar and took the incense thurible. He stood before the altar cross and allowed the incense smoke to move heavenward toward the cross itself. He then blessed the altar by swinging the thurible over and around the altar. The clouds of incense smoke filled the sanctuary. He handed the thurible back to the acolyte. Steele bowed his head so that he too could be blessed by the holy smoke. The acolyte then did the same for the other ministers, the choir, and the congregation. Steele turned to look out at the congregation just as they began to sing the last verse of the hymn. The organ, brass and timpani introduced the last verse with great fanfare. *Yea Lord, we greet thee, born this happy morning.* For Steele Austin, it was that verse that always brought Christmas to him. It was during the singing of that verse that he was assured that God was present with them.

Steele had thought about his sermon for weeks. He was anxious to share the words that he believed God had placed on his heart. "Think with me about the first Christmas. It didn't take place in a grand church like this one. No, it was in a stable. It was a place to keep the farm animals. The first visitors were shepherds. They were common people who were doing the most menial labor for a living. Oh, for sure, kings did come to worship the Christ Child. We celebrate that event on the twelfth day of Christmas. We call it the Feast of the Epiphany. I would ask you to keep in mind that those kings were not white Anglo Saxon Protestants. No, the kings were from the east. They were not blonde and blue-eyed. Their skin was dark.

On this night in our little family, young women are serving at the altar. This is a first for us at First Church. Without the cooperation of a woman, the Blessed Mother, there would have been no Christmas, but then again, none of us would be here had it not been for our own mothers." A slight and uncomfortable chuckle rose up from the congregation. "If we look at the life of our Lord, we will see that women played an indispensable role in His life and ministry. We must not ever forget that, save the apostle John, the only followers that remained with Jesus at his crucifixion were the women. Three days later the first witnesses to the resurrection were women. Yet, for two thousand years, the followers of Jesus have gone to great lengths to keep women subservient in the church.

Without the ministry of women, the Church would not have been able to achieve all that it has achieved. Yet, we have gone to great lengths to build walls designed to lock women out. The messages have been consistent through the ages. Women cannot sit on Vestries. Women cannot serve as ushers. Women cannot serve as acolytes. Women cannot be ordained. And lest we forget, we have scripture passages to justify this behavior. It's in the Bible. Do we really want to be a part of a Church that seeks to elevate some at the expense of others? Do we really want to be a part of a Church known for the people that it excludes, condemns, and judges as not quite good enough? Or perhaps, the more stirring question finds its origin not in our preference, but in the intention of the Christ whose birth we celebrate this night. Would Jesus Christ, who opened his arms to all and turned his back on none, want to be part of such a Church?

There is a large portion of the Church that tells married men that they cannot be priests. But did you realize that for the first twelve hundred years of Christianity, many priests, Bishops, and popes had wives? When the Church of England permitted married clergy, they were only overturning a tradition of celibacy for clergy that had existed for a mere three hundred years.

My hunch is that about ten percent of the people in this congregation are left-handed. Do you realize that, six hundred years ago, you would not have been permitted to be a priest if you were born left-handed? In fact, you would have been considered suspect. The Church declared that left-handed people are servants of the devil. Even until recent history, by that I mean the late 1950s; school students were forced to become right-handed.

If you have a wedding ring on your left hand, it's on the left hand instead of the right to chase away evil spirits that might haunt the marriage. If a husband discovers that his wife is left-handed in Japan, he can divorce her. In Arab nations, the right hand is used to touch parts of the body above the waist and the left hand is used to touch the parts of the body below the waist. And have we forgotten the Biblical imagery, even the words of Jesus Himself that honor the right and condemn the left? *Don't let your right hand know what your left is doing.* And in the parable of the last judgment, sheep are lined up on God's right hand while the goats are lined up on His left. Now do you understand why I find the phrase, *it's in the Bible* an insufficient answer to any complex question of faith? We Anglicans have a long history of refusing to give simple answers to complex questions. It's an honorable tradition. It has gone to make us a great Church in the worldwide family of Churches.

I am very much committed to the heart of what it is to be an Anglican. I am committed to a tradition that is not afraid to ask questions. To the contrary, we are encouraged to examine our faith in the light of the new insights that God reveals to us through science, medicine, and psychology. These disciplines are not at odds with spirituality, but an integral part of our spirituality. The opposite of faith is not doubt. The opposite of faith is fear. We are a people of faith who are not afraid to ask questions.

You have heard it said that we are not a Bible Church. My friends, we are a people deeply devoted to the Holy Scriptures. We are so devoted that we refuse to treat them lightly. We refuse to reduce them to a literalism that can only be understood by utilizing our heads, our brains, for a hat rack and nothing more. We are a thinking person's religion. You do not have to leave your ability to think on the sidewalk when you enter the doors of an Episcopal Church. We are committed to interpreting the scriptures in the light of tradition and reason. Our system of faith development will not allow us to use the inspired Word of God as a weapon. The loving words of Jesus contained in the scriptures are words of invitation. Anglicans are an inviting people. We do not make demands and issue ultimatums."

Steele stopped to look out at the congregation. You could actually hear a pin drop. There was no emotional wall. The people were open, receptive to what he had to say. "If this congregation is typical, and I believe that we are, fifty percent of us are divorced. Is our memory so short that we have forgotten the judgment that our Church, the Episcopal Church, placed on divorced people? In my lifetime I can remember that the Church ruled that divorced persons could not receive communion in an Episcopal Church. If you married a divorced person you were excommunicated. Divorced persons could not be remarried in the Church. And divorced persons could not be ordained. If a priest did get a divorce he could be deposed. Not only would he find his marriage and family in ruins, but the very Church he had loved and served would turn its back on him in his hour of need.

Jesus lived out His ministry caught between two very different understandings of God and God's people. The one understanding was built on the concept that the only way a person could attain salvation was to perfectly keep the religious laws. In fact, the only hope for the nation of Israel was if every adult male would keep the religious laws perfectly for twenty-four hours. Those who failed to keep the rituals and laws were not only labeled as sinners, but they were treated as public outcasts. Jesus rejected this understanding of God.

You have heard it said from this very pulpit that the Episcopal Church has lost her moorings. You have heard it said that if we welcome everyone, we will mean nothing to anyone. When Jesus stretched out his arms on the cross, he did so in a loving embrace. He did it to draw all the people of the world to Himself. Jesus invites all people to be full members of His Church. The Episcopal Church can do no less.

Jesus revealed God as Father. He told us about a Father that would never turn His back on any of His children. Rather than excluding, judging, and condemning those that the religious of the day found so unacceptable, Jesus ministered to them. We must never forget those that Jesus reached out to. The leper, the tax collector, the adulterer, the prostitute, and the common people were all a part of Jesus' congregation then, and they remain so today.

First Church has taken a baby step forward tonight by opening the ministry of the Church to these young women. Now we must ask ourselves if First Church is going to be like the Prodigal Father in the familiar parable. Will we open our arms to all wayward sons and daughters that want to come home? The Church is continually caught between two opposing understandings of the Gospel. On the one hand, there are those who would say that we exist only for those who believe that they are without sin. They have a corner on God and possess the only understanding of the Bible. Such a Church exists to exclude those they deem as unworthy. Its message will be to exclude, judge and condemn.

In two very memorable parables Jesus taught us about these two opposing expressions of faith. In the one, He told us of two men who went up to the temple to pray. The one was a Pharisee and the other a publican. The Pharisee stood and boasted of his righteousness before God. The other knelt quietly in a corner and prayed, *we do not presume to come to this thy table trusting in our own righteousness.*

In the second parable, Jesus tells us of a Prodigal Son that wasted his inheritance on worldly living. When the prodigal came to his senses and returned to his father, the father received him with open arms. The prodigal's older brother resented the grace and mercy that the father was showing his rebellious brother. The prodigal, however, knelt before his father and prayed, *I have done those things that I ought not to have done and I have left undone those things that I ought to have done.*

It's important for Episcopalians to remember that two of the greatest evangelical hymns ever written were written by Anglicans. "Amazing Grace" and "Just As I Am" are both products of Anglican spirituality. They are at the very heart of what it is to be a Christian who lives out our faith in the Episcopal Church. Our focus needs to be on seeking forgiveness for our own sins and forgiving those who have sinned against us. Our spirituality doesn't afford us the luxury of sitting in judgment on sinners that we don't even know. Our primary focus needs to be on seeking forgiveness for our own sins. These we know all too well. Would our spiritual energies not be better spent repenting of our known sins versus speculating on the sins of our brothers and sisters?

It appears that Americans have developed a fondness for quoting the Bible. The quote chosen at a given moment is the one that best suits the purposes of the person making a point. I have a point to make tonight. So please allow me the courtesy of quoting a passage of scripture that helps me make the point. I want you to remember it when you think about the birth of Jesus. *God did not send His Son into the world to condemn the world.*

As I came into this parish tonight, I saw the people carrying signs that condemn me and First Church for our ministries to the outcasts in today's world. Some of them had Biblical quotes on them. But then remember the Biblical quotes that condemned left-handedness. I know you also saw and read these signs. But, I also noticed another sign. I noticed the sign that hangs just above our entry gate. It reads, *The Episcopal Church Welcomes You.* There are no footnotes on that sign. There is no fine print. There are no conditions on the welcome. It doesn't exclude women, people of color, divorced persons, left-handed people or anyone else. However, I think it just might suggest this footnote. *If you don't feel good enough to be a member of any other Church, then the Episcopal Church welcomes you.*

On the lawn of First Church there are two types of signs this Christmas Eve. There are signs that exclude, judge, and condemn, complete with legitimate Bible quotes. There is also a sign welcoming any whom God would lead to our door. The question that each one of us has to ask ourselves tonight is a profound one. On this Christmas Eve, which sign do you think Jesus would have you carry? Or even more important, as Jesus was carrying that cross up that ugly mount called Golgotha, which sign do you think he was carrying?"

Steele paused. His eyes had grown misty. He realized that sometime ago he had departed from his prepared text and was speaking from his heart. He knew only that the words he had been speaking were not his own. He was but a channel for a message that needed to be shared. He glanced down at his notes on the pulpit. They were a blur. He would not be able to find the point where he had departed from his prepared notes. He looked out at the congregation and waited for the words he needed to say to be given to him.

"It's so important that we understand that God uses imperfect people to accomplish his purposes on earth. God uses imperfect people simply because no others are available." A chuckle rose up from the congregation. Steele smiled. "Consider our Biblical heroes. Noah was a drunk. Moses was a murderer. David was an adulterer and a murderer. Solomon was a materialist. Simon was a coward who denied Jesus, not once, but three times. Yet, he became *Petros* - Peter, the rock, on which Christ built His Church. Saul was responsible for the Church's first martyr, but we don't remember him as Saul. We call him St. Paul. Some traditions question whether or not Mary Magdalene was a woman of the night. But she became one of the first witnesses of the resurrection. And let us not forget that on that awful Friday when Jesus was crucified on that ugly hill, he personally escorted into Paradise one of the thieves that was crucified with him.

There are plenty of Churches and an abundance of religions in the world that bask in their own self-righteousness. They delight in singling out those that they believe the Bible has defined as unacceptable. The question that I want to close with tonight is this. Do we want to be one of them? Would the ministry of Jesus Christ be advanced further if we spent less of our time and energy debating the faith and more of our effort went into sharing the faith? Which method do you think will lead the most people to know and love the Christ Child whose birth we celebrate this night?"

Steele ended his sermon. The silence continued. He knew that the congregation had listened to him. He didn't know whether or not they had received his message. He stood silently studying the faces of the people. From the pulpit Steele had an even better view of the congregation. Every space was taken. Folding chairs had been set up to seat people wherever possible. The rest were standing.

Almeda, along with her sons and her new stepdaughter, were sitting on the front pew. Rob McBride and Melanie Mason sat in the pew behind Almeda. They were holding hands and smiling back at him. Steele noticed that there were quite a few people in the congregation that had just a few weeks ago left First Church to go to St. Mary's. He wondered if this meant that they were returning. He looked up into the balcony. His heart skipped a beat. That familiar feeling of nausea returned. In the far corner on the very last row of the balcony sat a familiar face. There sat Ned Boone.

CHAPTER 31

A very unusual winter storm had swept across the southeastern part of the United States on Christmas morning. Snow and ice were reported from the Carolinas across Eastern Tennessee and all the way down to Atlanta. Frost and freeze warnings were issued for all of Georgia and Alabama. Even the citrus crops in Florida were threatened. The cold winter storm was felt as far south as the Florida Keys.

Steele and Randi welcomed the cold spell. It reminded them just a bit of Christmas back in Oklahoma. Steele built a roaring fire in the fireplace and they waited for Travis to wake to see just what Santa Claus had left him. They didn't have to wait long. Intuitively, the little three-year old awakened just a bit earlier than his normal routine. He was wide-eyed as Randi carried him into the living room. Santa had been extra good to him this year. But then, after all, he was a very special love child.

After they had opened their presents, Steele put the batteries in one of the toys under the Christmas tree so that he could play with Travis. Randi went into the kitchen to tend to the rib roast she had selected for their Christmas dinner. Melanie, Rob, and Rob's son would be joining them for the Christmas feast. The first telephone call of the day came from Almeda. Steele answered the telephone and heard her sing, "Merry Christmas to all of you!"

"And a Merry Christmas to you and Horace." Steele smiled. "I just know that this is a very special Christmas for the two of you."

"It has been absolutely marvelous." She cooed. "Horace has spoiled me with a new outfit, a beautiful new bracelet, and a nightie that can only be called naughty."

"Almeda," Steele interrupted. "Too much information. You've forgotten that I'm a priest."

She giggled, "And you've forgotten that I'm married to a priest. Don't try to pretend to me that you guys are above wanting to see your ladies in something just a bit on the skimpy side."

"Okay, you've got me."

"Horace and I have decided that we want to have a New Year's Eve party here at my house and we want you to attend."

"I'll double check with Randi, but I don't think we have any plans. We'd love to come."

"That's just great. I'm going to invite a couple hundred of my closest friends."

Steele had some second thoughts. While a lot of people had accepted Almeda's marriage to Horace, there were a lot in her former social circle that had not. He had overheard their comments and they were not kind. Oh, for sure, they had been polite to their faces, but he had his doubts as to whether or not they would accept an invitation to a party at her house.

"Steele, are you still there?"

"I'm sorry." Steele paused, "Almeda, I'm just a little anxious for you."

"My darling boy, don't you give it a second thought. Horace and I have already discussed it. I know what your concern is, but frankly, we don't care. The invitations are going out and if the excuses come in, then we'll know just who our real friends are."

"Well, as long as the two of you are prepared for some..."

"Please, don't concern yourself any further. We'll be just fine. But can we count on you and Randi?"

"I'll clear it with the boss, but I feel certain that we'll be there to welcome in the New Year with you."

"Marvelous. Now you all have a wonderful Christmas Day."

"You, as well. Give my regards to Horace."

Steele went back to sit on the floor by the Christmas tree with Travis. Randi asked, "Who was that?"

"Almeda and Horace are having a New Year's Eve party. They want us to come. I told her I would check with you, but as far as I knew we would be there."

The telephone rang again. Steele answered it.

"Merry Christmas, Parson. That was one hell of a service you put on last night."

"I'm glad you liked it, Chief. Did your officers have any trouble with the demonstrators?"

"No sir, no problem at all. In fact, after you started your service they started one of their own. They did some Bible reading and then offered some prayers for your salvation and the salvation of the Episcopal Church."

"Well, all prayers are appreciated."

"Your sermon was right on target."

"Do you think the folks really heard it?"

"Oh, they heard it. The question is whether or not it sank in. Only time will tell. I'll not keep you, Parson. I just wanted to wish you and Randi a Merry Christmas. Give her a big hug from me."

"That's real easy work. Have a great day with your family, Chief."

Melanie, Rob, and Rob's son arrived. After taking off their coats, Randi brought them all some warm wassail to drink.

"We've decided on a wedding date and we want you there," Melanie gushed.

"Congratulations and best wishes." Steele stood and hugged them both. Randi did the same. "Just tell us when and where and we'll be there."

"I want to get married in my home parish in Beverly Hills. Can you come, please?"

"When?"

Rob responded, "This woman is an undying romantic. She wants to be married on Valentine's Day. Steele, you and my son here will be my best men."

Melanie joined in, "And Randi, you'll be my only attendant. And we want Travis to be the ring bearer. Now, will you guys do it?"

Steele looked at Randi. She was smiling and nodding. "I believe the decision has been made. We would love to come. I'll check on airline tickets later this afternoon."

"No," Melanie interrupted. "My family will take care of all your travel costs and your hotel."

"Gosh, Melanie, that's really generous."

She laughed, "Listen, my Dad is relieved that the mess around Esther's death has been resolved. Now, he's happy to see me happy. I think he'll do just about anything to make this wedding happen."

Steele was thoughtful for a minute. "You know, Randi, we've never been to California. What would you think about extending our time there? Let's take Travis to Disneyland and then let's take a side trip up to San Francisco. I've always wanted to visit Grace Cathedral and that city that everyone describes as being so beautiful."

Randi reached over and hugged Steele, "I think that would be wonderful. Let's do it."

Just then the telephone rang again. Randi picked it up. She listened for a few minutes and then offered the phone to Steele. "It's Sharon Weller."

Steele whispered, "Does she sound upset? Is she crying?"

Randi shook her head, "To the contrary."

"Father Austin, this is Sharon Weller. I know that it's really cold outside and that it's Christmas Day, but is there any chance that you could come over to our house for just a minute?"

"Are you upset, Sharon? Are you having a difficult day?"

"No, Father, this just may be the best day we've had since Mandy died. You have just got to come over. I have to show you something. I promise it won't take long."

Steele was silent for a minute. "Is it really that important to you?"

"Yes, please come. Do you have guests there at your house?"

"Yes, we do."

"Please bring them with you. I promise you won't be sorry."

"All right, we'll be over within the hour."

After explaining the telephone call from Sharon Weller to his guests, everyone got in Steele's car and drove over to the Weller's house. Sharon was waiting for them at the door. She had a big smile on her face. Max came from the back of the house to greet them. He too was smiling. "You just aren't going to believe this. It's a miracle. I'm so glad that all of you came. Please follow me."

They all walked through the house and out the back door. He led them across the back yard to a creek bed that ran behind the house. They had to climb up a small embankment so that they could see down into the creek. The creek itself was dry, but it was in full bloom. Easter lilies filled the little creek bed immediately behind their house. The smell of Easter lilies filled the air. On the other side of the creek bed, two small magnolia trees stood. They too, had blossoms on them. They stood like lit candles on either side of a floral display. On this freezing cold Christmas morning, Easter lilies and magnolia trees were in full bloom.

"How?" Steele looked at Max.

"Do you remember all the Easter lilies that people sent us for Mandy's funeral?"

"Yeah, the church and your house were filled with them."

Max nodded, "When they began to die, I didn't know what to do with them so I just brought them out here and tossed them in this dry creek bed. I hadn't given them a second thought since then, but this morning when I brought the dog out here for his walk I smelled them. I first saw those two magnolia trees in bloom, so I thought it must be them. But then, I walked up here on the embankment and this is what I saw."

"Incredible." Everyone stood silent looking at the flowers and taking in the fragrance. Then Steele continued, "I can't figure it out. Why would they bloom today? I mean, it's so cold out here. I just don't see how they could bloom in this frigid temperature. It was close to freezing last night."

Max put his arm around Sharon. Tears were streaming down her face. Tears welled up in Max's eyes as well. Then with a broken voice, "You don't remember, Father, do you?"

"Remember? What? I'm sorry. Is there something that I forgot?" Steele studied the faces of the grieving parents.

Max pulled his sobbing wife closer to him and smiled. "Father Austin, friends... today is Mandy's birthday."

CHAPTER 32

Steele, Randi, and Travis had to take a commuter plane from Falls City to Atlanta. There they boarded a direct flight for Los Angeles. After the plane lifted off the runway and leveled at its cruising altitude, the steward served beverages and a light lunch. Travis settled back in his seat and went to sleep. It was then that Steele shared with Randi a letter that he had retrieved from the mail that very morning. He reached into his briefcase and pulled the letter out of its envelope.

"This came in the morning mail." He handed her the open letter. "I think you should read it."

Dear Father Austin,

We at St. Jude's Episcopal Church are in the process of searching for a new Rector. Our parish is but twenty-five years old. We were started by the Mother Church of our Diocese to serve a rapidly growing suburb of San Antonio, Texas.

Our previous two Rectors were instrumental in leading us to be a strong, vital congregation of 2,500 baptized members. Our congregation is composed primarily of young families, but we also have a few retired people as well.

We have just dedicated a new worship facility that comfortably seats 600 worshippers.

We are looking for a young, dynamic leader with strong pulpit skills. Our preliminary research indicates that you are just such a person. Enclosed please find our complete parish profile and a questionnaire that we would like for you to complete. If you're in agreement, we prayerfully welcome you into our search process.

Faithfully,
Charles Gerard

Randi sat quietly staring at the letter. "Steele, what do you think? I mean, this is really flattering, but... I... uh... I just don't know. Are you ready to leave First Church? Have you thought about it like that?"

Steele put his arm around Randi. She lifted up the arm rest between them and snuggled up to him. "I haven't thought about much else since I read that letter this morning."

"So, what do you think?"

"I know that I'm getting tired. First Church is a very difficult congregation. It just seems like it's been an uphill battle since the day we arrived."

"But Honey, you're winning a lot of them over. Look at the change in Almeda. I mean, even Howard Dexter and his family have warmed up to us."

Steele nodded, "I know that you're right about that, but there's still some very strong opposition in the congregation to me and my leadership." Steele shook his head, "I just don't know how much energy I have left to deal with the Mudds, Ned Boone, Bishop Petersen and all the rest of them. I wonder if it's even worth it."

Randi sat up so that her eyes could meet his, "Listen to me, Cowboy, look at all the good you have done. You have left your mark on First Church and there are plenty of people in Falls City that are grateful to you for what you've done."

Steele laid his head back on his seat. "And that's just the point. Maybe I've done all that I can do. As the song says, *you need to know when to fold them.* Maybe this letter is God's way of telling us to look at other possibilities."

"I'll not stand between you and God, but if you decide to take a call to another parish, I think you should realize that not everyone at First Church is rushing to plan your farewell party. There are a lot of people who would hate to see us leave."

Steele pulled her close to him once again. "And you, my darling, can't be objective when it comes to your husband. But you're probably right. I think there would be some people who would be hurt if we left. At the same time, I don't think any of them would blame us for doing so."

Randi read the letter through one more time. "But this is only an inquiry, right?"

"Yeah, this could be the end of it. I mean, I could answer their questionnaire and they might not like my answers to their questions. And then of course, they will need to run references."

She sat up, wide-eyed. "Would Bishop Petersen be one of those references?"

"For sure, they'll talk to him."

"But Steele, he can't stand you. What do you think he'll say?"

"There's no way for us to know. In fact, we'll probably never know."

"But he could ruin your chances."

Steele looked out the window of the airplane. "Chances are he would. On the one hand he wants to get rid of me, but obviously this is a better call. It's a better situation in a larger city. The parish is twice the size of First Church. I pray to God that I'm misreading the man, but I don't think he'll give me a favorable recommendation."

"You mean, if it were a tiny little parish in the swamps he would recommend you?"

"Oh, I think in that situation he would sing my praises, but then again, I sometimes get the feeling that the only thing that would make him happy is if I weren't a priest at all."

"Ladies and gentlemen, this is your captain speaking. We are sixty miles from Los Angeles International Airport. I'm going to turn the fasten seatbelt light on and ask our flight attendants to make final arrangements for landing. It will please you to know that it's a beautiful 72 degrees in Los Angeles today. The sky is clear and the blue Pacific is right in front of us."

As Steele fastened his seat belt, Randi put the arm rest back down between them. Steele checked on Travis to make sure he was secure in his seat. He was still sleeping, but beginning to stir. "Let's just agree to think about this letter while we're here in California. I don't have to give them an answer until we return to Falls City."

The next week went by so fast. The wedding was all that Melanie and Rob had hoped it would be. The retired Bishop of Los Angeles and a long-time family friend of the Masons, presided at the wedding. Steele, dressed in a black tux, felt strange standing in the place of the best man. With a little coaching from his mother and some come hither gestures from Steele, Travis walked down the aisle. He was dressed in a white suit with a red bow tie. He carried the cushion with the rings on it.

He maintained a perfect processional pace until he got within running distance of Steele. He broke into a full run and leaped into his father's arms to the smiles and amusement of the congregation.

When Randi came down the aisle Steele's stomach filled with butterflies. She was absolutely beautiful. He felt himself falling in love with her all over again. At the reception he held her close as they danced. "It's not fair that the bride's attendant is more radiant than the bride."

"Why, Misturh Austin, you make a lady blush." Randi faked her most persuasive southern accent. "If I didn't know better, I would think that you're just trying to have your way with me."

Steele followed suit by pretending his own accent, "Madam, that's exactly what I have in mind. In fact, I've reserved a room in this very hotel for that very purpose." He chuckled and squeezed her even more tightly.

Rob and Melanie left for a honeymoon in Tahiti. They had shown Steele and Randi the house that they would live in. "Rob doesn't have to work, but he says he wants to do something. My father said he would introduce him around. There are lots of possibilities."

"Melanie, I love you and that's enough for me, but I just have to do something to make me feel like I'm pulling my share." She hugged him. "Whatever makes you happy, Rob. Whatever makes you happy."

Steele rented a car so that he could take his wife and son to Disneyland. Travis understood Mickey Mouse, but Disneyland was only a vague concept until they walked through the gates. They were met immediately by a larger than life costumed Mickey and Minnie posing for pictures. Travis ran from his father's arms to hug Mickey. Mickey responded as Randi snapped pictures.

Travis made quite a scene on the Dumbo the Elephant ride. He was riding with Randi. He screamed his displeasure when the ride stopped. He fought his mother's efforts to lift him out of his seat on Dumbo. The young attendant allowed Randi and Travis to ride again for a second and a third time since the crowds were light. He was no less happy, however, when he was forcefully removed from Dumbo. He cried for Dumbo as Steele carried him toward another attraction.

When the parade came down Main Street Disney, Steele glanced down at Travis, who had been sitting on the curb. When he saw the characters, he jumped up and started laughing and pointing at them.

Steele realized that his son's eyes had grown wide. It was an expression that Steele had fallen in love with several years ago. Travis had inherited his mother's eyes and her facial expressions. It always delighted Steele to see Randi's eyes widen in amazement when she was surprised or pleased. Their son shared that facial expression with his mother.

Mickey and Minnie were at the end of the parade. Their float was just passing them when Minnie spotted Travis sitting on the curb. The float stopped and she stepped off. She came over to Travis. She was carrying a big red balloon on a string. She tied the string of the balloon around his wrist. Steele and Randi both were so surprised and pleased with the gesture that they both almost forgot to take pictures.

Travis found a Mickey Mouse doll in the gift shop that was as big as he was. Once again he let his determination be known. Steele relented and bought the stuffed animal for his son. Back at the hotel, a very tired little boy lay on his bed sleeping soundly on his stomach with his arm wrapped around Mickey.

Their weekend in San Francisco was equally wonderful for Steele and Randi. The city was every bit as beautiful as Steele had imagined it would be. They rode the cable car from Fisherman's Wharf to Union Square. They wandered through Chinatown and along the waterfront. Travis particularly enjoyed riding the carousel on the pier. They had high tea at the Fairmont Hotel and hot chocolate from Ghirardelli. It was a perfect time together. It was also time to do more than just talk about having a little brother or sister for Travis. "If we don't want him to grow up thinking that he is the King of the Universe, we had better bring a little competition into his life." Randi was more than willing to cooperate with Steele's suggestion.

On Sunday morning they walked up the steps to Grace Cathedral. After they left Travis in the church nursery, they found seats on the aisle near the front of the nave. The choir was absolutely magnificent. On this particular Sunday the combined Men and Boys Choir led the worship. Their clear tones echoed off the Cathedral walls. The Dean preached a moving sermon. Steele and Randi both felt challenged by it. It was as though he was talking directly to them. He spoke of Jesus leading his disciples from town to town. He suggested that we keep in mind that Jesus is always leading us. We must not grow too comfortable in any situation. We must always be ready to follow Jesus to the next phase of our lives. We must always be prepared to go where He leads us.

"Do you think he has been reading our mail?" Steele whispered to Randi. She looked back at him with that same wide-eyed look that he loved seeing on her face.

Steele held Randi's hand as they went to the communion rail. They knelt together and made the sign of the cross in unison. After receiving communion they returned to their pew and knelt on the cushion to say their prayers of thanksgiving. Steele sat back in the pew and began watching the other worshippers return from the communion rail. He was sitting quietly when his heart skipped a beat. He punched Randi and whispered, "Look! Look at that man!"

"You mean the young Adonis in the white turtleneck and blue blazer?"

"No, look at the guy walking with him. Do you see the man with the black hair and moustache? Randi, he looks just like Chadsworth Alexander."

Randi grabbed Steele's arm. "My God, Steele, that is Chadsworth."

As the two men walked past them, Steele met the older man's eyes. The man slowed as he passed Steele. Steele turned his head to follow the man down the aisle. The man turned and looked back at Steele. The couple didn't return to their pew. The older man took the arm of the younger and directed him to the exit.

"Randi, I may be crazy, but I think that was Chadsworth. I'm going to try to catch him." And with that Steele left his seat and hurried down the aisle to the front steps of the Cathedral. He looked for the two men, but they were nowhere to be seen. Soon, Randi was standing beside him. "Did you see him again?"

"No."

"Steele, Honey, Chadsworth is dead. You did his funeral. You buried him. They say we all have a double some place in life. Maybe we just saw someone that looks an awfully lot like Chadsworth."

Steele relinquished. "You're probably right. It's just so weird. He was talking to the young blonde guy when he passed us. I swear to you Randi, it sounded just like him."

"Come on." She took his hand, "We've got a plane to catch."

"And a big decision to make. How we answer that letter from San Antonio just could change our lives forever."

Randi smiled at her husband. "San Antonio would be closer to home. It's a bigger city. The people sound more like our kind of people. Maybe we should at least give it a look."

Steele put his arm around her and hugged her. "Let's go get Travis. It's time for me to take my little family back to Falls City. And you know what?"

"What, Cowboy?"

"Right now, Falls City feels an awfully lot like home."

EPILOGUE

After Steele and Randi had checked their luggage at curbside check-in at San Francisco International, they turned to take one more look at the beautiful city by the bay. The sun felt good on their faces. The houses on the hills surrounding the city, the flowers in bloom in the middle of winter, it was all very satisfying. As they surveyed the city one last time, neither of them took notice of the black limousine parked at the curb just a few feet from them. The back passenger window of the limousine lowered. A man in dark sunglasses peered out.

The muscular young blonde sitting next to him asked, "Is that who you thought it was?"

The man sat silently watching Steele and Randi.

"Well, is it?"

The man lowered his sunglasses further down his nose so that he could get a better look. After a few seconds, he laid his head back against the seat. He closed his eyes. He was quiet.

He lifted his head from the seat and looked at the young man sitting next to him. He smiled and took his hand. He then looked out the window yet one more time. He took a long, lingering look at Steele and Randi. And then, as though satisfied, he pushed his sunglasses back up on his face. He rolled the window up and motioned to the driver. The limo drove away.

COMING IN 2007

Pruning the Magnolia

Book Three in the Magnolia Series

By

Dennis R. Maynard

Was that who you think it was in the limousine?

How will Steele and Randi respond to the letter?

Father Austin's vulnerability increases dramatically when he uncovers a scandal that will shake the very foundation of First Church.

A most unusual pastoral situation cements the young priest and one of his most outspoken antagonists in an irreversible bond.

Young Father Austin's idealism continues to confront the prejudice and bigotry that tries to disguise itself as tradition. In the process, more secrets of sex and greed are revealed, giving his foes even more reason to attempt to remove him from office.

It is said that the only way two people can keep a secret is if one of them is dead. What if the other person is your priest? You won't want to miss the third installment in the Magnolia Series.

ABOUT THE AUTHOR

The Reverend Doctor Dennis R. Maynard has been a priest in the Episcopal Church for thirty-six years. He has served parishes in Oklahoma, Texas, South Carolina, and California. The author of six books, he is often requested to be a guest speaker or preacher in congregations and communities throughout the nation. He has also served as a consultant or retreat leader to some sixty parishes and dioceses.

Doctor Maynard and his wife Nancy have parented four children. He retired from full time parish work in 2003. He lives in Rancho Mirage, California. Daily visits to the local gym are an integral part of his life plan. He does concede that he has reached the point in his life that he has to restrict his snow skiing to what he calls *ballroom skiing*.

All of his books can be ordered through his website at www. Episkopols.com, through Amazon.com, or any of the online bookstores. If you want to have Doctor Maynard visit your parish or organization as a guest speaker or preacher, please visit his website.

WWW.EPISKOPOLS.COM

BOOKS FOR CLERGY AND THE PEOPLE THEY SERVE